MW00978788

Michael Meehan gre
novel, *The Salt of Br*
Prize for Fiction in the 2000 New South Wales Premier's Awards. He lives in Melbourne. This is his third novel.

DECEPTION

MICHAEL MEEHAN

For Michele Sommer

First published in 2008
This edition published 2010

Copyright © Michael Meehan 2008

All rights reserved. No part of this book may be reproduced or transmitted in any form or by any means, electronic or mechanical, including photocopying, recording or by any information storage and retrieval system, without prior permission in writing from the publisher. The Australian *Copyright Act 1968* (the Act) allows a maximum of one chapter or 10 per cent of this book, whichever is the greater, to be photocopied by any educational institution for its educational purposes provided that the educational institution (or body that administers it) has given a remuneration notice to Copyright Agency Limited (CAL) under the Act.

Allen & Unwin
83 Alexander Street
Crows Nest NSW 2065
Australia
Phone: (61 2) 8425 0100
Fax: (61 2) 9906 2218
Email: info@allenandunwin.com
Web: www.allenandunwin.com

Cataloguing-in-Publication details are available
from the National Library of Australia
www.librariesaustralia.nla.gov.au

ISBN 978 1 74237 264 8

Set in 11.5/17.5 pt Fairfield Light by Midland Typesetters, Australia
Printed in Australia by McPherson's Printing Group
10 9 8 7 6 5 4 3 2 1

Mixed Sources
Product group from well-managed forests, and other controlled sources
www.fsc.org Cert no. SGS-COC-004121
© 1996 Forest Stewardship Council

The paper in this book is FSC certified. FSC promotes environmentally responsible, socially beneficial and economically viable management of the world's forests.

He wrote of stones. Sebastien Rouvel. In one fragment after another he wrote of stones drawn deeply from a country of felled walls and scattered rocks. He wrote of how he walked hand in hand with another across fields of broken stones and fresh growths of crumbling rock, stooping now and then to break bright flowers from fragile stems, handing as a bouquet to the one who walked beside him nothing but sharp stalks, thrust like jagged spikes from a burning fist, the stone petals breaking into dust upon the touch.

From the earth they drew a harvest. There being once a presence in that place and a voice which told of order. All these stones they now discovered just fragments of that image, shattered wreckage from the fall. Believing that if the stones were put together they might again make the image, and that the voice might speak again . . .

It was in the dust at Mount Deception and across these scattered stones that the children played for that last time, the dust coursing in the confused winds that skipped about them as they arrayed their final ring of stones. So it was, as Agnes later told, on that day when her mother and her sisters, Colette, Geneviève and Clémentine vanished in the storm. She spoke of the children gathering the stones, of a dying lizard and a circle of bright rocks, of how the wind blew up and the earth began to run and the fire flickered and died and then flared again.

She told of the lizard clinging in terror to the end of a stick, the pup yelping and snapping, the children shrieking through the wind. She watched the three of them playing in the dust, a half-grown girl with two younger children, struggling to light a fire in the heat of a windy February day, the fire and the dust running about them not in steady sheets before the wind but in circles which chopped this way and that amid the flaking trees, the fire struggling to take hold and the lizard still clinging desperately, its jaws clamped to the far end of the stick.

Then fifteen and always a reckless tomboy of a girl, Agnes had ridden out along the creek bed on her horse, a biting hard-mouthed brute misnamed Princess, scaring rabbits with the gun, the rusting relic of a police pistol her father mostly used for scaring crows. So hot and blistering a day it was, with the sounds of doors crashing in the wind and windows slamming shut, the sky darkening against the flying dust and the loose iron beginning to flap and shriek. She soon brought Princess back, nostrils flared, neck arched as always against the dragging of the bit, back through the wind and shrieks and laughter and the yelping of the pup, to be tethered at the garden gate. She took the pistol to its place behind the kitchen door. In the distance she could see the smaller girls still trying to feed the fire, their pinafores dragged and tossed about them as they picked up sticks and tufts of withered grass, with Colette gone off perhaps to fetch some larger wood. Agnes knew the fire would never catch because the wind was far too strong, and the little ones, Geneviève and Clémentine, were now giving their attention to the stick and to the lizard, and the circling yelping pup.

Then it was that something happened.

This, so many years after, was what old Agnes told. There was the sound of a door crashing violently in the wind, and the sight of Monsieur Rouvel breaking from the house. In blurred and moving shapes, obscured by the wind, she saw him stumble, crouching and limping as he always did, but this time almost falling from one verandah post to the next, staggering out across the stonewalled garden, steadying himself for a moment on the far gatepost. The children stopped tormenting the poor lizard, and all began to watch him as he peered across the yard. As though trying, through his one unshattered lens, to make some sense of what he saw through the wind and dust and debris. Then he stumbled through the gate and began to untie the pony, pulling and tearing and cursing at the tangled reins, shaking his head and shouting something to them that they couldn't hear.

All things became uncertain in the storm, and even more uncertain in the long tracts of time that ran between that time and the time of telling. Princess began to rear and sought to bite as he struggled with blinded awkward fingers to release her from the post. Agnes saw him move in front of the plunging horse and then to the wrong side, hopping and straining for a stirrup that was far too short, the saddle straining perilously against the girth, the unwilling pony twisting and stooping into the weight of his foot so that he was forced to turn within the arc of the straining horse, her eyes rolling in dread and anger as she twisted and plunged about him in this wheeling and ridiculous cursing coil of man and horse and dust.

He managed at last to rise into the saddle, with a last look to the girls, to Agnes with the pup now squirming in her arms, to the two younger children standing by their ring of stones and to their wretched captive lizard still clinging to its stick. He dragged Princess's head around, half falling in the saddle, his feet not yet in the stirrups, cantering at first towards them and then down into the bed of the creek, which led off towards the north and to the west.

> Some fragment of a hand, a shattered shoulder, some edge or chisel's mark, as the pilgrims came to scour the deserts for these scattered scraps of stone. All knowing in rage and sadness that the more they picked and foraged, the more fragments they discovered, the less truth they would find . . .

He rode out into the desert. Into the emptiness. His bones at last to join the scattered rocks. The remains discovered, 'disturbed by native dogs', months later. There being no-one to go after him, no-one to look for him, with all others soon vanished in a rush of baggage and the gig brought to the front, her mother's cheek wet with tears in a last rushed kiss, the gig then beating out and over the toppled gate, and off towards the south.

One

Just outside the long grey walls of the old Bibliothèque Nationale, there is a little garden. The square Louvois. A place of refuge and fresh air for weary scholars, of gravel paths and flowerbeds, shaded by giant chestnut trees. There is a large and ugly fountain at the centre, with four half-clothed amazons in stone, the Loire, Garonne, Saone and Seine, holding the waters aloft. Within days of my arrival, I'd set up a routine, taking something from a patisserie in the colonnades of the Palais Royal, and coming back to eat alone and watch the old women—war widows, I was told—shuffling about and feeding the sparrows. The iron benches were mostly occupied by readers taking a few minutes of air. There was the odd *clochard*, those scrounging tramps in dark and ragged clothing, a few local workers, van drivers, local shop assistants and staff from the Bibliothèque, lazing over their lunch. Summer. Nineteen sixty-eight. The square Louvois, still a tranquil refuge from the rage, the stones, the burning in the streets.

Nick Lethbridge. Lawyer. From the far side of the world. A student now, in England, putting together a thesis on international conventions, in the first days of what I planned as a summer spent in France. Already rattled from misunderstandings in shops. Already exhausted from edging my old right-hand-drive Renault through the streets, and hunting for spots to park. Already upset from a sorry battle with the library, a misunderstanding over my application for a reader's ticket, and I with scarcely enough language to sort it out, much less—it was tersely pointed out, as tempers frayed—take up scarce space in the Bibliothèque.

My arrival was soon noticed. A bundle of rags from an iron bench on the far side struggled up and began to trudge towards me. I judged what loose change I had, what fumbling would be needed to separate out a couple of francs. The rags, though, did not ask for money. He flopped beside me in an outrageous stench, and cleared his throat in a harsh roar of mucus.

—*Salut.*

I knew the stench of bodies long unwashed, how it

invades the nostrils, the mouth, in too-familiar ways. How it clings to the hair and clothing and runs about the body, expelling other smells, all pleasing inhuman distant things like perfume or soap or flowers. How it assaults all the deep commandments of childhood, all the dictates of social life, carrying dread reminders of the club and bearskin, the fire and ring of stones.

The rags grinned. There was a cheeky tongue just visible, quivering between yellowed and broken teeth. Eyes peered out at me through a ragged thatch of hair. The rags moved and parted, and disgorged a grubby hand.

—*Monsieur.*

And that was how I first met Lucien.

I'd seen plenty of *clochards* around the streets before. There are thousands of them in Paris, begging in doorways, sleeping over the pavement grilles and stretched out along the benches in the metro, catching a few hours' sleep during the daylight hours, roaming the city at night to prey on the tourists and scavenge in the bins.

—What are you doing, in the library?

I had expected him to ask for money. My scruffy jeans, my straggling hair, my student air made me an easy target. I'd once been told I had a hungry look myself, with my dark hair and pale skin and hollow cheeks. A look to draw on the blind, the halt, the lame.

I replied tartly, before I'd properly heard. I scanned the square for some escape, my nostrils narrowing against the stinks that rose about us.

—But what is it that you are studying, exactly?

I looked at him more closely. I couldn't guess how old he was. Somewhere between thirty and fifty. Much of his face was covered by hair, a thick, uncut and uncombed tangle that had hardened into spikes; hair that had probably once been light brown but which had darkened in grime and oil into a dark and knotted mass. The part of his face that was not covered in hair was seamed and blurred with ingrained filth. I expected to see the red and weepy eyes of the helpless drunk. Instead, the eyes were bright, inquisitive, insistent.

—Are you an historian?

—Not really. I'm a lawyer. A sort of lawyer. A student.

The rags was still unsatisfied. I tried to pass him off with a few more hazy details, about my doing a bit of special research in Paris. The nineteenth century. Politics.

The rags asked for names, dates, further places. Pressing always closer. Reeking with intent.

I mentioned the Paris Commune and my interest in the fighting in Paris. I talked about the thousands of exiles who were sent out to the South Pacific and my part of the world in the years that followed.

—But who, exactly?

—My great-grandfather. It's a family thing. He was there. He was deported.

—A name, a name!

—His name was Duvernois.

The *clochard* edged even closer, the smells thickening with excitement.

—Duvernois. Duvernois? That tells me something, that does tell me something!

He scratched at his hair, his hands in fraying mittens. He started to scrape fearfully at his face, as though in search of something there.

—*Australie*, you say?

And at length, he offered a triumphant sigh.

—I know this Duvernois. I know about this great-grandfather. Duvernois. I've read things. He was a writer. Not an important writer, but a good one. Very young. Rochefort found him, building barricades. Had him write pieces for *Le Mot d'Ordre*, as I recall. Good pieces. He was an engineer—an architect? He might have been very good, had he not been shot. No, of course Duvernois was not shot. Of course—or you would not be here, no? Deportation. He was, of course, deported. Do you know much about the deportations? The thousands of political prisoners, after the fall of Paris, that were sent out to rot in New Caledonia? There's more, there's more.

His eyes were tightly closed. He ran his fingers even more fiercely through his awful thatch of hair, mumbling to himself, as though sifting through a set of files.

—New Caledonia. The Isle of Pines? Probably the Ducos Peninsula. If he had once been sentenced to death, it was most likely he was sent to Ducos. *L'enceinte fortifiée.* Not that Ducos was really fortified. Sharks, and tales of cannibals. That was all that was needed. Young Duvernois. Who was imprisoned and exiled, and escaped from New Caledonia with Henri Rochefort and the others. The one important escape. Duvernois was the silent one on the boat, the one we don't know much about. He was the one who did not come back, with Grousset and Ballière and Jourde and the others, to fight for the amnesty. He simply disappeared. The others were all famous in some way. They all wrote books, when they got back. Histories. Even novels. But no-one ever asked what happened to poor young Duvernois.

He shuffled closer and put his hand on my arm.

—Why didn't he come back with the others, with Rochefort and Jourde? They all came home to France. Why didn't he come home?

—This is what I'm trying to find out. Why he stayed.

Duvernois, young Duvernois. Ballière and Jourde. The famous Rochefort escape. The ragged bundle shook with enthusiasm. He said he would soon tell me more.

Mumbling, more to himself than to me, that he would have to go away and think about it, and that soon he would be able to tell me much, much more. That he had read everything written by Duvernois. Everything they had in there. He gestured across the road, to the Bibliothèque. The famous escape. The famous Marquis de Rochefort, who wrote a book about it. Three books.

—*Australie*, you say?

He chewed excitedly on the filthy rats' tails of his hair.

He would soon tell me all that I could wish to know. His name, he said, was Lucien. *Enchanté.* He grinned, and offered me, again, a filthy hand.

There is a further, a more distant beginning. The leather trunk. The trunk that my grandmother Agnes had kept up in a loft in the hayshed, on the far side of the world. Just outside Gladstone in the mid-north of South Australia, amid the flat and yellow wheatlands that ran down from the deserts in the north. The trunk that was brought down from the ruin of Mount Deception, up below the Flinders Ranges, many years before. It was full of dress-ups for me and my sisters when we were young: with high-heeled boots with long rows of buttons up the sides, leather leggings and wide straw hats with faded ribbons, dark floral dresses that smelled of must and damp, long coats with collars of fur gone stiff and rank, and piles of ancient yellowing underwear that had frayed and cracked along their folds and broke in pieces when we spread them out. There were bags of trinkets, necklaces and bangles and medals and small metal caskets full of buttons and broken beads, ancient books with damaged spines and curling photographs and bundles of letters and small piles of documents all bound in strings and ribbons.

And with these things, the manuscript. In one of the large cotton drawstring bags were the bits and pieces left behind by the last visitor to Mount Deception, up beyond Quorn and Hawker and much further to the north, where our grandmother Agnes had spent her childhood. There was a long pipe with a broken stem, a folding knife with a wooden handle, a pair of spectacles with only one lens, and a tobacco pouch, long gone stiff and fissured, with a dry and hard-caked crumbling knob in it that might once have been tobacco. And with them, the yellowed pages, the hundreds of written pages of his manuscript, bound together with faded ribbon and stiffened lengths of string.

The paper was brittle with damp and age. Each page was covered with tiny handwriting, almost impossible to read, the writing running not just across the page but up and down the margin and sometimes in great circles that ran out from the centre, in widening loops that were finally lost at the far edge of the page. Stories there were, or poems perhaps, that filled the page and then continued in a thin and snaking scrawl that ran back to the top, turning upside down and then running in between the lines, so that you were forced to search between them for the way the story ran. And often, too, there was writing on the reverse, the ink seeping through to the first side, the jumble of letters then impossible to read and the writer seeming not to care but stabbing rather at his page, the nib dragging through the surface as he wrote.

He was a visitor from nowhere. Old Agnes told of how he stayed, of his writing in the half-darkness of his stone shelter down by the sheepyards, the hessian curtains drawn against the light, with this Monsieur Rouvel, locked in with the heat and always working, as it seemed, on the same small piece of paper. Writing quickly, as though knowing his time was short, with Agnes and her younger sisters watching sometimes from the window, his thick hair falling over his face as he sat scrawling away, squinting at the page, groaning and mumbling strange things under his breath.

The language had been lost, decades ago. The family kept a few familiar phrases, some letters, some old books. Agnes had once spoken a kind of French but had never learned to read it, and never passed it on. And even when I could read a little—schoolboy French, and not much more—I could make little sense of most of what he wrote. Even when I had worked out most of the words, the writings still held no kind of meaning, with each wild idea slipping off into another almost the moment it began. I read about silver obelisks of salt and iron, and voices crying from caverns or cellars far below the earth, about the partitions of the heart, and castles made of frozen tears.

While my sisters would play with the beads and buttons, the pipe and jewellery and old clothes, I used to take the papers to the shade of a pepper tree, and think of this visitor with the straggling hair, of the heat, the smells and hessian curtains. Unable to make much sense of the words, I'd explore the patterns, trace the jagged lines of thinking, hoping that these designs might hold some kind of meaning that was lacking in the tangled words themselves.

I felt always that the crumbling paper, the strange patterns on the page, the words that slipped and coiled and broke or seeped slowly into other words, must hold something that was closer, more like speaking flesh and blood, than the scattered stones far to the north at Mount Deception. An escape from all that was flat and empty, the dry rectangle wheatlands that were the lives of those to follow. The curiosity only grew with obstruction, the infection only spreading with each tangled fragment that

I couldn't understand. Imagining, against all the protests of loving but puzzled parents, alarmed at these signs of deep distraction, that somewhere amid these shreds of yellow paper I would learn something of this family lost to silence; something about a house that was quickly abandoned and a family divided, and then all gates shut on the past.

Against the ruin of Deception and Agnes's stubborn silence, against all the dry unpeopled country to the north, the vast plains of time and distance that now stretched between me and Mount Deception, I imagined that these shreds of yellow paper would one day help me put it all together. Thinking always, and against my solid and steady flatland childhood, that there couldn't be such wealth of mystery without some kind of meaning. That the less the bits and pieces seemed to hang together, the richer the whole pattern had to be. That one day when I'd gathered all the pieces, when I'd found out all there was to know, it would at last speak for itself. My world would then be whole, as solid and sure and seamless as it seemed to be for my parents, and for my sisters, climbing and shrieking and calling loudly to me to join them, in their gaudy fraying dress-ups from the trunk.

My new friend Lucien was a famous man. A famous scholar. Everyone who worked on French history found their way to the Bibliothèque Nationale, and everyone who worked at the Bibliothèque Nationale soon came to know of Lucien. In former times, they found themselves next to him under the huge cupolas of the *salle des lecteurs*, and were soon forced to move upwind. More recently, they would have seen him in the square Louvois, as they came out for air and exercise. And those who took the trouble to speak to him—those who clenched their nostrils and risked just the few short moments that it took to find out just who this Lucien was—would take back stories of him to others, who came in turn to the Bibliothèque and the square Louvois to keep an eye out for this tattered encyclopaedia expelled so roughly from the *salle*. Not that there was ever any move to have him reinstated. But popular indignation at what had happened had only added to his fame.

I was told the story of Lucien by another scholar, a foreign researcher I had met by chance, the day I got my reader's ticket at the Bibliothèque Nationale. I was working in the vast chamber where they brought you the old newspapers, turning the pages of the Marquis de Rochefort's *La Lanterne* as carefully as possible, when two pages stuck together. The deep silence of the room was broken by the sound of tearing paper. Across the table, another reader—the only other person working in the room—gave a loud and amused 'tsk, tsk,' and we began to talk. He was Canadian, a professor. His field, he said, was Condorcet.

He suggested coffee.

—Lucien? So you've met old Lucien? Well, perhaps he's not all that old, you know. They don't live long, these *clochards*. Lucien would not be forty. But he's an institution around here. I hope you didn't tell him that you thought he was a tramp?

I had not.

—Good. He calls himself a private scholar. But it's a long time now since he's been allowed in any library in Paris. He's living off the twenty years or so he spent here in the *salle des lecteurs*, reading every article, every piece of newsprint, every book in the whole goddamn library.

The Canadian was big and bluff, very formally dressed for library work in a grey business suit and escutcheoned tie.

—He used to be a scholar. In the normal sense, I mean. He wrote a doctorate for the Sorbonne. The big doctorate. On Auguste Blanqui, I think it was, and the Paris Commune. He became more and more involved in his work. Then he began to smell. It all got very difficult.

The Canadian paled at his own stinking memories of poor Lucien. He took a long gulp of coffee to steady himself.

—I should warn you, it can get on top of you, this sort of work. Month after month of it. It's a professional hazard. The boundaries get confused. You lose distance. Sometimes, he thinks he's back there, in the thick of it, the barricades, the smell of cordite. Happens to all of us. Sometimes I think I'm more like Condorcet than myself.

He laughed heartily at his joke.

I looked at the Canadian, with all his comfortable distance, his suit and clean shirt, his insistent deodorant, his spotless tie. I thought of Lucien reeking on his bench, over in the square Louvois.

He sipped his coffee, and went on.

—One day, they told Lucien that too many readers were complaining. That he could clean up, or stay away. He chose to stay away. For a time, he was a kind of wandering scholar, moving around a shrinking stock of libraries that would let him in—the Bibliothèque Arsenal, Sainte Geneviève, the Comédie-Française, and finally the libraries of some of the religious houses, until he let them know his religious views. Lucien is one of your old republican anti-clericals. Have the heads off the lot of 'em in a trice.

—When the Arsenal finally caved in to the protest and threw him out, he gave up altogether. He keeps up with things by picking the brains of people like you, over in the square Louvois. Out there, and in a dozen other spots all over Paris. Gives as good as he gets, too. Lately, the rough living has been catching up with him. People say he's getting a bit confused. One thing running into another.

I told him of my talk with Lucien.

—The Commune. Eighteen forty-eight. The Prussians. Dreyfus. You try him on anything. He's told me things about Condorcet that I never knew. Way outside his period. Way outside his field. He'll pick up a hint of something, and a few days later he'll be back with a mine of information, just dredged out of some dusty corner of his own brain. Or maybe he's got it all filed away, in garbage bins all over Paris. Soon, he'll start asking you to read things for him. You just wait and see. Always interesting things. Articles in obscure political journals that ran for a few issues somewhere in the early 1830s or 1870s, and then simply ran out of ideas.

The Canadian was plump and rosy. His admiration for Lucien, though, was unbounded and sincere.

—Oh yes, our Lucien is quite a character. Has he told you about his trips up to Montmartre? To the Basilica? Usually, he begins by telling people that. Something he's now quite famous for, as well.

—To Montmartre? Does he go there to pray? Some kind of commemoration?

The Canadian went off in hoots of laughter, sending

his coffee splashing and putting the fine tie at risk. He mopped up with his paper serviette.

—You could say that. Some kind of commemoration! Yes, I guess you really could say that.

He saw that I was getting annoyed.

—Look, I'll let him tell you about it. I'll leave it to him to explain.

I am, I think, an Ishmael. A bit like poor Lucien. A wanderer. Born of a stolid race of stayers, but with some remote infection, some taint of long meandering in the blood. Teased from contentment by the spaces left by my grandmother Agnes, the oldest of the girls, the one who was left behind. Drawn by the gaps, the sudden awkward endings in what she told of Deception. Wanting, from early childhood, to know what really happened. Wanting to understand, indeed, why I should be the one to care.

I spent a lot of time with Agnes. More than any of the others. We would sit out on her verandah. She would work with her needle, measuring each careful stitch, and I would sit alongside, just swapping yarns, as she would call it, she in her bagging orange chair and me chipping at the edge of the planks of the verandah with my pocket knife, or fooling with a kitten and a bit of string. Often, we said nothing. Agnes seemed to feel it was enough just to sit and watch the plants grow, to watch as, day after day, the tendrils from the mile-a-minute would swing and coil and find their place—a branch, a nail, a string of wire—to twine and dry and harden, with another wandering tendril soon reaching out and searching for a hold. This, and watching the summer flowers, the geraniums, daisies and petunias turning to the sun, and the yellow patches slowly spreading in the lawn as the summer heat beat on, the sandy patches that always dried out in the summer, no matter how much she sprinkled and watered in the evening shade.

Her usual place was in her sagging canvas chair, sunning herself in company with the cats, often with Tinker, the big tortoiseshell, basking in her lap. She would stroke him with her old and mottled hands, the cat kneading in bliss the cushion of her heavy thighs, his claws breaking on occasion through the dark floral of her summer dress and the thick weave of her stockings, to score the skin and break the summer peace. After a fond scolding and a heavy shake, the old woman and the cat would rearrange themselves, with the cat beginning then to purr again. Thoughts turning upon little. The cat kneading her thighs.

There was a bond between us. Not one we ever talked about, but one that she acknowledged in the things she did not tell the others, of her riding out on Princess with the crow pistol and her times down at the camp, her secret places along the creek where there was almost always water that the others never knew about, and the big rock where it was said the blacks used to go to die, long before the white men came. At those moments, she would speak in a voice that was scarcely her own, a voice retrieved from long ago, and together we'd swap tales of nests and conquerable trees, and she'd tell me more of the hills around Deception, and her sisters and her father, and the droughts.

Agnes's stories came in jagged fragments, rising out of nowhere and with no special end in view. In tales of how the sisters had played together in a barricaded yard, hemmed in by slabs of native pine. In stories of the old house at Deception, the shutters closed against the midday sunlight, and in the story of how she was once chased by a wild cow she'd shot at with the crow pistol, the shot just angering it with all that noise and smoke, the sharp thump and the sting of the cardboard wadding. Agnes could tell a good yarn, giving you the yard itself, the rough bark on the slabs, the cranky cow with its wet nose and heaving flanks, her horse run off and she left hanging from the branches, scraping madly for a toehold on the trunk. It was always like that. She liked to keep things simple. She shied away from explanations. The pain of the family's sudden leaving was real enough, and she could talk about that. But she couldn't tell why it happened, or why she and her father were left behind.

Agnes's childhood had ended on that dusty day in February 1893. Waiting in an empty house for her father to return, with nothing to tell him other than that she had stood by the gate and watched them go. Just once, she told me something more about this leaving, of Monsieur Rouvel limping along the verandah and clambering awkwardly onto the sweating horse. It was something she saw through the dust, the biting sand that forces you to close your eyes or watch through slotted fingers. She remembered a door slamming, and her mother bursting from the house, striding over to where the younger children played. She saw the children called back to the house and, at last, her mother, her long dark hair unpinned and her burning cheeks striped by dust and tears, suddenly wet against her own in a last rushed kiss, telling her to wait, that she must tell Papa, that she must wait, and come with Papa. She saw a horse, strapped into the gig by Fritz and brought up to the front, the gig quickly loaded and the horse flogged on one flank and then the other with the loose lick of the rein, her mother standing unsteadily with the whip coiling and cracking high above her sisters' heads, the horse then twisting and stumbling its way over the toppled gate and out into the storm of whistling sand.

Within weeks of Marie-Josèphe's leaving Agnes was sent down to the nuns at Port Augusta, who began with strict determination to tame this odd creature, wild as a young rabbit, her father a foreigner, and with a mother who'd committed the one sin that could not be forgiven: to run off in hard times. This was the end of childhood, with nothing left that you could call childhood, not the rapping of knuckles across the piano keys, the evening rosaries and the dressing screens, the white beds set out like slabs in a mortuary, and the hot tears going cold against the chill starch of the pillow. Wondering in the darkness where the others were and why she was not with them, what curse it was that had sent them away and what even greater curse had left her behind. Wondering about her sisters and Maman, about who was looking after Princess, and why Papa had sent her there at all, to learn things she would never need to know when everyone came back to Deception in the end.

I was the curious one. I've spoken of infection. Was it what Agnes told, or what Agnes failed to tell? I felt I'd spent my life as Agnes spent that lonely week after they left, moving through an abandoned house, following an absence that roamed from room to darkened room, peering into ransacked drawers and unmade beds, lying awake and listening in futile hope for the sounds of the travellers' return, as she must have stayed awake in the darkness of those seven uncertain nights, listening to the cracking of the cooling roof, hoping for the friendly sounds of dogs and harness, for some familiar form of movement at the door. Waiting in the empty house, with a saddled but riderless horse limping back from the west, and with no sign of Monsieur Rouvel. Waiting with all the windows closed and the shutters locked against the wind, the beds strewn with clothing and all the detritus of a rushed departure, the wardrobes gaping open and drawers dripping with abandoned clothes. Learning how to live without explanations, to concentrate on the things you could know and smell and touch, the banging shutters, the creaking iron, the horse with saddle twisted, its reins dragging, limping back into the yard.

A week it was before her father finally returned, making his way back with a hungry and depleted flock, threading his way back through orchards of hot rocks that stretched for miles about them, making his way through wide and open fields that bloomed in red fragments, through broad paddocks richly sewn with stone. Back to the silent girl who waited in the shuttered darkness of the house, listening to the creaking iron, trying over and over the words which would tell of all that happened and still tell nothing, words which broke in pieces even as she spoke. Leaving me, so many decades later, still adrift among the fragments, amid the fag-ends of her stories, still struggling through a thousand further repetitions to peer more clearly through those cracks and broken edges. Leaving me to look again, from the very corner of Agnes's uncertain eye and through that one fraction of telling, towards the children and the lizard, the man struggling with that resisting horse, and the scattered ring of stones.

Two

I WENT DOWN, FINALLY, to Saint-Germain-sur-École. Uncertain of what I might find. After two weeks of hesitation in Paris, two weeks of lonely confusion in a city sunk in disruption, with buildings closed and traffic blocked and fire and violence in the streets, shops closed and library hours erratic and the nights filled with tramping feet, sirens and smoke and angry shouting. Something I felt I should somehow be a part of, but most of which I did not understand. After two weeks of excitement but of quickly fading hope, of fragile leads that went nowhere and archives closed and interviews refused, I went down to see what traces I might possibly pick up at Saint-Germain-sur-École.

Two weeks of hesitation, after waiting for so long. I

was nervous about this visit. Anxious at what I might, or might not find. I went, in the end, at Lucien's insistence. My new friend Lucien, who felt there must be some better way of picking up the thread, someone who might recall their living there, perhaps even one of the great-aunts themselves, or some further descendant like myself, still close to that address. I knew where to go. Agnes once showed me an old envelope with *Inconnu à cette adresse* scrawled across it, from three parts of a century before. The last moment of contact. A farewell to all connection. Unknown at this address.

Saint-Germain-sur-École is a hamlet in the southern Île de France, on the margins of the Forest of Fontainebleau, a pretty place, with its old water mill and ancient sheltered wash-house, its tiny spartan church and winding stone-walled lanes. A house there had been left to my great-grandmother, Marie-Josèphe, by an uncle, along with the land that ran along the stream towards the neighbouring village, Dannemois. This, my family knew from Agnes, who had heard her parents speak of it; of a large house, the grandest in the village, empty and waiting, with her mother arguing and protesting, wanting to go home.

Saint-Germain-sur-École. They had lived there at least for a time, on their return to France, my great-grandmother Marie-Josèphe and her daughters. The family had known that because a lawyer from Port

Augusta, sorting out Deception's tangled affairs, managed to pass on to them the news of my great-grandfather's death. Marie-Josèphe then wrote at last to Agnes, who was already losing her French, unable perhaps to read it at all and determined now to stay in Australia. Agnes had shown me that letter too, just once and long before I could hope to understand. At the time of her death, the letter disappeared. The income from the property in France had been enough to allow Marie-Josèphe to pass what was left of Deception over to Agnes at the time of her marriage. Her new Australian family promptly grabbed the stock, the curtains, glass and roofing iron, surrendered up the lease and closed the gate behind them. It is possible that Agnes never replied to her mother's letter. All links just died away.

I found a lane blocked by a tractor, but the tractor driver helpful, showing me by a simple gesture the way to the house. It was the grandest in the village, as Agnes had been told, but was now in grander disarray. The high walls had toppled here and there, and across a ragged screen of trees and bushes I could see the wretched state of the upper storeys, the deeply fissured façade, the shattered *œils-de-boeuf* peering out from the high, mossy-slated mansard roof.

Still, the place was impressive. The tall windows on each floor were imposing despite the broken panes and clumsy patching, the boards and loss of paint and fallen stone. More signs of disrepair stood out starkly as I came nearer, with downpipes that had parted from the gutters, eaves prised apart by the ivy that had climbed, twisted the timbers and then died, leaving matted, greying runners that ran like raw nerves across the walls.

The gate was open. It was a huge wrought-iron tangle, crowned with imposing coils and spikes but now sadly awry, its left side hanging from a single hinge, its lower edge half buried in the gravel and the weeds. I swung the Renault into the gateway and looked along what had been the drive, leading to a set of mossy steps before the house. It was blocked by low branches, a wild flourishing of weeds and tangled grass. Not far from the gate I could see the rusting skeleton of an early 2CV, its roofing fabric torn and stretched low with the weight of fallen leaves, its tyres flat and weathered, its remaining windows smeared opaque with grime and spiders' webs. It now served as a dovecote, with grey and white heads popping in and out of the raised side-flaps, and droppings cascading, layer upon layer, down the grey and rusting doors.

The house was battered enough, looked at from the gate. Closer up, the disorder was worse, a clutter of old furniture spread about below the steps and along the deeper reaches of the drive. What had once been a garden was strewn with dismantled appliances and splintered fruit boxes. To the left lay the spilling innards of a discarded mattress, its sodden kapok spread like soiled and melting snow across the grass. Further down the side of the house, there was bank after bank of bird cages, ramshackle structures of wood and wire and netting, interwoven with the branches and tacked down around other household remnants: rain-warped chests with yawning drawers, old sideboards and bookshelves—anything that could block a gap or shelter nesting birds.

My ageing Renault made a commotion in the stillness of the place. The crackle of the exhaust caused chaos in the cages, where battered racks of pigeons, parrots, ducks and even sparrows and starlings began to protest at my arrival with a sudden outburst of shrieks and angry twitterings, and a furious beating of wings. When the motor stopped and the commotion settled, there was nothing but a dead, damp, dripping silence, the house as though deserted, with no living thing to be seen.

I wandered to the nearest of the cages, and called down the side of the house. There was no response. The only sign of movement was a large orange cat which appeared through the leaves, slinking along a low wall to his right, its eye fixed on the beating wings in the first of the ramshackle cages.

I walked over to the wall, and reached up to it, the

cat stretching forward at the prospect of a chuck under the chin.

—*Go! Get out of here!*

Something struck me on the shoulder and glanced off, clipping my ear in its path. It was an old shoe, or perhaps a block of wood, solid enough and flung with enough force to bring water to my eyes.

—Out! Go! There's nothing for you here. Go home!

At the top of the steps stood an ancient woman bound up in a filthy green overcoat over a sagging cardigan, her long grey hair straggling like antennae from a tangled, drooping bun. As I turned, she came quickly down the steps with an unsteady hobbling gait. She was brandishing an old single-barrelled shotgun, waving it recklessly in my direction, but shouting, as it happened, at the cat.

—*Sale bête.* I've warned that cat!

One of the aunts, perhaps? Colette? Or Clémentine or Geneviève? I could not have asked for richer promise in her age, the wandering hair, the sheer oddness of it all. She expressed no surprise at finding me there. She showed me the gun. Still looking for the cat.

—I'll use it. I told her, Madame Fromentin, the next time that cat comes over the wall, I won't be afraid to use it.

I nursed my injured ear. She hobbled over to the side of the house to prop up the gun, and began taking birdseed from the bottom of an old and once-ornate commode that lay gaping against the wall.

I made an offer to assist with the bucket. What I was about to say now seemed rather silly, my whole momentous tale of distance and exile and the loss of generations quite muddled by the birdseed, the bucket, the business with the cat.

—Madame. Madame? My name is Nick Lethbridge. *Nicolas.* Your nephew, perhaps? Great-nephew. I am from Australia.

She paused in her work. She peered not at me, but into the depths of the garden.

—We were all born in Australia.

—Yes. I think that you are perhaps my aunt. My great-aunt, that is.

—I've told her. I'll use it. *Sale bête!*

—I'm Agnes's grandson. Agnes. Your sister?

She did not respond. She filled the bucket, and I carried it to the cages for her, holding back a jagged flap in the netting so that the dangling tatters of her coat would not be snagged. When the bucket was empty, the feathers brushed off and her boots wiped, she turned and squinted up at me, her eyes red-rimmed, sceptical.

—If you are from Australia then you must talk to our sister. You must talk to Colette.

She gestured towards the house with a shrug of her shoulder, and turned back to her birds.

I climbed the steps. The front door was wide open. I could see into the hall, and partly up the stairs. The interior seemed in better order. It was still elaborately furnished, the lower floor at least, despite the wreckage strewn around the steps. The darkly papered walls were draped with pictures, sombre portraits and country scenes encased in dully gilded frames. In the dim salons that opened to the right and left, I could see further signs of a remote way of living, in heavy mantelpieces laden with a fine clutter of tarnished *ormolu*, ornate clocks and intricately sculpted objects, straining nymphs and startled reindeer, and glass-fronted cabinets preserving racks of porcelain. Old. Dusty. Not like any house I had been in before.

The bell no longer worked. I knocked and waited for a time, and then knocked again. There was silence, apart from the sound of singing and the beating of wings back at the birdcages. I stepped inside and hallooed feebly up the stairs. Then I called more loudly, my voice echoing from the first and second floor. Above, there was a sound of banging doors and female voices, and then a series of demands, not questions, came beating down the stairs.

—Who is it? Say who you are! What is it that you want?

I called my name. There was a long silence.

—Your great-nephew. From Australia.

There was a longer silence.

It was some minutes before the hem of a dark skirt and a thick-heeled shoe appeared at the top of the stairs. I could hear a stick cautiously placed, a slow movement down the steps.

—Australia?

—Yes. Your great-nephew, I think. The grandson of your sister Agnes?

I saw the feet, the dark skirt, the careful probing with a stick. She came down to my level, edging her way down the stairs, feeling her way cautiously but with her eyes alert, searching, firmly fixed not on the steps but on this stranger waiting below. The stick a firm support. Perhaps a weapon.

She was tall, taller than me, her grey hair drawn severely into place, her back stiffly straight despite the stick, her air collected and intent.

—I am Colette.

We peered at each other in the half-light. I searched for some shred of likeness, some touch of mind or body's kinship with my grandmother, old Agnes, with her sunflowers and geraniums and cats. This same Colette, whom I knew of only in those brief eluding glimpses in the stories Agnes told, the young girl who appeared suddenly from nowhere on the verandah, her hair moving about her in the wind. The tall young girl with freckles and with auburn hair, the last to be called by her mother to join them in the gig, the horse and cart then running out across the fallen gate and out into the dust that blew up along the Hawker road. Hatless, unlike the others, with her hair still blowing in soft clouds about her face as she looked back for one last lingering moment to the house.

When she arrived at the base of the staircase, she offered me a hand that trembled, yet had strength in it, drawing me around so that the weak light fell more strongly on my face. For quite a time she did not speak a word but only examined me, as a statue, or a photograph.

—Nicholas, you say? It is not a family name. *Nicolas?*

Without waiting for an answer, she moved across to the salon on the left, motioning for me to join her with an elegant sweep of her hand, showing me into a darkened room rich in dim mementos and muted portraits and medallions and cabinets of dusty bric-a-brac. She showed me to a seat that was carefully positioned, positioned out of the light, and more for listening than for speaking. She looked me over, closely, before taking her own chair, near the window. Her eyes, grey-blue, still searched my face as she began to speak. As though seeking some known shape, some familiar expression.

She began by marking distance.

—If you are Agnes's grandson, then I am indeed your great-aunt Colette. I hope that you speak some French. We do not speak a word of English. We have not spoken English since we left Mount Deception. Not a word.

Mount Deception. Our family knew the basic story. It was the tale of a whole landscape that was cleared and ploughed and sown and soon abandoned. At the time when that part of the country was settled, everyone knew that it was just a desert, a dry land shooting tips of green with each chance rain that passed, but then slipping back to rock and shale as the heat and dry returned. Those who had passed through it, for thousands of years before, knew this was no place to stay. The explorers and surveyors who then rode up from the fertile plain of Adelaide, across the plains and towards the ridge of barren hills that marked the route to the west, could record nothing but ungenerous withered trees and blasted grass and endless space for bitter disappointment. They turned back, leaving their advice behind them in names like Mount Hopeless, Mount Misery, Mount Deception.

Paul-Auguste Duvernois, we knew, had come across from Sydney in the mid-1870s, and had taken up a small block at the furthest margin of the newly opened wheatland regions, just beyond Wilpena and the northern Willochra Plain. It was a modest beginning, but enough to set the imagination running, with Paul and others like him soon caught up in the excitement of a string of lucky years. Chance must have seemed like destiny, good luck like just reward. The settlers pushed further into the wastelands until 1879, the year that followed Marie-Josèphe's arriving to join him, in time to see the last good harvest and the beginnings of decline. She arrived in time to share a decade of wasted hopes and thankless effort and desire tamed into failure, with the rain simply giving out, the rust coming on and then the locusts, the plagues of grasshoppers that soon drove most of them back in ruin to the south.

About Paul himself, my family knew little. There was little that even Agnes could, or was prepared to tell. We knew of a dour and silent Frenchman, appearing from nowhere with no past he cared to speak of, to take up the run, with his wife and the first of his daughters arriving some time later. Speaking to almost no-one. Listening to no-one's advice. Building, in the years of growth, a house that was aggressive in its grandeur, in the foolish scale of its conception. We knew little of the early years of labour, of felling trees and piling rocks. We knew that Paul had managed somehow to pay his deposit and buy the tools needed to clear the land and harvest his first crops. That the crops were successful, and that he cleared and planted more, and soon bought out his neighbours, and then cleared and planted even more. We knew that, as others began to drift away in the early 1880s, he was able to convert his holdings into pastoral leases, to take on the wreckage of his neighbours and to lease a larger run.

But about this, there were few records. Few letters, documents, no reports from friends. There is a Frenchman's Creek among the dry gullies that cross Willochra Plain, and a Frenchman's Peak on the low range named Mount Deception, which may have been named for him. The main monument though, after generations of slow decay, lies in the ruins of the house. Paul's grave is not far distant, on a low rise above the flat where he laid out his house. The stone is still standing, his name, dates and *Requiescat in Pace* already fading in the softness of the stone. From there, you can still view the layout of Deception, the low toppled walls and outbuildings, its immense chimneys alone intact. You can look out across the plain towards the mountains, towards Mount Deception itself, or to the south, into the country where the trail of ruins begins, and threads its way through the broken country that leads back towards the south.

In my childhood, the family made just a few trips up to the place. It was a long passage through what nature itself had appeared to deem a no-man's-land, a long slow trip which traced the scale of the disaster in sluggish dusty stages, a dry scene of devastation that for practical and cautious farmers like my father just meant mistake and misdirection, dismissed with a shake of the head as something just Too Damn Daft for words. With our tents and waterbags, my sisters quickly restless and wanting to go home, we made our way north by gravel roads and through the choking dust into a ghost terrain of ruined stone cottages and abandoned town sites, past road signs pointing only to further road signs that pointed back the way we came. We passed by abandoned farms and ruined cottages, twisted windmills and broken fences, and wondered at the towns that were laid out but never built, the bridges and cuttings for railways that had never run, the parks that saw no children, and the cemeteries marked out amid the saltbush and still yawning for their dead.

Of all those who knew Deception, it was perhaps old Agnes who understood it best. Agnes who, unlike the rest of us, had lived up in that country where so little ever ran to ready answers, to neat and pleasing endings. Perhaps Agnes, with all her gaps and sudden silences, was the best keeper of the past, standing back from fuller stories, cautious always about rising beyond what she had touched and felt. It's the mystery that is concrete, the explanations that are abstract. That's what she seemed to say. That's what she seemed to tell me, through all her fragments of stories, those teasing Deception glimpses that would last a certain distance and then fade off into others. I might have listened much more closely and, demanding less, learned more. Perhaps Agnes showed the best path to knowledge, when it comes to bringing back the past, in tales of the bite of sand, of the crash of a door, of old things in a trunk, of ancient clothing, newspapers, a pipe and tobacco pouch. Of that hatless girl with auburn hair passing over the toppled gate, her hair still tossed about her face as she looked back for that last moment to the house.

She sat me down amid the musty cushions, the deep uneven folds and bare threads of fraying tapestry, the past she spoke of pressing on us from the worn textures, the paper curling and discolouring from the walls, the clutter of old photographs and other dry mementos of the dead, the weakness of the sun now shining as a brittle glare upon the grime of those few windows left unshuttered against the day. There was no sign of freckles. No relic of auburn hair. Her skin was pale, almost translucent in the pale reflected light.

She asked me, first, about Agnes. Of her living, and her dying. A necessary telling, but one, I could see, that she read as a form of accusation. *Inconnu à cette adresse*. I did all I could to reassure. I told her the full story of a good marriage, of children, of the marriages of those children and even of those children's children. I spoke warmly of how Agnes's life was, in the end, a happy one.

—It was never our intent—never our mother's idea—that she should stay. You must understand. Only that she should wait. Wait for our father. That was all.

There were obstructions, I should understand. Long delays. And then their father's death. It seemed better, then, that she should stay. A cruelty, but perhaps a cruelty that was needed, to ensure that happiness?

I told her then a little of myself, of my parents and my own childhood on the farm just out of Gladstone, and of our trips up to Deception. Of the time I spent with Agnes in her old age, of the verandah, her cats, her stories of Deception. Colette's manner seemed to soften as my life took on more shape and more connection, as we moved away from Agnes and the time of their leaving, to speak more broadly of her father and Mount Deception, and Saint-Germain-sur-École.

—I thought, perhaps, you would help me. That you could tell me more about those times, Tante Colette. More than the archives, the papers.

She smiled now, and warmly. Tante Colette? Her hand trembled on her stick.

—Your Tante Colette, indeed. And Tante Clémentine, whom you met in the garden. And your dear Tante

Geneviève, too, who is upstairs. Whom you will meet, as soon as she is well. We are not accustomed to many visitors. We live so privately. *Tante Colette*.

She toyed with the words, almost as though they were an object to be measured and enjoyed.

—There is so much I would like to know, Tante Colette, about Mount Deception. The old house. And your father.

She moved at last from searching my face, and off towards some more distant place. She was silent for a time. Looking about her and to the middle distance, as though there was something of Deception still lingering in the air. As though choosing where to grasp, at what point to begin.

—We always thought that someone would come. I always imagined someone older. Someone my own age. Until, of course, that became unlikely. Then impossible. In time, I think, we simply forgot about your country. Though not, I should tell you, about Agnes. You ask about Deception. Is it not better, though, that I should begin much earlier, with the story of my parents? It is surely better, Monsieur—*Nicolas*—that you understand why they came, as much as why we left. Is this not one of your questions, why they came?

She smiled, now more fondly, as she pronounced my name. So often, she said, they had sat in this same room late into the night, she and her mother, when neither of them could sleep, and especially in the early years when they were still waiting for Agnes and her father to join them from Deception. So often they had sat together on that same *canapé* where I now sat, where they would drink chocolate together, and talk of Agnes and the girls' father, and what they had left behind.

—Your great-grandfather, you may know, was a captain in the engineers. Paul Duvernois. He was an architect, at the head of his class at the École des Beaux-Arts. It was then he met my mother. Your great-grandmother. It is the story of a young woman, up from the country, from Provins. In Paris to improve herself. Of an apartment in the avenue de Tourville. Of the affection, and the watchful eye, of her Tante Agathe, in whose care she was placed. She was no more than a girl, you understand.

I watched her closely, as her eyes strayed off again. The intricate cameo brooch set high at her throat, the sudden whiteness of her collar and cuffs against her dark and well-worn velvet, her grey hair fixed back with fierce precision. Had her mother looked like that? Not in the photograph that stood above us on the mantelpiece. Paris, 1870. Studio Penot, rue Richelieu. Blurred sepia. A tall dark-haired young woman, boxed up in a stiffly tailored dress, her hair piled high, her brown eyes framed by brows a shade too straight; handsome, expressionless for the camera, book in hand. A gentle face, uncertain of itself.

Colette saw where I was looking. She gestured towards a second oval frame, set up beside that of her mother. A young man.

—Twenty-three years old, he was, when the photograph was taken. You can see how fine he was, even when so very young, and in that splendid uniform. Enlisted in the Emperor's army to save Paris from the Prussians.

She turned her head and looked at me across the half-light of the room. Searching my eyes as though for some trace of reflection, some shadow from these lives that went before. Paul-Auguste Duvernois. I looked at the thin-shouldered but handsome youth with sad eyes and an impressive waxed moustache, with a collar and a bagging coat that was far too large, as though he had been thrust into a uniform that was made for someone else.

—My father. Your great-grandfather, Nicholas.

The dark, straight hair. The lick of hair that strayed across the forehead, even in the formal studio pose. The thin face. The long neck. The boy clothed as a man.

—Like you, when at your age.

I should know, she said, of her parents' first meeting. As a place to begin. It was another time like this, of violence and disturbance in the streets. Her mother had been brought by her Uncle Claude, the brother of her Tante Agathe, to the house of one Madame de Verneuil, just one among the many grand houses so recently thrown up on the old plain of Monceau. It was a time of war, the very beginning of the war against the Prussians, and all was still excitement, all gaiety and thoughts of glory, the men parading in their splendid uniforms, the conversation full of tales of easy victory, the glories of Empire.

Her mother told of the excitement of a vast and coiling staircase with marbled steps and gilded ornamental foliage, of entering on the arm of Uncle Claude. She told of wearing for the first time a dress that fell low across her shoulders, and of the splendid jewellery that he had bought her just days before from a friend newly established in the place Vendôme. It all began in brightness, with the hiss of gas, the shifting colours, the glittering chandeliers. With the carriages arriving, the servants in livery, the lights that glimmered in reflection in the puddles in the boulevard de Courcelles. With splendid people crowding up the stairs and spilling into the vast and bright-lit rooms.

And then, there came a sudden darkness. An unwelcome presence, a stranger's body coming near. She told of how her uncle had turned away into conversation with another, of how she was left alone for just one frightening moment at the centre of the room. Of an approach from the depth of shadow, of cruel eyes and lank and greasy hair, of a face too close, of intimate whispers and of warm stale breath upon her face and neck and naked shoulders, and she remembering, only then, the tales of Madame de Verneuil's foolish flirtation with the fashionable Opposition. How all that festered in the north and on the far side of the river had come to haunt the new world of Monceau.

—It was then that my father rescued her. As she would often tell. Of how he pushed his way between them, speaking to my mother as though to a close acquaintance, pushing the other aside. It was then that he took her by the arm and led her away, across the room and back to her uncle Claude, distracted and laughing in a far part of the room. That was how they met. My parents. It was then that it began. A wonderful story. With so many secret meetings, beyond the watchful eye of her Tante Agathe, such happy times to follow. Even in such times.

Tante Colette fell silent.

That warm breath on her breasts and naked shoulders. It seemed to me an odd detail for Marie-Josèphe to tell her daughters, so many years afterwards. It seemed an even odder thing for a daughter to want to pass on, and to someone still a stranger. That old Colette, her own body so closely buttoned against any such intrusion, so stiff and unsmiling in the half-light of her dusty salon, should choose something so fleeting, so young, so very fleshly, as the best point to begin.

—There is much more. This is a detail. No more than a beginning. You will of course come again. And I will tell you much more of their early times together. Such romantic adventures they had together, even in those troubled times.

She rose awkwardly from her chair.

—You will come again, and meet Monsieur Jalabert. Our lawyer. As his father was before him. And who is now our oldest friend. There is much that he can tell you. So much he knows. The history of those times. The grand events.

She brushed away assistance, and reached for her stick.

—Clémentine, as you have seen, is quite confused, and our sister Geneviève is ill. I am older than the others. I can remember more. I was my mother's confidant. We were always close. I am the best one to tell you the story of what happened. Of my parents, and Deception.

She took my arm, and smiled. There was real warmth now in the firm grasp of her hand. As though I had passed some test, or had answered, perhaps, to some shadow of what she felt she saw in those parental photographs?

—When you come again, you must stay longer, *Nicolas*. When you come, I will tell you more. We will show you the things we have from those times. From the time of Tante Agathe. And later. The letters and old photographs. And I will tell you stories, all my mother told me, here, in this very room, when we talked about those times.

She led me towards the door, the hall, the steps that led down towards the gates. We ignored a distant crashing from the direction of the cages. She drew me to her, to place her cheek against mine. Holding her face to mine for quite a time. Letting the body speak, in that moment. She still held my hand.

—*Nicolas*. Our new nephew. Nicholas! It is important that you know. You must come many times. It is important also that the telling match the happening. So many things that are strange, without reasonable explanation, are sometimes less so when you come to know them in slow stages, in the way they came about. This house. Our lives. So that with the knowledge will come the understanding that is needed. So that you may pass it on to your children, for them to tell their children the stories that my mother told.

I drove back to Paris, the light rain falling on the windscreen, amid the fading scent of lavender and a remote memory of some other ancient perfume, one that brought to mind Tante Colette's careful story, the light of gas that fell upon the whiteness of bare shoulders, the glint of splendid jewels, the swirl of precious fabrics and the motion of fans against the heat from the vast fires that were lit against the rain that fell outside, the soft light that dropped from chandeliers that floated like bright suns above those gilded rooms. Seeking to bring, as Colette had insisted, the understanding up to match the telling. To know, to feel, to draw, almost as distant and fading memories, on all I had seen or read or had been told.

Early nightfall it must have been at the new house of this Madame de Verneuil, with the carriages arriving in the wet beneath the deep red glow of Chinese lanterns, the liveried footmen in cloth of gold waiting at the doors, the light that played in soft shadows on the columns and ran in glittering motions across the shining frames and gilt cornices and deep into the gleam of lacquered furniture, the rich mix of Japanese screens and ornate chinoiserie and silken hangings in red and gold, to be swallowed at last in the deep Genoa velvet curtains, the dim retreating pigments of ancient tapestries and the darkened portraits that looked down from the walls.

She stood at the centre of the room, suddenly caught up in this struggle, and with no help to be found. Feeling for the first time in all that perfumed circus of rouge and painted beauty the true breath of the wilderness. Finding in these barbed and whispered compliments her first knowledge that men could act like beasts, that all the care and order she had to that time known was just a fragile artificial thing bred out of good intentions and long years of cultivation and delicacy and respect and care, her father presiding in dark suit and strictly tied cravat, the old *curé* at the Provins dinner table, the music lessons and the strict regimes of Tante Agathe; an eggshell world that broke apart in moments before the cruelty of a laughter which mocked at every word she uttered. Laughing away her family and the old *curé*'s blessing, her father's fine cravat and the genteel life of Provins and all hopes of victory and the Empire itself and even Tante Agathe. His hands playing on her in ways that might not have been offensive were it not for the insinuating smile, the play of words as though across her body, and those dark and calculating eyes that swam within the deep pools of his heavy spectacles, and circled like a pair of feeding sharks.

Taking her arm, a gesture appearing to all others harmless but with those fingers biting deep into her flesh, he now forced her to turn her eyes towards the long gilt-framed mirrors, asking that she should see how every effect, each solid and luxurious impression, each bright ornament and even the dancers themselves were just reflected from one glass to another, challenging her to show what was real and what was mere illusion, where so much that milled about her was made up of fragile melting light that ran from one side to the other.

And it was then perhaps that she first saw him, the tall and pale young man with loose collar and sad moustache and badly tied cravat who caught her frantic looks, who of all those in that overheated room seemed to understand, touching her on the elbow and then moving his body half between her and that of the other on some pretence of a familiar greeting, forcing this rough intruder to move away. In turn, his adversary just laughed and reached across, touching her arm once more, with a breezy *Au revoir, chère Mademoiselle de Provins*, until we meet again, as though some malign prediction. The intruder then pushing his way through the crowd, snatching quick glasses of champagne from the trays of startled servants as he went.

Three

WE ARRANGED TO MEET in a café in the place de la Bastille, not far from my hotel in the rue de Jarente. Julia Dussol. I was early. The streets were deeply disturbed, the place the site of gathering for a new phase of the violence. The waiters were abrupt and hurried, and the clientele rude and nervous. My coffee arrived, swimming in its saucer. Not far from where I sat, I could hear the sound of shouting and see the first signs of drifting smoke. The air was full of news and rumours, with strangers talking in the street to strangers, of universities closed and barricaded, of fire and destruction on the far side of the river. Of hundreds of arrests and, again, death in the streets.

She had told me to watch for someone in spectacles,

fairly tall—too thin, perhaps—wearing a tweed jacket and carrying a bag with lots of books in it.

Julia Dussol was Sebastien Rouvel's great-great-niece. The granddaughter of the daughter of his brother. A brother he despised, by all accounts. Hers was one of the few names I knew, when I arrived in Paris. I had talked to a friend in England about the Rouvel papers, an historian who knew of others with an interest in such things. One call led to another and, finally, to an expert in the field. The expert was extremely rude—how had I got his number, anyway?—and put me off before I even mentioned the papers with the name of this Julia Dussol. Some French woman, he said dismissively, a purported descendant who'd managed to persuade some commercial operation to bring out a book on Rouvel. He muttered something about wrong-headed and careless work, and fashionable topics. He hung up before I could say more.

I was told more about Julia Dussol by the same Canadian professor who told me about Lucien.

—There's someone you should meet.

The Canadian seemed to know everyone and everything.

—Someone who is working over that period. She's working on the life of another Communard—some rogue called Sebastien Rouvel—who also found his way out to your part of the world. Died out there, too. She knows that period backwards. I think she's working on some kind of book. She comes to the library quite a bit. I could point her out to you.

I asked if she was a friend.

—Well, let's say she was. She's very strong. That's all I'll say. Has her own way of doing things. Rouvel was some kind of relation, I believe, or so she claims. I think sometimes it clouds her judgment. She loses distance. I told her so. It was not appreciated. She's very, very strong.

When the Canadian gave me Julia's name I mentioned the cantankerous scholar. The expert. The Canadian was nastily amused.

—Did he mention the review?

There had been no talk of reviews.

—It's a very good story. He published a book a few years ago on this Rouvel's attempts to set up a Committee of Public Safety, during the Commune. Eighteen seventy-one. The 'Commune's Neo-Hébertists', he tried to call them. She shredded it, in a major journal. Only a young student at the time, and she shredded it. Presented all sorts of things he had left out. Dates, names, times he had got wrong. Even so, she did go overboard. Wrapped it up in some wild assault on institutional scholarship, and truth, and where they parted company. There were complaints. No-one gave a damn about the expert, particularly, but everyone felt threatened. There were letters to the editors about the thin line between academic critique and straight-out libel, between decent reviewing and personal abuse. He's probably waiting in the wings for her own book to come out. A dangerous enemy. I'm surprised he even mentioned her.

—So you knew her well, then? You know about her work?

—I know a little. And a little, too, about this man she talks about, this Sebastien Rouvel. He escaped from the city just before the end, while the fighting was still going on in the east and to the north. One story has it that he disguised himself as a priest—that's a good one for you—and was recognised on a train, somewhere in Normandy, making his way towards the coast and probably England, like others who had talked of revolution and resistance just a few days before. A priest, of all things! Try that one on Mademoiselle!

The Canadian swallowed the last of his coffee, and began to look like a man with more important things to do.

—You should meet her. You say you have her number? Great-great-niece, I think she claims to be. You must call her. Don't be shy. She wouldn't be. I could introduce you, but it might be better if you just ring her yourself.

There was a sudden clatter. A metal chair toppled onto the paving stones, scurrying waiters and a flushed apology—*Oh, pardon, pardon, suis desolée*—and a heavy bag, stuffed with books, still swinging threateningly upon her shoulder. I saw other customers, edgy, uncertain, looking about them, even leaping to their feet. There was the sound of a cup and saucer clattering to the ground.

Julia Dussol was around my own age, somewhere in her early to mid-twenties. Her face was nervous, her features fine, almost severe, with the beginnings of crow's-feet at the corners of her eyes, her long, light-brown hair drawn back gently, coiled behind. She wore a tweed jacket with a burgundy pullover and a neatly tailored skirt. Simple, well-cut clothing. She wore no make-up at all.

She took my hand with a beaming smile, while peering steadily into my eyes.

—Julia. I'm Julia Dussol.

She had the look of someone torn from a strict routine, not wanting to waste time. Her eyes, though, were curious, welcoming behind the metal rims. She surveyed me closely, frankly. Looking over my hair, too long, the jeans, too rumpled, the bagging green pullover, the canvas satchel.

Anglais, sûrement.

But also saying, I must get to know you quickly. The times, this movement all around us. We have things to tell each other. Please don't be disappointing.

She was still flustered from the business of the chair,

the spilled coffee and the poor fellow who had taken it in his lap.

She lit a cigarette and ordered a *menthe à l'eau*.

—He has, of course, been much misunderstood. I hope you understand that.

Her first words. Almost the first words she spoke. She drew deeply on her cigarette. Did I too misunderstand?

—Misunderstood. By everyone. People will always need a scapegoat. An evil genius. Someone to blame.

Which was what the Condorcet man had told me she would say.

—You'll find it in all the histories. Sebastien Rouvel. He was one of the most powerful members of the Commune. Chief of Police, at only twenty-four years old. I'm sure you will have read these things. Even in the English histories.

I had read the English histories. I knew all they had to say of Sebastien Rouvel.

—Of course, everyone has blackened Rouvel. He gives them what they need—someone to blame. The execution of the Archbishop. The slaughter in the rue Haxo. The Martyrs of Auteuil. All these, the few atrocities the Commune did manage to commit, have been blamed on Sebastien Rouvel.

I had read of this. The Paris Commune. With the rest of France surrendered to the Prussians, and Paris still up in arms, and this time against the rest of beaten France. It was almost exactly a century before. I read of the fall of the Commune, and the notorious Bloody Week to follow. How the city defenders, many of them demobbed soldiers, like my great-grandfather, left stranded in the encircled city, were lined up in rows and shot, and piled up in the Parc Monceau, the Buttes-Chaumont and the Jardin du Luxembourg. I had seen the engravings in the press, and photographs of young men, mostly my own age and younger, rotting in their open packing-crate coffins or just scattered like piles of rags across the street. I'd read of corpses piled up in every dark corner of the city, and carted out in wagons in the night. The parks and gardens of the city had been turned into gory abattoirs, with bodies floating in the fountains and ornamental lakes, and rivulets of blood, so it was claimed, that flowed down the Seine towards Rouen and all the way to Le Havre.

The second cigarette went the same way as the first. Stubbed and twisted, and replaced with another. She gazed out across the place, fiercely, at all those who had written about Sebastien Rouvel.

—You will have read bad things about him. I'm sure you have read bad things. Even serious historians need someone to blame. An evil genius. Someone to take the wrinkles out of history, just by being there. To exonerate the others. To idealise the cause. To shape it as a moral story. Do you know what I mean?

She stopped and searched my face for any signs of dissent. She glared around her at the crowds scuttling past, at an armoured van that had just parked nearby. At the heavily armed police who now spilled from it, lining up, stroking their batons and flexing on their toes. In the distance we could hear the sounds of shouting, of sirens and of breaking glass.

—This was a time of war. A time of revolution. Just imagine. The Prussians, parading on their horses in Paris itself, if only for a day. Paris barricaded, and with the real slaughter then beginning. There were thousands shot—some say more than thirty thousand people shot—and all after the fighting stopped. It is hard to imagine now, is it not?

I looked around me, at the restlessness, the anxious movement of people through the streets. Passing in the places des Vosges earlier, I had seen the *paniers à salade,* the long lines of police vans and heavily screened vans of the CRS, the police lined up in long ranks along the gravel paths and around the fountains, helmets. I thought of the barricades and banners—*De Gaulle: Assassin! Sois Jeune, Tais-Toi*, the bloodied heads, the overturned and burnt-out cars I had seen the night before on the other side of the river, the coursing groups of thousands of shouting students, the piled-up paving stones, the stark graffiti, the battered rows of pillaged shops.

—And the papers?

Julia's eyes moved to my satchel and back to me again. She stubbed out another cigarette and fumbled nervously for the next.

—You did speak of papers. You did speak of things that were his. The things he left behind.

I produced the papers from beneath the table, still in their original wrapping of crumbling newspaper and faded ribbon. I slapped them down between my coffee and her *menthe à l'eau*.

—You say I may take these? Read them?

Her hands hovered over the package, itching to pull on the loose end of the ribbon and dive among the sheaves.

I invited her, by a gesture.

The long slim fingers plunged. She turned the pages, saying nothing for a time. Turning through them hurriedly, as though there was some risk that the lower ones might be blank. Disturbing her hair in a nervous and agitated gesture as she read, her hair escaping in soft brown strands that tossed about her in the hot unsettling winds that blew about the place.

She sat back. Excited, almost tearful.

She smiled at me with deep warmth and gratitude. She reached across and squeezed my hand. Her eyes glittering with pleasure. Almost a kind of greed. Not letting go of the papers.

—Yes. It's him. Monsieur–*Nicolas*. I know the handwriting, almost better than my own. It's really him. All of it. I can hardly believe it. Every word!

The winds troubled the papers in her hands. One or two pages blew from her grasp. I scampered after them, crawling among the legs of tables and chairs. She extracted further pages with greater care, turning them in her hands, seeking to follow the winding sentences, peering more closely at others where the seeping inks had blurred the words. She tried to neaten the pile, shuffling the ancient pages awkwardly, the filth falling about her, the red dust clinging to her pullover and her coat. We did not speak for some time. It was difficult for us to hear each other anyway, with the growing movement in the place, the agitation of the waiters, the movement of the police vans.

I watched her as she read. Julia Dussol was beautiful, almost, with all her troubled intensity, her lips pressed taut with concentration, those bright, searching green eyes. But with little interest in being so. She adjusted her spectacles, and held a page up to the light. She glanced up at me now and then, smiling as she sifted through the papers, catching my gaze, happy enough to be looked at in this way, I thought, as long as I didn't distract her from her reading.

Her eyes again moved from me to the manuscript, and then back again.

I hadn't expected her to be attractive in this way. Was it because of the dismal picture that the grizzling expert had given? Was it because I was told she was some sort of scholar, who spent all her time in mouldy archives? I'd really only thought of what I was doing in terms of documents and papers, old photographs and files. Yet here was the same story, or part of the same story at least, but now marked out in flesh and blood. In the beating of the pulse. In passion, curiosity, excitement. In the adjusting of spectacles, the crossing and recrossing of legs, the furious fossicking through the papers, the sudden flash, now and then, of a warm smile.

I must have been so disappointing. She looked up at me from time to time, as though to see if I might in some way match what she was reading. I began to wish I had scrubbed up a little more. That despite my jeans and grubby canvas satchel I looked just a little more the part. The bearer of a major revelation. Hermes, incarnate in modern Paris? I dusted stray breakfast crumbs from my pullover, and tried to hide my scuffed elastic-siders beneath the table.

She searched on through the papers, passing hurriedly from one batch to the next. Shaking her head in amazement, and now and then mumbling something to herself. Looking up at me occasionally, though, as if I suddenly might not be there when the next wreath of smoke had passed. As though the seat might suddenly be empty and the whole thing, me and the papers, the canvas bag they came in, vanished back to where they came from, to the far side of the world. Back to where he died. Back to this place called Mount Deception.

> *So she is all future and all past as she waits with arms that extend in nakedness across the blistered land . . . She is the mountains and her teeth the stones. Her tears the only waterfalls. Her shoulders the barren slopes . . .*

She asked me, now and then, about Deception. About Australia and the desert. But each time as I began to tell her, her attention would slowly fade, and she would soon be foraging deeply in the Rouvel papers yet again.

About us, there was a strange mix of the everyday, people still taking coffee and trying to read their morning papers, yet nervously aware of a menace gathering in the place; the police vans moving in procession, the rising sound of sirens, the acrid smell of burning rubber. The waiters were starting to move the tables, the moment they were free, into the restaurant. Standing over the patrons, eager to grab their cups and saucers. The smoke was increasing, borne on the winds from other parts of the city, and across the river.

—Why was he there, Nicholas? To die so all alone in such a place? So far, as you say, from anywhere? Your great-grandparents, I can understand. An opportunity, perhaps. But Sebastien Rouvel—this was all he knew. These streets. This city. This was his world. What we see around us, here.

She read on, flicking from page to page.

Her hair the one thing that still grows in this place where the earth cracks and hot winds strip shards from broken rocks . . .

She read aloud, carefully, very slowly, in French and then in a simple English. As though pausing on the edge of making sense. She raised an inquiring eyebrow. I simply shrugged my shoulders. I had no answers. It was for this I was in Paris.

—I think I should read it all, Nicholas. Properly. Before we talk further. So I'll know what questions to ask. May I?

She put the papers down, and smiled. A friendly, indulgent smile. Her face was alight, her intense gaze softened by the gentle wrinkles at the corners of her eyes.

Looking at me, for the first time, with real attention. And with some amusement, or so it seemed.

—But you. What do you want, Nicholas? What do you want to find?

—I want help. To understand what he has written.

—What will you do when you have finished? When you know?

—I don't know, Julia. I thought perhaps a book. A family thing.

I knew it sounded weak. I might have asked, why does it matter, all this fuss about your own great-great-uncle? Who cares if he's considered good or bad, generations beyond his time? Was it because as a sort of lawyer I was trained to put the case in order, to pull together all the bits and pieces, so nothing could slip through? Someone once told me that I'm a lawyer and a dreamer, and that it's an awkward mix. The dreamer opens gaps where no-one else can see them. The lawyer goes in search of all that's needed, to close them down again. Perhaps it's what makes some people good at history. But does it make for better living, all these openings and closings, while more sensible people simply get on with the job at hand? Can it really lead to better thinking? Or only to the likes of Julia Dussol and me, adrift amidst the smoky chaos, a society and a city all around us breaking open at the seams, the two of us in deep toil over something that might perhaps have mattered a hundred years before?

A police van, its siren blazing, went hurtling through the place.

—Perhaps I'll write a proper history. Depending on what I find.

She made no comment. Just a further sympathetic smile.

—I just need to know, Julia. That's all.

What I really wanted to talk about was Agnes. About the stories that ran up to a certain point, and then abruptly fell away. About ways of telling that just seemed to push out further questions. About how hard it was to conceive of a decent future when you couldn't even manage a version of your past. How hard it was to put your best foot forward when the other was on such slippery ground.

I said nothing. Julia had the air of someone quickly bored. We looked to the documents.

—Have you shown this to many people, Nicholas? These papers?

I had not. I would have told the expert about them, except that he hung up on me. I did hope one day to raise it with Colette. When we knew each other better. There was some shadow, in the stories Agnes told, that made me cautious. Some constraint. I'd decided not to raise it until she herself made mention of Sebastien Rouvel.

She reached across the papers and placed her hand on mine. Almost a caress.

—I'll help you, Nicholas. I'll help you to translate. To find out what it means. But there's one condition. I hope you won't mind. I want this to be a secret. Our secret. Don't show the papers to anyone until later. Until after my book is published.

I agreed. A shared secret. I liked the idea.

—It's important. Trust me, this is far more important than just your family story, interesting though it is. We'll work on this together. I know we can help each other.

The wind was strengthening. A student, shouting, his shirt almost torn away, ran through the place. Pausing by our table, the last table still set out on the pavement, yelling something at me that I did not understand. At the tables, at the waiters and then, with a clenched fist, at the long rows of waiting riot police.

Julia looked about for her bag, and I watched nervously as the Rouvel papers vanished into its depths. The waiters came at speed the moment she stood. Taking the chair, even the table.

She smiled, her hand again on mine.

—I'll help you, Nicholas. You can't imagine what this means. I know this writing better than my own. Though this is new—the poetry. And so much of it!

She scribbled her address and telephone number on

the back of a used metro ticket. I must ring her. She would contact me, soon, so we could talk further. We would meet for a coffee. I must come to her apartment, in the rue de la Clef. We would talk more about Rouvel and the papers. And of course, about this Mount Deception. She would need just a day or so to read. To talk to her publisher. Editions Grandet.

—I'll show you all my things. There's so much more I can tell you. My papers, photographs. Everything. You must come very soon. Rue de la Clef.

She kissed me goodbye. Warmly, on both cheeks. She caught my eye moving to her bag, the vanished papers. She laughed, and caressed her bag. Hugging it to her side.

—Don't worry, Nicholas. I can see you are worried! I'll take good care. I promise. With my life!

She left me. To a new kind of loneliness. The papers, stuffed into her already overloaded bag, disappeared with her into the troubled crowd, into the movement of a city suddenly flung from all routine. I sat down again. It was as though the city had for a moment gained then lost a face. The waiters did not disturb me. Perhaps simply forgetting, in the agitation of the moment. Or deciding that in a time of revolution the loss of one chair was really no great matter.

I sat, exposed and alone on the pavement, watching the growing movement in the place, the swirling smoke, the first glow of a fire, a car burning in the distance along the boulevard Henri IV, towards the river. The traffic had stopped. There was a new roadblock, further down the rue Saint Antoine. And suddenly, a strange quietness. As though all those fleeing some sudden outbreak of violence had now fled. There were only the distant sounds of shouting, and of breaking glass.

I thought then of something I had seen—a book, a film?—proposing ways in which we might hope to move about in time. That time ran in steps from start to ending, like writing running down a page, or like a list. That such a page might one day be folded at a point of choice; that once it had been folded, you could simply pass across the shortened distance that then ran between the present and the past. That you could simply step, as through a door, from one side to the other. The streets were now almost deserted, the police dispersed, the vans gone off to another part of the city, the traffic barred from entry to the place. This no-man's-land that now ran between the present and the past. This city which seemed to fold itself with each new generation, touching yet again the violence that had been. I looked into the emptiness, the sudden silence of the place. Looked into the space, the path, the doorway in the perturbed crowd through which Julia had just passed, carrying my precious papers. Left with just her scrap of paper in my hand. A tattered metro ticket, with her name, number and address. Julia Dussol.

As though by some malign prediction. I thought of how it must have been, these same streets folded back one hundred years, touching again the fire, the rage and violence in the streets. I thought of a bull-like figure in wide hat and ancient coat, bracing himself against the cool night winds, his pockets filled perhaps with pillaged fruit, his hand grasping still the last glass of champagne. I thought of how he must have passed quickly from the ordered gardens and clean new stone of the boulevard de Courcelles and towards the older city, through the insistent drizzle and tangled maze of streets that led across the rue du Faubourg Saint-Honoré and through the walled and sleeping passages that led towards the river and his own familiar haunts.

There once was a city. A city that was made of words. A city built of stones that once were words. A city built of towering tenements with unlit squares below and dark and narrow streets that ran between. Built as the legends told beside what was once a river and on green fields that lay between green forests. A city circled by walls which were higher than the highest tenements, with no gates to be found.

A city long deserted at this hour, as this same man strode through the glistening puddles that crossed the place Vendôme and past the carriages as they waited in a sodden line along the western side, their attendants swathed in heavy capes and sitting as a dank cortege amid the dripping rain, the horses stamping against the cold, the jingling harnesses heard above the hissing of the gas lamps and sometimes the sounds of voices. He listened to the laughter from the windows above and the splashing sound of his own feet as he made his way towards the river, taking a pleasure in the deepening shroud of darkness, in the faintness of the streetlamps with their yellow auras streaked by rain, in the sounds behind him of horseshoes beating on the cobbles and the brisk sudden clatter of passing cartwheels, some late-night reveller retiring or some early-morning traveller out to defeat the day.

They were told the stones were found out in the fields and that they came with the streams and fruit and trees. That new words and decrees came with the spring, and grew like fruit and changed into stone each year as the trees lost their leaves and summer fell into autumn. Until one day a traveller who had entered through a crevice in the wall told another story. That once there was simply cruelty and speechless barbarians with their random acts of torture. Then the word was invented and the word was given force and all the unspeakable acts were turned into speech and orders and decrees.

He drew his coat more closely against the soft fall of beating rain, drawing away from this unfamiliar quarter with its grand buildings and its new and widened streets and making his way down to the river by the allée d'Antin, down the steps and then along the quays and past the forbidding walls of the Tuileries palace, striding against the sharpness of the winds that ran up from the river. Was his mind still moving perhaps upon a young woman in a warm and brightly lit salon? Upon her naked shoulders, the lights reflecting in the darkness of her eyes, the pleasure of her sudden anger and the part-pleasing sting of insult, the flinching of her bare arm and shoulders so moulded in light satin and softened by candlelight?

These acts of torture were turned into laws and the laws turned into poetry and recited in the forms of art and beauty. The city spread across the plain and rose with high walls to block the light, in stones of words like Curses Lies Abuses Satires Condemnations Denunciations Sentences Prohibitions Proscriptions

Decrees Enjoinments . . . tenements were thrown up with Imprecations Fabrications Mandates Regulations Consignments Writs Embargoes Instructions Maledictions Charms Falsehoods and Untruths and the walls soon mounted higher to conceal with each new stone that was sung.

He came now to a more familiar world, along the stone banks of the river where the city's lost and ragged huddled by the braziers that burned below the walls, his own name now rising here and there in greeting as he pushed towards the spitting coals. Hands reached out to seize his own, with bottles passed from hand to hand, fruit, caviar and cake hauled from his pockets and shared around the coals, all toasting soon in laughter their friend, this ragged man of revolution.

Then came another poet late into this world. He found the stones ill-fitted and scarce mortared to each other. He watched the graves now full and overflowing with the bones of the departed creeping upward with each generation that passed. He saw the mounds of corpses threatening at last to overreach the walls . . . the chance had come at last to mount the ladder of bones that rose above the rocks and walls and toppled tenements and to create new words too soft for stone.

Leaning into the coals, looking into the blazing heart of fire, he thought perhaps once more of the fear and anger in her eyes when he had tried to tease her, this mere provincial schoolgirl from the grey depths of Provins. Why should he think of her again? He glanced across at the heavy mass of the Conciergerie, and in the dark streets far behind it, the Préfecture. Looking into the fire, his mind moving to thoughts of some grander adventure soon to come, the Prussians moving closer and all things about to break, the chance to climb at last beyond all Embargoes and Prescriptions, the confident stone mansions on the old Plain of Monceau, the clean regime of that same girl and all the Tante Agathes that ever were, his thoughts soon teased in easy stages beyond ladders of bone and toppling stone towards a young *grisette* who huddled shivering at the far side of the fire, a childlike novice to her trade half clad against the bitter cold of night and clinging to the warmth and laughter of the fire, her red painted lips and flushed tubercular cheeks telling of some chance of brief forgetfulness, before all things began to break.

Four

Lucien took me out into the throng, the open spaces. He told me that I must know the streets. That we must first set out to do what my ancestor did and see what he had seen. To understand what happened from the ground, the time it took, the distances covered, the toll of sweat and dread and leather.

—A stout pair of boots, *mon vieux*. That's what you need. It was one of your English historians who said that. The first thing you need for writing decent history is a good stout pair of boots.

We must go, he said, to Père-Lachaise. The cemetery, where it ended. But only at the end of a long day's walk. Only after we had traced the scenes of invasion and of killing, past the barricades and toppled ruins, of burnt-out palaces and teeming slaughteryards. Only when we had followed the path westward across the city of the invading troops from Versailles.

We would begin at the site of the porte du Point-du-Jour. Far to the west. The National Guard was celebrating at some festival in the place du Châtelet at the time. The gate was undefended. The army from Versailles had simply walked in. We would, Lucien insisted, tread the same paths that the invaders had taken as they fought their way eastward. So I would understand how long it took to walk from the porte du Point-du-Jour to the Palais Royal. From the avenue de Tourville to the Hôtel de Ville. From the Préfecture de Police, or from the place du Châtelet, right up to Père-Lachaise.

We walked for hours. The day was hot and troubled. I soon felt the heat of bitumen and concrete burning through the thin sole of my shoes, tormenting the blisters that soon formed on my feet. Lucien was relentless, shuffling through the streets at speed in his oversized and flapping clogs of rope and unlaced leather, and his ragged streaming coats, his smells increasing in the maddening heat. We were threatened. Sworn at. Detoured by police barriers and by flung-up barricades. Buffeted by the angry crowds.

I was already tired as we came to the Etoile, and down to Champs-Élysées-Clemenceau. Lucien seemed to take on energy from the heaving crowds that swirled around us, the police barricades, the shields and swinging batons, the clouds of smoke and shouting crowds that surged about us as they came nearer to the centre, to the place du Châtelet. It was an odd moment for a tour. I passed through crowds of people, mostly my own age and younger. In anger for the present. In arms for the future. While Lucien and I crept through them, passed around them, part of the crowd but never with them, as though lost on our far side of the folding, a hundred years before.

We crept through the disorder all around us, visiting the sites of the Commune, the Bloody Week, as though they were religious shrines, with Lucien describing how the barricades were thrown together with cobblestones and pillaged furniture, of how the invaders moved through the houses, breaking their way through the adjoining walls, running through the rooftops and firing down on those below, beating the city's defenders steadily to the west. We pushed on through police barriers to see those places where the most famous of the Commune barricades had been: the rue de la Paix, the place Vendôme where the column had been toppled, the rue de Rivoli and, later, the rue Sainte Antoine.

We stopped for a time in the Tuileries gardens. Here, the place was strangely deserted, except for a few nervous police. Normally, on such a warm day, the lawns were crowded with sunbathers, canoodling couples. We sat on a bench. Towards the western end of the gardens were signs of a fairground, a brightly painted merry-go-round and a small Ferris wheel. Not moving. The gardens, set up for a summer's pleasure, now closed against the violence in the streets.

We sat quietly for a while. Lucien, though, had something special in mind. At length, after much scraping and snuffling agitation, he waved a contemptuous hand towards the vast enclave of the Louvre, looming on three sides around us.

—You must realise, *mon vieux*. Most of what you see here is built to stop you understanding. None of this gives you the past. Most of it is here to make sure you never see.

He scraped his fingers fiercely through his matted hair.

—It's not the real past. Not the past that you really need to know. It's all there to stop you knowing. That is the truth. It's actually a veil, between us, and then. A curtain.

I asked him to explain. He sighed contentedly and lay back upon the bench, opening his coats, his stinks, his ideas, to the bright sunshine.

—So much of what they call 'historical' is put there to

prevent history. To stand in the way of knowing. You look at the Hôtel de Ville. We'll pass it soon. So very beautiful. So very old? It's all just reconstruction, my young friend. Put back together, block by block, to mask what happened there. The fire, the blood, the dying in the streets.

Lucien closed his eyes, still disentangling his thoughts.

—History? The history of this city? Just here and there it can be seen. This, where we sit, is my favourite spot, the best spot in the city. But it's what's not here that holds the truth.

—What do you mean, Lucien?

He grinned. His moment was carefully prepared. He snuffled again, cackling triumphantly. He began to scrape at my knee, as well as his own.

—I talk about the power of absence. This spot, where we sit. This was once a palace. This very spot. The Tuileries Palace. Burned down, during that same week in 1871. Ha! Did your ancestor Duvernois set fire to it? I would say not. It happened, though, while he was fighting in the streets. Burned down, and in this instance, not rebuilt. A space, a telling space, young Nicholas. The power of emptiness!

I looked around, at the towering pavilions of the Louvre, still indicating the dimensions of the palace that had been.

He chuckled hoarsely, rubbing me on the knee.

—If this Mount Deception of yours was still in good order, do you imagine you would be here? Would you be wandering the world, trying to find your answers?

He clenched my arm in his ragged mitten. Still smiling, but with deep intent.

—Do you think you would still be curious? Isn't it the ruins, my friend, the scattered stones, empty spaces, the running wounds, that have brought you here?

He leaned closer. He waved his hand across the empty lawns and benches.

—Most people don't know the gaps exist. Most just get on with the business of living. Do you think we are better off than they are, you and I?

The scattered stones. Our shuffling, dodging ramble through this landscape of forgetting. Past the marks of ancient gunfire on the Madeleine, the yawning spaces where palaces once stood, past scenes of massacre and counter massacre, the slaughteryards of Luxembourg, the scenes of slow and ordered murder around the Tour Saint-Jacques. Through all these absences. I looked at my ragged friend. Drawing in his smells. Lucien as a fleshly reminder. Lucien, the reeking wounded body. The accumulating, unsponged human truth. The stinking bearer of all true forms of knowing.

Lucien hawked and coughed and spat rich mucus into the gravel.

—Come, come. It will be dark before we get there!

We made our way down the rue Saint Antoine and to the place de la Bastille, the soles of Lucien's oversized boots now beating loudly as we veered off towards the north, passing around the place de la Bastille, following the desperate path of the last defenders as they fought their way up along the rue de la Roquette, towards the north and up to Père-Lachaise.

The cemetery was quiet, the noises of the street dying away as we passed through the southern gates. Below, we could see the smoke from fires on the far side of the river, the muted sounds of the city, the wail of distant sirens. I slumped, exhausted, my legs quivering with fatigue, on the nearest tomb. Père-Lachaise. It was not actually the last battle of the Commune, Lucien explained. Only the most famous of the last battles, with some later skirmishing still further to the east, even after the notorious slaughter in this place, of the last surrendered *fédérés*.

Lucien wanted to move on, below the vast trees that lined the avenues, that blocked the light and protected a midsummer growth of moss, along the winding paths and beds of flowers, past the last small groups of summer tourists struggling back along the slippery paths from visits to the tombs of Balzac and Chopin, of Corot and Wilde and Delacroix. We moved up past the grander tombs, the monuments of the imperial bourgeoisie, the mausoleums and cenotaphs, the caryatids and marble angels and veiled and weeping virgins and Gothic palaces and pyramids, the columns and obelisks. Lucien telling me with each step of the fate of the last of the defenders of Paris, fighting in the darkness and harried from tomb to tomb. Pressed steadily up, towards the waiting ditches in the north.

I thought of Paul in this same place—another escape, indeed—in the spare stories Agnes had told. Of a bullet, a wound, a ricochet from a tomb. Of his being hidden, out of sight. I thought, too, of what Colette had told, of how Marie-Josèphe and Paul sometimes evaded the watchful eye of Tante Agathe and had met at strange times and in the most unlikely places. I had read of how the mood of the city darkened as the war began to slip away, of the defeats at Froeschwiller and Wissembourg, the first sight of the wagons carrying the wounded back through the streets of Paris, and then the humiliation of General Bazaine and his vast army trapped in Metz. Of how soldiers like Paul returned to Paris to build the barricades to defend the city itself against the Prussian threat, with all those who just short weeks before had cried *à Berlin, à Berlin* in the streets now fleeing from the city in long lines up towards Versailles, with stray shells launched by the Prussians from the captured fortress of Mount Valerian reaching even the home of Tante Agathe and the avenue de Tourville. Of how lovers like Paul and her mother still met under bridges and on barges on the river, in secret and forbidden places in Charonne and Ménilmontant and perhaps even here in Père-Lachaise itself.

We climbed the wandering pathways towards the famous wall where the last of the National Guard, the famous *fédérés,* were shot. Where Paul-Auguste Duvernois ought to have been shot. I chose a dozen different tombs on which he might have been hidden, if the brief story passed on by Agnes had any kind of truth. Lucien followed, now short of breath himself but still chattering excitedly, pointing out to the east and into the falling light, to where the Prussian camps had been, and then leading me towards the wall where the final shooting had taken place.

It was growing cold. Before us lay the city, now grey and fading with the light. We sat on the edge of a tomb, looking towards the famous wall. Listening in silence to the muted sounds of the city.

Until Lucien spoke at last.

—Why do you need to know?

It was the same question that Julia Dussol had asked. The kind of question you only ask, I do suspect, when you've felt the need to come up with some answer of your own.

—I thought perhaps a book, Lucien. There isn't much to draw on. No letters, few memories. It's as though that's how they wanted it. The silence. What I do will depend on how much of the truth of it all I manage to find out.

—That's not an answer. It just brings up a further question. Why do you need a book? What will it really tell you?

—I don't know, Lucien. I just need to tie it all together. To fill in the gaps. It's about being able to move forward.

Lucien laughed. He was laughing at me, but it was not a cruel laugh. He got up and walked to the wall where the shooting took place. Testing the pitted surface with a grimy hand.

—You say you want the truth?

Beneath the stinking thatch, the bright eyes seemed still to be teasing.

—There, you do need to be careful. Some of us are stuck with this truth you talk about. Some of us live it, every day. While not exactly moving forward. My life is full of truth. And, as you can see, not too much else.

Lucien spread his filthy hands in an expressive gesture. He may even have winked.

There was a café just outside the cemetery gates. The *patron* scowled, but let us stay. The place was almost empty, anyway. We were directed to sit outside. Lucien eased his feet out of his flapping boots. He ordered a steak and chips.

The name Rouvel came up. It was Lucien who raised the spectre, not me. Had any of the Communards really deserved such brutal treatment? Lucien told the story of how Rouvel had insisted that the innocent director of the Hôtel de Ville be shot, a man called Chaudey, despite his pleading that he had a wife and children to support. Rouvel, who then escaped unharmed while others suffered.

I longed to tell Lucien what I knew. I thought of Julia's embargo. I opted for the distant scholar's gaze.

—But you know, Lucien, this Sebastien Rouvel. I've read of him. He must have had abilities of some sort. He was only twenty-four years old. That's younger than I am. Chief of Police. What sort of person was he, Lucien? What was he really like?

Lucien tore at his steak. Blood ran into his whiskers.

—Rouvel was bad. Notorious. Some say that if the Commune was really a revolutionary movement—and there are many who doubt that—then Sebastien Rouvel was its leader. The true Blanquist, through and through. Steeped in revolutionary lore. In totalitarian revolutionary terrorism. To the doctrines of Hébert, Saint-Just, Jacques Roux and *les Enragés*, all of the extremists of the 1790s. Steeped in them, he was. A right stinker, in all.

—But why do you say he was a terrible person? Perhaps he was just a true revolutionary? Doing what he had to do?

—The reports are mixed. Perhaps even confused. Some who met him spoke of a disarming charm. You've probably seen the photographs. They don't tell you much. The large, dark beard, the long hair, all neatly trimmed. Normally, it ran wild. Some complained of that. The filth. There were stories of his success with women; rich women, beautiful women. Tales of splendid humiliations, of night-time visits to his stinking hole in the Latin Quarter. Women with carriages, and servants waiting below, and Rouvel sending them away in bitter tears. Many stories of this kind.

Lucien fossicked more deeply in his hair. He said that there was something special about this Sebastien Rouvel. The way he seemed to know what everyone was thinking before they knew themselves. It wasn't just his files, the secret dossiers he had collected from the Préfecture. He seemed to know the worst, the weakest in people. You could see it in the memoirs of some of the other *déportés,* like Bauer, and Chapotel. There was admiration, but also a kind of dread. He had a strange gift. He would nudge others into those forbidden places where he moved with ease, places where others were cautious, embarrassed, ashamed to be found. A dangerous gift. Henri Bauer had written about it, from the islands. There were hints in Ballière.

Lucien became agitated, began to scratch at his hair,

at his face, sinking deeper into memory, chasing elusive fragments. He shovelled a greasy handful of *pommes frites* into his mouth.

—There was something about Rouvel, though, that didn't fit. Something that no-one ever quite felt easy with, even his supporters. As though the whole thing, revolution itself, was some sort of game, some kind of theatre where he just played a part. From which he could simply move on, to play other rôles. That all the talk of revolution was just a mask for other things. Something his escape seemed to confirm.

The escape. The priest. I thought of my Canadian.

—Rouvel disappeared from Paris on the Thursday of the Bloody Week. He was meant to report to a barricade on the rue Saint Antoine, but he had disappeared. Many thought he had been shot. Anyone out on the streets, anyone captured by the Versaillais, was liable to be stood up against a wall and shot. The slaughteryards were already in full motion, in the Parc Monceau, and down at the Tour Saint-Jacques.

—And then?

—Two weeks later, on a train, on the way to Calais, someone recognised him. Dressed as a priest—a priest! The man who signed the death warrant for the Archbishop. The most violent anti-cleric of them all. On his way to England.

—So it was seen as a betrayal?

—I can tell you, if it were not for that escape, you'd be reading a lot more about Sebastien Rouvel in the history books. In many ways, he was more important than any other—more than Rochefort, more than Blanqui himself, more than poor Ferré or Rossel, shot at the stake out at Satory.

Lucien covered the last of his steak with thick mustard, and filled his frightful pockets with bread.

—There were always rumours. The light sentence he received. His treatment on the boat, the notorious *Danae*, and the easy time he had of it later, in Nouméa. The house on Mount Coffyn, and the servants. There were stories of secret dossiers, of friends, perhaps even victims, in high places. Not heroic at all, *mon vieux*, when you think of the thousands who were shot in the streets, and another thirty thousand or so who were locked up in filth and misery in the prisons out at Versailles.

He burped loudly, and wiped the mustard from his whiskers with his sleeve.

—And not one of them half as guilty as our good friend Sebastien Rouvel. But why do you ask? Why this interest in Rouvel?

What is it really—this reluctance to live within the present, within our own truncated stretch of territory, within the body's narrow bounds? Our need for some extended drama, some out-of-body experience to relieve the narrow burden of the fragile elusive present, some longer passage across the future and the past? It was something I had just come to know about. I was browsing along the book traders' boxes on the boulevard Saint-Michel. Just days before. I stepped out into the road, with a bus bearing down on me. The traffic was moving, of course, down the right-hand side. The driver slewed and shuddered to a halt. The passengers were flung off their feet.

I scurried off, followed by a busload of curses.

—*Espèce d'idiot!*

A half-second from death. From being squashed and smeared along the boulevard Saint-Michel. Fragility. There one moment, and able to announce my name and passport number. Gone the next. Dead, like all the city's dead beneath my feet. If the bus had hit me, how would they have found out who I was? It would have been at least a week before the *patronne* back at the Grand Hôtel Jeanne d'Arc reported an absconder to the police. They would have found some scraps of paper in my room. Perhaps my passport, with a photograph to match the mess in a bucket somewhere in a Paris morgue.

—*Espèce d'idiot!*

I'm from another country. From the far side of the world. We do things differently there. What use to talk of right- and left-hand drive? I sat by the side of the road for a few moments, to steady myself. I went back the next day. And the next. To the same spot. At the same time. Watching the same crowd moving about the book tables, the same bus—even the same driver—roll by. Who did not, of course, know me. But how different would it have been, if I'd actually been squashed? Within an hour or so, the road would have been hosed down. The driver would perhaps have been sent on leave for a week or so, to Trouville or Deauville or some place to the south. The book stalls, the street, would all be the same. Those who called me an *idiot* the day before would be back at their routines, with no lack of new idiots to harry. Can you wonder that we don't want to live within the short lease of the body? Naturally, we struggle for some form of extension, beyond the flickering candle flame of our own poor parting space. Into other times. Other bodies. Into books, memories, dreams, exotic scribblings, even old photographs.

My thoughts ran back to Père-Lachaise, to the Emperor's soldier laid out as though already dead across the damp moss of the tomb. I thought of Agnes's spare stories, of how her father was badly wounded, and how his friends hid him high up on a tomb. Of how it was his blood, seeping down the monument, that betrayed him in the end. I thought of how his thoughts then slipped in slow and chilling stages to the thinkings of dead men, the pain turning to numbness and then to the nothingness of stone, all things receding in a liquid motion as he sank in slow stages from the deep red of the burning sky, from the mud and rain and blood that ran in rivulets beside him, untroubled by the sounds of dying battle, the last shouting and the screaming to the north.

Did he think perhaps of this last day that had passed, of how they fought their way to Père-Lachaise, the stragglers from all parts of the city streaming through the southern gate, to watch the distant dying fires of the Palais de Justice, the Tuileries Palace, the Hôtel de Ville, the flames sending rich waves of light across the graves and casting crimson shadows across the tops of the trees? Père-Lachaise, walled cemetery and now walled killing ground, last refuge for this ragged beaten remnant now creeping up the shaded paths past watching angels, urns and obelisks, towards the northern wall.

I thought of a city burning and of the mounting piles of dead, the carnival continuing in this sudden feast of blood, the bodies rolling down the river and in rotting mounds in the streets, with troupes of crazed children sporting with severed limbs and well-dressed women urinating on the faces of the dead. Of the Versaillais, moving slowly eastwards through the city, the rage of a broken nation finding release in wholesale slaughter, the defenders of the city now the hunted of the city, scuttling north and westwards through the streets, fighting street by street, fired on from the rooftops and with all doors closed against them, with word passing back in frantic rumours that in Belleville to the north the fighting was still strong, that in Belleville there was some chance of resistance amid the crowded tenements and narrow curving streets.

From the heights he must have seen the troops approaching, must have seen his own death approaching along the mossy walks and flickering in the darkness as they ran from tomb to tomb, the blue jackets massing below and just within the southern gate, the fighting beginning just as the darkness fell, an inglorious slithering battle between the tombs in the fall of steady rain. Then feeling at last the hard blow to his thigh, the numbness and the pain to follow, the Chassepot bullet ricocheting from a tomb, flinging him into the mud of his own blood and the blood of others, his friends helping him and he begging at last to be left, to be helped to a hiding place on a large stone casket, under the heavy canopy of a grand family tomb.

Waking at last to the shouting, a different kind of shouting. Hearing the voices raised, some screaming in protest and others gruff in abuse. Hearing the sound of soldiers moving below the tomb where he lay, the sounds of jeering, in accents from the south and from Bretagne; country louts, brought in to ensure that the righteous Expiation should be merciless and complete. Feeling at last the darkness come on again, another kind of darkness, the cold creeping up through his body, taking on the thick texture of stone, the deep cold of the tomb now coming over him again, this time wrapping itself about him like a thick and darkening blanket, this time bearing him beyond sight and sound, beyond the tombs, the fires, the cries for mercy and the blows to follow, beyond all familiar feeling and connection, into the deep heart of a special silence from which no-one, and not even those to go on living, could ever hope to return.

Five

THERE WAS A MESSAGE for me from Julia waiting at my hotel in the rue de Jarente. I must come to her apartment in the rue de la Clef.

But not for two days. Two full days. I realised I had nothing to do for those two days but wait for our appointment. Two more days of confused shuffling through the city and trying to stay out of trouble. Days of pretending to be busy, and hot on the track of things. Days of watching the violence in the streets increase. Days of watching the strikes begin to spread. Days of batons, barricades, shouting crowds. Nights spent lying under the sloping ceiling of my tiny room in the attic of the Grand Hôtel Jeanne d'Arc, rehearsing the last moments of my conversation with Julia, and wondering, imagining, practising for what the next phase would bring. Her place, in the rue de la Clef. Inside, inside! Away from the buffeting. Away from the crowds and the confusion. Inside Julia's apartment. That was suddenly what really mattered. Inside this troubled city. Inside the thoughts of Julia Dussol, inside this rich and intriguing story we were about to put together. This city of closed doors, of queues and regulations and testy librarians and barricades, had suddenly become a city with a face. A smile. An invitation. And just as suddenly, my history was a history with a purpose. My story, a story with a reader, with an audience, even a new teller of its own?

As I arrived, she came to the door. Looking down over the bannister, three flights up, as I came past the concierge who watched in frosty silence, scratching her elbows at the door. Her eyes were glazed over with excitement and fatigue. She had just showered. As I approached I could smell the warmth, the fresh smell of soap. She was still dragging at her rucked-up pullover with one hand as she met me on the stairs.

She was barefoot, wearing jeans not yet properly zipped up at the front, and a baggy green pullover. Her hair was loosely bound up, behind. She greeted me as almost an old friend, a dear friend.

—Come, Nicholas. Quickly. I have so much to show you. Oh, such wonders. Do come.

She was holding a clutch of papers.

—It explains everything, Nicholas. I haven't read it all, but so far it seems to explain just absolutely everything! Now we can show everyone what he was really like. How he was misunderstood. Misrepresented. Blamed for all.

With scarcely a further greeting, without bothering to show me in, she drew a page from her bundle and read it to me slowly, with deep emphasis.

Her tears the only waterfalls. Her shoulders the barren slopes. Her hair is the only thing that still grows in this place where the earth cracks and hot winds strip shards from broken rocks. She alone casts a strong shadow across the tortured earth . . .

—What do you think of that?

—It's certainly very rich, Julia. Very dense.

—Dense?

—Fantastic.

—Yes, that's it. Fantastic!

—Well, poetic, somehow. Distilled. Strange.

—Yes. Yes! It's so very, very strange! You can see from the way he wrote, just the way he filled his pages, that he was writing in a private sort of way, in a language of his own.

Julia caressed the page before her in wonder. Tracing the patterns with her finger. Nodding her head in silent reverence.

—Nicholas, it's all there. The whole story. It's just what I imagined. It's uncanny. I can't tell you. I just can't thank you. There's no way that I can thank you.

She broke off and clasped my hand.

—Not quite French. Using French words, but even so, sometimes a language all of his own. He wants us to translate, to interpret, to struggle in some way, to earn our understanding. You will help me, won't you, Nicholas? Explain to me the details, all the things that I don't understand? I'll translate. I'll tell you about the city. You'll tell me about the desert. I don't know about deserts.

She laughed.

—You see, Nicholas, how we'll help each other?

She grabbed a handful of my clothing, and drew me in.

Julia lived in the rue de la Clef. On the edge of the present violence, alongside the rue Mouffetard. On the very place, she soon explained, where the prison of Sainte-Pélagie used to stand. The main prison for crimes with words attached, for what Julia called 'writing crimes': libels and blasphemies, satires and frauds and seditions. It was the place where all the truly exciting writers were sent, the Blanquists and members of the Internationale, and errant artists like Courbet, and of course Sebastien Rouvel himself, who moved straight from his studies at the Lycée Louis-le-Grand, she said, to those in Sainte-

Pélagie. To what he always called the 'best university in Paris'. By his twenty-fourth year, the time of the Siege and Commune, he had served three sentences.

Julia's building was not old—Sainte-Pélagie was only demolished in the 1890s—but it had been remodelled and subdivided, with doors going off the landings at odd angles and a noisy wood-and-rattan lift that ran loosely up and down the middle of the stairs with a grinding of ancient engines and the crash of concertina doors. She had a studio bedroom and an alcove kitchen, with a tiny bathroom tacked on to one side, jutting out into what once must have been a wider landing. The whole place, even the bathroom, was awash with papers, notes and files and bits of typescript. There was one large window which opened onto the place Monge, overlooking a large marketplace with much crashing and bustling, and long lines of tooting traffic banked up and down the narrow streets that ran beside the rue Mouffetard.

The window had just been opened. I could still smell the fumes of concentration that clung to the scattered papers and the vast piles of unsteady folders that threatened from all sides. The smell of cat food, and worse. I surveyed the notes, the toppling cartons full of used exercise books and manila folders, the maps sticky-taped to the walls with lines scrawled across them, the old photographs and charts, the spilling typescripts and the dog-eared, open books, peppered with torn strips of paper and handwritten notes.

Julia laughed as she steered me further through the chaos to the bed, the only place in the room that was almost free of clutter. Even then, she had to clear a place for me to sit. She pushed some papers aside, and dislodged a large white cat. Mouffe, she said. His name was Mouffe. After the street.

The cat settled itself again into a nest of papers at the far end of the bed.

—I'm sorry, Nicholas.

She made a vague gesture with her hand.

—I'm sorry that things are in such a state. I haven't had time. My sister comes down sometimes. Catherine. She lives up at La Villette. She makes me organise myself. But I've been up all night. Again, Nicholas. Just reading. Every word. I have put some bits of it into English for you already—a sort of English. It gets better, though. It is very, very exciting, Nicholas!

She stooped and hugged me. Hugging the papers. She knelt beside me on the bed, thrusting a bundle of pages into my hands and hovering over me closely, intently, as I began to read.

—A coffee. But of course, you must want a coffee!

She slapped me on the arm, and laughed. She leapt up and threaded her way through the papers to the kitchen. In moments, though, she had forgotten the coffee and was back with some further sheets of typescript she had retrieved from the kitchen, fitting her spectacles to her nose.

—Do you think they are in their proper order, Nicholas? As he meant them to be?

There was never any order. I remembered pulling out bits that looked easier to translate, and then sticking them back on top of the pile, sometimes even throwing away pages that seemed too torn and crumpled to be of use. I recalled an awful carelessness, with whole handfuls blowing out across the paddocks behind the machinery shed.

—There's an awful lot here about deserts, Nicholas. Pages and pages of it. Mixed in with other things. Sometimes it seems to make no sense at all.

She read them carefully, in French and then in English.

> *I cannot speak of deserts. I think of all the flags of blood and the banners of flayed stretched skins that I have seen shaken by the winds that blow amid the cruel amber light of these dry places. I see them decorate in taut and tortured Abyssinian hieroglyphs the impregnable castles of our expectation . . .*

—Some of the sections don't make even as much sense as this bit, when you first read them. It's only when you've looked over the whole thing that you start to see the deeper meanings. I can really feel it, Nicholas. It's like a process; more like some kind of psychological process than just some ordinary book or poem. Just listen again!

And speak much less of forests. The forests that grow beneath the earth with all their nests of worms and bark of decaying flesh and shrinking marrow trawled by the sharp keel of those dreams that still traverse those floating orchards of roots and tangled fragments.

She looked at me expectantly. I did think for one treacherous moment of what old Agnes had once said when I read her a piece I had translated. That it did seem like an awful lot of talk that went nowhere.

—Well?

—Do you think that it was ever really meant to be read, Julia? I've always wondered. Perhaps these were just drafts, just personal thoughts. Rich. Provoking. Unfinished. That it was perhaps just an accident that it was ever kept, for anyone to look at.

—No, Nicholas. This is the inner voice. Of history. It doesn't matter that it's not finished. That it doesn't make sense in the usual way. It's true intimacy. Real knowledge, Nicholas.

Julia took up the cat, stroking it abstractedly. There was, she said, so much work still to do. More work now than ever. She smiled with vast pleasure at the thought.

—Unfortunately, the contract for my book has a short submission date. My editor at Editions Grandet wants it on the streets as soon as possible. While there is still a whiff of tear gas in the air. Those are her very words. The real job of sorting it all out might not be finished. I—you and I, Nicholas—might have to do a bit of guesswork, for this first edition. A bit of hypothesis. 'Informed conjecture', my editor calls it. It's not a problem. Historians do it all the time.

She suddenly cleared a space around her on the floor, thrusting her cups and papers into perilous piles on either side. Sending Mouffe scampering. She stripped a street plan from the wall, with routes marked out in red and blue, and spread it out across the floor, over the scatter of papers and filing cards.

—A map, Nicholas. The first thing that you need. To understand the city. To get to know what really happened.

We lay alongside each other, propped up on our elbows, and she traced it, street by street, the life of Sebastien Rouvel. She showed me the Lycée Louis-le-Grand, the rue de l'École de Médecine and the site of her apartment, of Sainte-Pélagie. There was the vast church of Saint-Eustache, where Rouvel often spoke, and the site, too, of his tiny rooftop apartment in the rue Saint-André-des-Arts in the Latin Quarter, of the Hôtel de Ville and the Préfecture de Police on the Île de la Cité. She showed me other places, too: the road to Satory and Versailles where the prisoners were kept, and the Château de Vincennes, the military archives, where she did much of her research.

It was the trouble in the streets, Julia explained, that provided the opportunity, that declared this to be the moment for Sebastien Rouvel. She had been criticised—even laughed at, she admitted—for what were described as 'extreme views'. But now the chance had come. It was Editions Grandet who first had the idea. A book. A quick book, by someone with the knowledge, someone with the time for fast, concentrated work. She was happy to set the doctorate aside, with the universities being closed and the libraries in turmoil, in pursuit of the book, with Anne Thieulle at Editions Grandet now ringing her almost every day.

So much, she whispered, was now slipping apart. Couldn't I just see it? So much was changing. So very quickly. This, I could surely see. The whole fabric, all those old forms of knowledge that were not really knowledge; all was coming apart in the fire and violence in the streets, in the universities, everywhere around them at this very moment. It had happened in this city so many times before. But then, without the leadership. Without the insight or the knowledge. Without access to the deeper understanding, Julia seemed almost to be saying, contained within the rich symbolic reaches of these newly discovered writings, this wisdom and direction from Sebastien Rouvel.

Julia suddenly rolled over on her back and looked up at me.

—So tell me, Nicholas Lethbridge. Really. Who are you?

In what was almost a whisper. And out of nowhere, as we lay spread across the maps. As though there just had to be some further thing, some exotic revelation to match the papers I had brought, to rival the fantastic legacy of Sebastien Rouvel.

Her smile was friendly but still cautious, a touch inquisitorial, as though this whole thing might yet be some massive trick, some cruel stunt of her enemies; as though I and my precious trove of papers were part of some vicious ruse, some fragment of the present violence, of the disorder in the streets. This halting voice from nowhere, on the telephone. This improbable tale about old papers. Though with some seal of authenticity, perhaps, in my bad French, my awkwardness in the ways of waiters and tables, my head still spinning at each disturbance, at each new sign of turbulence in the streets.

Who am I? I rose to my knees to answer her. What could I say? That I was, like her, still a student. That when sensible people gave up such things and turned aside to work, like her, I simply went on studying. Went on seeking to find out. I told her a bit more about my work on international conventions, and the scholarship that brought me to England. She yawned, just very slightly, behind a discreet hand. I told her of my years spent preparing for the chance, of my long hours of struggling to learn French, my saving for funds to fix up the ageing Renault for the trip across to Paris, to see what could be found.

Should I have told her more of my first weeks of loneliness and confusion in Paris? Of the days I had spent just waiting for this further meeting with her, the chance to talk to someone other than my new friend, Lucien? Of all my poor attempts to break from the present moment back into the lives of Rouvel and Duvernois? I told her of useless days spent in the Bibliothèque Nationale, waiting for books and journals that were rarely delivered, the library disturbed and threatening closure from one moment to the next. I told her about my few meagre leads that in all cases went nowhere, an article or two by

Paul-Auguste Duvernois in Rochefort's *Le Mot d'Ordre* and then no more to follow, with clues leading only to further clues and vanishing in mounds of further paper, in indexes and archives and bad handwriting and court and army processes that I could not hope to understand.

Who was I? The more I talked, the further I drifted sideways, lengthways, away from what she sought. Julia raised a hand to my cheek, as if to bring me back. Who was I, indeed? That's what I'd come to Paris to discover. How far can you really know yourself, where memory is blocked? How far can you hope to explain yourself, where so much of your own history is a blank? She'd need to know more of where I'd come from, of sheds and plains and open wheatlands. She'd need to understand more of Agnes, who never deigned to ask the question, in spite of all the closed doors and toppled gates and gaping ruins of her past, who seemed to take all the knowing that she needed from the familiar things around her, who'd learned to live within a present that simply rolled on to other present spaces. Who just passed the question on, in tales that failed quite to come together, and in trunks and ageing papers, telling papers, hidden papers, never read but never thrown away. As though something she vaguely knew as History might have some claim of its own.

I told her more of what I knew of Deception, of the threads that seemed to lead somewhere, and the stories that were blocked. I told her more of Paul, and the battle in Père-Lachaise, and his subsequent exile. I talked of the escape with Rochefort, and of my great-grandparents' time at Mount Deception. Of how her ancestor Sebastien Rouvel had arrived, at the very end of their time there, sick and exhausted, with nothing but his papers.

I told her more of those last moments, all that Agnes ever told. Perhaps more than I'd heard. I told her more of the uncertain story of her great-great-uncle's death, with the body discovered in the desert some months after, a notice in the *Port Augusta Express*, the remains 'disturbed by native dogs'. How Agnes had kept his writings in a trunk, and the trunk down in the machinery shed. Reluctant, for some reason, to keep it in the house. Not wanting to know what was in it, but keeping always one step back from having it destroyed. With the trunk being closed and locked, as the beginning of a long dry season, through the barren years that followed the droughts that brought Deception to its end. A long time of careful forgetting. Of doors being closed. Of trunks staying locked. Of curtains being drawn against the past.

I was about to tell of Saint-Germain-sur-École. Of the three sisters, still living, who had spoken and had listened to this Sebastien Rouvel. Of my time with Tante Colette. To keep up Julia's interest, to feel her hand reach again for mine. But the thing stopped, somehow, on my lips.

I thought of what Colette had said, about the need to tell such things in slow stages, about making sure that the knowledge came with understanding. The facts, with proper feeling. Saint-Germain, the three sisters. Colette, Genèvieve and Clémentine. Tante Colette's memories could perhaps wait for a better moment. In time, when she was ready, Julia must surely ask me. Was *inconnu à cette adresse* the real end of it all?

Julia shuffled her way deeper amid the papers, now examining the ceiling, as though she might find her history there. She told a little of her own story, mingled with fragments from a much remoter past. A long narrative of exile. A long tale of denigration, of some extended family humiliation. Her edgy nervousness came on in bounds. She told of a forced migration, of the family having to leave Paris in the late 1870s, after the fall of the Commune and the deportations. She spoke of childhood and schooldays in Grenoble. Of their name being tainted by her great-great-uncle's activities. With the dark shadow of his life, his distorted reputation, falling heavily on them all. For more than two generations, she said, they had felt safer far from Paris.

She told of a *maîtrise* in English from Aix-en-Provence. Of two years in California, at Berkeley, studying and working as an *assistante*. Of her own interest in her family's past, probing through the suppressions, the discouragement of her parents and, later, the scorn of colleagues, content to take the high ground, and let Rouvel bear the burden of the worst sins of his time. She told of later studies, and then the beginnings of her doctorate, on the leaders of the Commune who escaped to London.

It was the first time that she had met anyone from my part of the world. A part of the world, she admitted, she had scarcely thought about until she received my call. There was always some notion that Sebastien Rouvel had spent time in Sydney, that he perhaps had business interests there, even during his time in the prison islands to the north. She knew, too, that he had died in a place she knew vaguely as *le centre de l'Australie*. That if she had really thought about it, she might have known. That the far side of the world was exactly the place where the answers would be found. Instead, she tried to find it in letters back in London. Or Paris. Or Switzerland. Months lost in fruitless searching.

—If only we had met sooner, Nicholas.

She gestured towards a photograph of Rouvel, an enlargement of a portrait I had seen before, pinned askew on the wall, above the bed. The famous photograph, the one real photograph. Taken when he was Chief of Police. Still only twenty-four years old. Had I seen it before? The one true photograph that had survived. Had I really looked at him? Really thought about what he was trying to say? Julia pressed herself against me excitedly. Urging me to look more closely. To see what she saw there.

The high forehead. The long hair and heavy beard. The disdainful gaze. Sebastien Rouvel had been still at school when his revolutionary career began. He was still very young at the height of his power, under the Commune, of which he was, Julia insisted, the true leader, the true spiritual force, the one true heir to the spirit of '89. Of this Rouvel, very little had been recorded. Most of his writings were lost or, more likely, suppressed. The execution of the Archbishop of Paris, the death of the hostages at la Roquette, the shooting of poor Chaudey from the Hôtel de Ville, still begging for his wife and children—these were events to catch the headlines, but left untouched the other story, the vision and the heroism that led the city through violence and through revolution. The magnetic power of his orations in the clubs. Like all true visionaries, he was perhaps extreme, but this at a time, Julia insisted, when the hard crust of imperial corruption could only be broken in violent and symbolic ways. When whole shapes of thinking, so long entrenched, so much a part of habit, needed to be destroyed before reconstruction could begin.

—They need to know more about Sebastien Rouvel, Nicholas. Everyone. They need to know what you and I now know. What we have now seen.

She pressed closer, in what might have seemed an intimate approach, except that her eyes were focused so far away. Beyond and through the photograph. In distant reverence.

Editions Grandet had agreed. The contract had been signed. Delivery of the manuscript was to be no later than the first week of September. Julia was to present them with the lost Rouvel, the philosophic Sebastien Rouvel, the 'Cohn-Bendit' Rouvel who had always been there, if only in fragments, in his scattered notes and proclamations. But who would now be there for all to see within the glowing pages of this rediscovered masterpiece, his philosophic poem. Anne Thieulle, her editor, was as excited as she was. She had agreed that publication could be pushed back to the end of the year. The photographs were ready. Reproductions of pages of the manuscript would be included as part of the text.

Julia propped herself up on one elbow. Addressing the air, the photograph above. Admitting that his actions were extreme and sometimes bloody, but always with an eye to something more. Something she had detected in the fragments of his speeches, some new marriage of the ideal and the temporal, some tale of richer forms of justice which he had never, in the surviving papers, quite managed to articulate. Turning instead to silence, and to exile. Ceasing to communicate, as far as her research had shown, with anyone in France or London, Geneva or Brussells. Simply dropping from sight and then, after so long and mysterious a silence, the news arriving of his death, *au centre de l'Australie*.

—He lived so many lives, Nicholas. War, death, exile, love and cruelty. His own, and that of others. The desert, and his illness. It's a magnificent story. And it's all here. If we can only understand how to read it. If you and I can find the key. You just have to look at him, Nicholas. Look at him closely. It's something you can see. Can't you? It's all there, in the photograph.

It was almost time for the last metro. A minor decision. To bring on a major one? I made as if to go. Julia did not protest. She did, however, take my hand, and embrace me at the door. An intimate kiss. Her body was still taut, though, with other pressing matters. The kiss, a gentle kind of shove. Though not an unfriendly one.

—You can't stay, dear Nicholas. Not tonight. I have to work. I need to finish something. But you must come back. Very soon. I'll leave a message. We'll work together. It is exciting, is it not, putting these lives together? You and me?

I couldn't face the crush of the metro. I decided to walk. To risk the batons and the cruising security police, looking for more heads to batter, and to make my way back across the river, to the Marais, my hotel in the rue de Jarente. In an odd state of excitement. The story? Or was it Julia? That apartment with its cat and papers, its maps and photographs? The street itself, the burning cars, the shouting, the battered heads?

I thought of the old photographs, that image of Marie-Josèphe from the Studio Penot, of all it told of lives intact and ordered, the careful pose, the elaborate piping on her dress, the long diagonal slats of velvet that banded her bodice and met in plunging pleatings at the front, the minute covered buttons arranged in rows that ran down the lapels. A dark dress. High at the neck. A book clasped in her hand. The way those old photographs tease, how they resist; how one searches against the formal posture for the elusive cast of mind, for recovery of the shape of everyday living, the pressures of troubling thoughts, of physical discomfort, of heat and cold and all the fugitive living that is lost in the stiff dignity that those old photographs deliver.

The hair, drawn back and high behind her ears, falling over her shoulders in long, carefully turned ringlets. The hours of careful preparation. The practised look of seriousness. Was that what she was really like, the only face that she gave to the world? My mother, Colette had said. Years before she became a mother. Was it before she first felt the breath of the wilderness, the first hint of a disorder that would overtake her life? I thought of those straight and anxious eyebrows, the tightness of the bodice, the long rows of covered buttons, the brooch at her throat. The same brooch, perhaps, that Tante Colette now wore? The book in hand. A book not to be read, an emblem rather of order and seriousness, of a life properly constrained. And yet, not quite. Was there a hint of resistance in her expression? Some part still her, the person, not the posture, the frames, models and patterns of the Studio Penot? What could those brown eyes tell? What kind of feeling? What kind of passion? A young girl, determined to be more than just the Young Woman, Photographed?

Had she met, by this time, the young man in the photograph that sat alongside hers on the mantelpiece? Paul-Auguste Duvernois. The loose collar, the bagging coat, the embroidered képi and sword. Still in the national army uniform. Or was he as I had seen him in another photograph, one that was also on Colette's mantelpiece, the young man in greatcoat and undercoat and waistcoat, thin and weighed down by his clothing but proud before the camera, the moustache finely waxed and pointed but only sadly flamboyant against so serious a face?

This second photograph was taken from a low position looking up, the coat, the moustache, the hand thrust deep in pocket, holding the left side of the coat open as though for some form of action, the chin raised against the camera as if to rebuke some impertinence in the photographer, the impudence of the awkward machinery that peered from its dark cloth. A handsome face. A delicate face, its finesse lost to the family since; the face of an idealist, an artist not a soldier, the moustache too fine, the hair hanging too long, too finely, over his ears and curling. Yet still, like her, more than three parts the Young Man, Photographed.

I thought too of the portrait of Rouvel. Lit by the soft light that flowed in from the place. I'd seen the political cartoons, the caricatures in the broadsheets and newspapers in the Bibliothèque Nationale, done in the style of the time; the tiny bodies, the huge distorted heads, the beard black and ragged, the hair in disarray. But the photograph, the only one that remained, was a deeply formal, studio-posed vignette—showing Sebastien Rouvel with a high, intelligent forehead, a heavy brow, with thick dark hair that hung long about his ears, a strong, authoritative gaze. A handsome man, in fact. The beard in the photograph was thick, but well trimmed in a heavy, spade-like fashion, unusual in the age of the waxed moustache and neat imperial, lending solid weight and authority to his mere twenty-four years.

The photograph was taken in times of deep disorder, when he was already the Commune's Chief of Police, consigning hostages to the stake. The old portrait trick, the taking from below, left him looking down at the camera with an air that was masterful. Belligerent. In command. The eyes were steady, dark and coolly appraising behind his fashionable pince-nez. His air was confident, decisive. A man to lead, in times of disruption. There was talk of fanaticism, of cruelty and a quick resort to extremes. But talk too of charisma, of intellectual power and strong sexual allure.

I read, against the photograph, all of what Agnes had said, who had known this same Sebastien Rouvel, who had seen him stumble down the verandah and ride off into the storm. I thought of what I had not quite passed on to Julia: the shattered lens, the straggling hair and awkward limp, the silence he brought to Deception, and of the dread of four young girls. How much did you really need to tell? If you are trying to draw out a decent ending, if you're on the track of vision, then perhaps you can't include real memories, of flies and weevils and falling teeth, of a man gross and seeming old before his time, of the visionary losing himself in the bush just a few miles from home, wandering around in a daze until the heat and thirst beat him down. You look for space and distance. Look to the formal poses. Cling to the documents, and the symbols, to history's own forms of resistance. To the stately photographs.

Agnes spoke once of the day of his arrival. Of the lives of three young girls, who played within sight of the house in the deep heat of early summer, until this breaking of the long vacancy of the day. A man with horses and cart stopping for just a moment by the gate. A visitor at Deception always being news, always something to note. The girls, three of the girls, watching as the dust settled. Watching as in the distance a ragged and unfamiliar figure descended from the cart, slowly and unsteadily measuring with care his foothold on the earth as though the earth were fluid and might shift and part beneath his feet, edging his way around the cart to draw a satchel of some sort from the back, the weight of the satchel threatening to topple him as he slung it over his shoulder, the cart then moving steadily away and up towards the northern road, the visitor now fumbling awkwardly with the gate, slumping heavily against the gate so that his own weight for a time prevented it from opening.

They watched him as he stumbled to the house, measuring each footfall and moving more and more slowly, as though the energy required for each new careful step was all the energy he had. Down to the house he moved, the children standing now like mutes, ceasing their noisy games to watch his gradual progress across the yard, not running shouting Maman, Maman *as they would usually do when a traveller came, but waiting and watching in quiet fascination the slow measure of his ragged progress to the garden gate and towards the shade of the verandah and the long wooden bench which he had sighted from the gate. There he slumped or fell perhaps, with his grimy bag that seemed so heavy and a rolled blanket and he looking in that moment just like any other of the many that blew in off the roads, except that he was so ragged and so ill.*

The children watched him as he sat on the bench on the verandah with his head fallen on his chest, Agnes now joining the other three to watch this tattered intruder with his long hair hanging about his ears in knotted rats' tails and moulded about his head in a damp ring by the pressure of his hat. His boots were tall and badly broken, and what was left of his soles held to the boots by bindings of cloth and rope, his filthy toes able to be seen through the yawning crevices, the dog now barking and snapping about him as he sat motionless on the bench, beginning to snarl and to drag at his rags.

Their mother came to the door, ready to offer the usual words of cautious kindness, already suggesting that they should fetch water and that this visitor should take himself down to one of the shearer's shacks and rest there for a time.

And then he spoke to her in French.

He looked up and said something to her, and then he spoke her name. It was then that they all first saw the shattered lens, the mocking look in his eyes. Even then, dry and sick and filthy as he was, he seemed to mock them all. The sickness seemed to leave him for a moment as he looked at her in the strangest way they had seen.

She dropped whatever it was that she was holding—some kind of casserole, perhaps, that clattered and spilled out across the boards of the verandah with no-one moving now to pick it up, she raising her hand to her mouth as though against some infection in the odours of the road, against something far more disturbing than simply one more sick swagman collapsed on her verandah.

She looked about for help, as though now herself quite helpless, in a kind of panic, looking to see if old Fritz or anyone was about, looking back into the darkness of the house as though some help might come from there, and turning to the children with shouted orders, 'Agnes, did I not tell you to fetch water! Colette, why are you standing there, gaping like a fool!'. The girls were confused and too frightened to bring the water as she wept; and all this while, the visitor simply sat, his head on his chest, his face hidden by his falling hair, too sick even to move.

Then she told them just to leave, with a sharp and reproving tone as though they had demanded something that it was not their business to ask, as though they had seen something they should not see. They went as they were told, but not far, watching her from the corner of the house, watching as Fritz arrived and the two of them helped the visitor into the cooler regions of the house, with Marie-Josèphe gruffly sent back to fetch his filthy satchel and whatever it contained. They helped him, with Marie-Josèphe now murmuring to him and he answering something that they could only partly hear and never really understand.

Six

—VISITORS, *NICOLAS*. We have visitors. Someone that you must meet. Such an opportunity. Come! They will soon be leaving.

Colette had left a message. I was to come, again, to Saint-Germain-sur-École. This time, she was waiting on the steps. She came down eagerly, and took my arm.

—It is Monsieur Jalabert. Our dear friend, *Nicolas*. He will tell you many things. Of how our father escaped. Above all, about the escape. Your great-grandfather was far more important than the histories say. Monsieur Jalabert will tell you many things.

Much had changed since my first visit. I felt it in the warmth, the touch of her cheek, her hand, the way I was taken into the room on Colette's arm, as some new prized possession. The salon was in half-darkness as we entered, though I could see Tante Clémentine sitting in a large chair knitting, acknowledging my entry with a happy smile but continuing with her work. Two others were present, seen unsteadily in the half-light: a very old man, meticulously dressed with tie, handkerchief and cufflinks, though in a suit shining with age, and next to him a large and vigorous-looking woman of perhaps sixty, wearing an unseasonal overcoat. Her greeting was firm but none too friendly, as though she felt that there was world enough at Saint-Germain-sur-École, with these old people moving gently towards their end, without intrusions from the far side of the world.

This, Colette explained, was Monsieur Jalabert, the family's lawyer and friend together with his niece, Madame Truchet, who so kindly troubled herself to bring Monsieur Jalabert to them when he wished to visit.

Monsieur Jalabert was, I thought, perhaps even older than Colette, wizened and stooped, almost enveloped by his chair. The formality and elegance of his manner was betrayed by the awkwardness of advanced old age, the frayed collar and cuffs of his spotless shirt, the rattling of his cup as he raised it from its saucer, the slight movement of saliva at the corner of his mouth which he would touch, now and then, in an apologetic way with the corner of his handkerchief.

In his eyes, though, there was no trace of debility. His eyes were searching, sharp, recruiting. He examined me closely as we sat and listened to Colette, as she talked blandly of Australia and distance and the swift motion of time. All the while I felt him looking at me, watching across his teacup, across the movements of his handkerchief over his face.

—Some small things, already, I have told him, Monsieur Jalabert. Old stories. Things I had forgotten. Things I had never thought to tell to anyone. It is indeed, is it not, the audience that creates the tale? Is it not curiosity itself, Madame Truchet, that creates the history? Is it not our great-nephew here, from so far away, that gives us all our past?

Madame Truchet looked blank, then a little irritated. Monsieur Jalabert's eyes moved from Tante Colette to me, as though to measure my response. At length he smiled dryly, putting down his tea, steadying with two hands the clattering of the cup.

—Our young friend must find many things strange, many things a mystery; the Old World somewhat older, a little further in decrepitude, than he might have imagined?

He gave me the room, the mustiness, the dilapidation, the old women beside him, in an elegant motion of his hand.

Madame Truchet was restless with this kind of talk. She patted Monsieur Jalabert on the wrist, with a flat indulgent smile to all the room, and looked to her watch and her capacious handbag. Saturday. The day's good deed was done. She assisted Monsieur Jalabert as he struggled to his feet.

He shook her off, but gently, and crossed the room, taking my hand. He spoke in a low voice.

—I am pleased to have met you. We must meet again, soon. We had expected someone. Perhaps not quite so late, so very long. There were many details—the property—that were never really sorted out. You may be able to help. To complete my father's files. I have, you see, this passion for detail, a love of neat endings, with all the pieces tied together. An old professional habit. Perhaps we can meet again. There are many things that we can tell each other. I will tell you more of your great-grandfather. The famous escape. Of Rochefort and the others. You have seen the painting by Manet?

He looked about him, to see that Colette was now deep in polite but trivial departure conversation with the worthy Madame Truchet.

—Perhaps we may talk of Sebastien Rouvel?

I looked at him closely but he had looked away, attending closely to his coat, his hat, his stick. I could not be sure that I had heard him correctly.

—You must come to see me. And soon. Mademoiselle Colette will tell you where.

He glanced fondly in her direction.

—It is close by. You must come soon.

After they left Colette took me for a walk in the garden—or, rather, the ragged wilderness that ran around the house. We stepped around crates, bedsteads, rotting frames and cages. Here and there, I held back straying branches so that Colette could pass through.

—You must understand, dear *Nicolas*. Things like this—this disorder, this decay—don't happen in a day. Nor does it happen by design.

We stood before the tall façade. The cracks, the spreading lines of ivy.

—This house, with its closed rooms and weeds and broken windows. You are polite. You make no comment, but your thought is clear. It must all seem so very odd.

I merely smiled and led her towards an iron bench, part covered in twigs and debris from the trees.

—It is strange. Perhaps only, though, at this late stage, even then only to others, to outsiders, to those who have not seen how ordinary things on ordinary days—a small theft here, a breakage there, a drain left to overflow, the handle of a door that is never fixed—gradually lead across the years, *Nicolas*, to what you see today.

I cleared the bench of debris. Colette directed me to sit beside her. She took and stroked my hand.

Nothing, she said, had ever been sold. The land, yes, but not the house or furniture. And almost nothing bought. Their lives—the strangeness of their lives had come about in the same way. With their few friends from childhood dying, or moving away and never being replaced, and theirs never having been a normal childhood; never normal, despite all the efforts of their poor Maman. She could speak of blocked drains and creeping vegetation forcing the very walls apart, of rooms closed off because of damp and falling plaster, of other rooms closed simply because no-one had any use for them, some of them still containing her mother's things and even things of her Uncle Claude, which no-one had looked at for years. And all around them, as I could see, they now had Clémentine's foolish constructions—their very lives, it sometimes seemed, slipping piece by piece from the house and into Clémentine's piles of wood and netting.

—The old furniture is unsold, but I did not say unused, and still mocks us from those sorry cages that run around the house.

She seemed to want no comment.

—Your parents, Tante Colette. Your mother. How did she find it, coming back, and coming to this house? Was she happy here?

—There was hardship, *Nicolas*. The house was better, then. But I could tell you much of those early years, soon after our arrival, when she had to struggle so hard to obtain what had been left to her. I could tell you of her struggles with her brother, who saw her as an intruder, his mind poisoned against her in some way, poisoned by stories told to him in his childhood. Or perhaps it was just the money, *Nicolas*, the money he had thought would be his own with his sister and the only living niece lost to the far side of the world, as good or even better than dead, until she reappeared one day at the gates of his inheritance, with no warning and with three children, three freckled girls still wilder than young rabbits, to take possession of what he thought must be his.

—He came here once. Just one time that I remember. An awkward and ungiving man, much younger than my mother but with the air of someone old. We were still very young. He sat with my mother in the salon, in the chair where you have sat. Another man was with him. His lawyer, I presume. They talked to her of rights and lack of rights, with hints and then much more than hints that she should take herself and her bastard children—voices were soon raised and many bitter things said and I recall the bastard children—back to the far ends of the world and let them all live in peace, as they had managed to do since the time when she disgraced them; disgraced the family, as he said, more than twenty years before. I recall the threats and fingers being waved in menace at the door, and our uncle leaving with no goodbyes to anyone, avoiding us in the driveway as though we were some kind of infection, some malign infestation that had blown in from the south.

—Afterwards, I crept back into the house and sat there, where you sat, and watched my mother, silent, just staring out the window. She did not weep. There was almost a small smile on her lips, as though she was now strong enough to face anything that could happen, as though she now knew what she was, and what she had to be. And from that moment we saw no-one, saw no member of her family again. Not her brother, our uncle, or anyone, and never a word from her parents. All was done by lawyers. Who stole from us, like everyone else, until we met the father of our Monsieur Jalabert. And in the end, my mother kept this house.

Colette was silent for a time. She just sat, scarcely breathing, simply gazing at the past. My head was full of questions. Which ones to ask? Which ones to leave? I thought again of what she had said on my first visit, about time, and the slow path of feeling.

She seemed to see this. Suddenly, she laughed. I was, she said, far too curious. She had noticed from the first. The eagerness. The agitation. It was perhaps because

I had lived so far away that I did not understand how closely these things touched, how so much that was strange had simply run itself into the weft of the simple and everyday. She said that she had watched me, even in those first moments, had seen me gaze about the room, my eyes lingering on all the signs of decay, the state of the wallpaper, the broken panes. She had watched me as I left, standing for a time down in the wilderness of the garden, my eyes roving across the cracked façade, my thoughts sweeping up and down the walls with a kind of hunger.

—Wherever you see a lack, *Nicolas*, you think you need to fill it. Or repair it. With some story, some explanation. Am I right? Believe me, often there are just lacks. Holes. Gaps that you must live with. There is so much that you notice, dear *Nicolas*, that simply does not need to be noticed.

Then she had smiled at me again. She squeezed my arm, to fill this new lack her own comments had caused.

—Was our mother happy here? Happy is not the right word. No—my mother was never happy in this place. Not after all that had happened. In Paris. At Deception. But she could not bear to be elsewhere. That is closer to the truth. She had played here often as a child, on a swing in the garden. The swing is gone, of course, but you can still see the metal bracket, rusting deep into the branch.

She told us that she had often played here and was happy when she came here as a child, and so she thought we too would have a better chance of being content in this place. The place reminded her of something, of better days. I sometimes think—I sometimes wonder, *Nicolas*—if we have not lived all our lives, too much of our lives, in some sad attempt to trace the childhood, the lost happiness of my mother?

From the rear of the garden, we could hear Clémentine singing, together with much screeching and the wild beating of wings.

—Come. There are things we have to do. We do talk far too much, *Nicolas*. Perhaps we can help Clémentine.

She rose awkwardly to her feet, took my arm, and began to guide me back down the driveway towards the house, towards the cages of Clémentine.

—You said that your mother followed him, Tante Colette.

—She followed him, to the Ends of the Earth. It is enough, for now. Come. We will assist poor Clémentine. We can do that, at least.

I stood in her path. Helping Clémentine must mean the end of questions and of answers. This business of the Ends of the Earth? This convenient dumping ground, this place where memory and the telling of all stories must simply come to its own End?

I felt part of what was exiled. For perhaps the first time. Part of what was deported, of what was left behind.

—Please tell me, Tante Colette. I really want to know. Just this, at least. Why did she leave, in the end? Why did you all come home? I want to know about Agnes. Why was my grandmother left behind?

She was annoyed, even distressed. She took time to rearrange some wisps of hair that had strayed across her face. She looked up at the house.

—You would only be disappointed in anything I can say. You complicate your life too much with what belongs to the life of others. This house was waiting here, for all of us. You might better ask, why was it that our father stayed? That is perhaps the greater mystery. A mystery that you may one day understand better than we do.

—Tante Colette, you say she joined him there. Your mother. Do you know much of the time between? Before she followed him, as you say, to the far side of the world?

—To understand why she left—what she did, and why she came home you would have to understand why she followed him, and to understand that, you would need to know much more about what happened, all those years ago. In Paris, in those times. About Agnes, too. It takes time to explain, *Nicolas*. You have such a list of questions. I have no list of answers. I can tell you of people. Of how they felt. That is all.

She was silent for a time, looking over the façade of the house, and up to Geneviève's open window. Hesitating. But then looking to me closely, as though searching in my eyes for what I already knew.

—You ask about times that are long past. About things that happened long before even I was born. Why does it matter to you? I have told you already of my parents' youth, the times they spent in Paris. What more must you know? I can only repeat. My mother was sent to Paris for 'finishing', as her Tante Agathe would have it. She fell in love with my father. Then there was war. War with the Prussians, followed by civil war. What happened there did indeed finish her, as far as normal living is concerned. That much, at least, you must understand. The fire and violence in the streets. A time like now, but with greater harm. There was disruption to the lives of everyone. To those who were directly a part of it, and to many others who were simply swept up in the storm. Like her poor Tante Agathe, who refused to change her daily routines, in spite of Prussians, *fédérés* and Versaillais. And then it was too late for either of them to leave. Did I not tell you? The apartment of Tante Agathe was destroyed by a shell fired by our own troops from St Cloud. She was forced out into the street, and was killed in the avenue de Tourville, in the midst of the fighting. My mother was left completely alone in Paris, in the street, in the midst of it all. Did not your grandmother tell you this?

She had not. For Agnes, Paris was just too many worlds away.

—What kind of normal life could come out of that? Our mother almost never spoke of it, and why should she? In those moments, she could feel the whole of life going wrong. The rest of her life was spent trying to turn it back. To recover what was lost. Even up at Deception. These are the things you need to know. Not just the facts. Not just what happened, but the dreams. The illusions, *Nicolas*.

She led me up towards the steps. I thought of Lucien, ragged and raw, disdaining shelter from the violence, living still the passion of contention, dragging his ruins and his bloodshed across the shining boulevards. I thought of Julia, pulsing with excitement at this new entry to the lives of others. It had been my parents' view that if all the gateways to the past are blocked, then there is probably a good reason. That the dead do have some right of privacy. That we owe the past respect, not to pry or search too far beyond the boundaries that those who went before us have carefully set in place. That if someone had written *inconnu à cette adresse* on an envelope, if someone had written *inconnu* on a letter that had come halfway around the world, then there may have been a reason of a kind we should respect.

—I do recall the arguments, *Nicolas*. This much I will tell. The many arguments between my parents, and all about this house. I did not understand all that was said. I do remember a letter. A letter to my mother from her family, from that same brother. Finally, after so many years of neglect, so many years of isolation, a resentful letter from this long-forgotten brother telling her of the death of Uncle Claude. The letter was cruel. The kind of cruelty that was only possible for those who feel they have God on their side. The kind of cruelty that can only come from the righteousness of devotion. With the letter, the suggestion, perhaps an instruction, that this house should quickly be passed over to the family in France. Our mother considered an offer from the brother, with the suggestion that the money might be used to help restore the shrinking fortunes of Deception. I also remember our father just taking up his tools again and walking out the door, leaving the suggestion unanswered, walking out into the blazing blast of light that caught him as he went through the door, into the heat and despair of yet another dry day's useless effort.

—And Agnes?

—Who stayed on to help our father. Until they could join us all in France.

She stood close. My hand still placed gently on the hand that held the stick.

—Enough of these questions, *Nicolas*. The questions that you ask will always be more complicated than any answer I can give. You never will be satisfied.

—I'm sorry, Tante Colette.

—I know. What I tell you is too simple for you to accept, perhaps, with all your books and libraries and dreams of faraway places. Life was difficult. The place, your country, was too difficult. Too difficult for all of us. Monsieur Jalabert will perhaps tell you more about Deception. That is all.

Colette was suddenly tired. She held my arm, tightly, now with tears in her eyes.

—This is why I tell you, dear *Nicolas*. It calls for more than knowledge. Do you not understand?

She looked up and down the driveway, then up at the broken shutters, the open window, the tangle of weeds and growth across the driveway, the buckled gate and the rusting body of the car. She gestured wearily towards Clémentine, struggling with her cages, as though to pass me over.

The last days of the Commune. The avenue de Tourville. The death of Tante Agathe. I found the street, in the late warmth of the evening, watched the lights that moved behind those curtains. I thought of new Tante Agathes and Marie-Josèphes immured within, of Colette's tales of this young woman sent to improve herself in Paris; thought for a moment of falling walls, of the impertinence of gunfire and obscene scuttling troops, and of all the secret life of Tante Agathe, the paintings, crockery, furniture and scattered clothing, set out in muddied display along the raw and shattered reaches of the avenue.

I wanted to know. Should I rather have said, I *needed* to know? To demolish those apartments that we all create, between time and time, and space and space, for new and even muddier displays of our own? But just how much, beyond the range of touch and sight, and memory, can we really hope to recover? How much will just be fantasy, the gaps topped up with spectres of our own devising, the need more than the knowledge still pushing the whole thing forward, no matter what we're told? How far could I really hope to pass across, in the way Colette had asked; to think myself among the thousands of the dead, to think of how her mother had roamed these streets alone, the piles of corpses mounting by the abandoned barricades, the courtyards turned to execution grounds, the cartloads of the dead already rolling to the west? To imagine how it must have been, moving through the side streets and sheltering in doorways to avoid the Versaillais, feeling her way in slow and cautious stages to the river, beating back towards safety and refuge in the apartment of Tante Agathe in the avenue de Tourville?

> *They watched them from the toppled banks and bridges, watched as they sang through the city, aided by the light of the fires that burned more brightly in reflection from the streams of boiling mercury and lead. They watched the floating barges with their cargos of doomed souls as they coursed below the bridges, the tattered sails still burning, the smoking cords still flickering and cracking through the heat and twisting winds . . .*

Through the smoke and falling light she must have seen the vast glow of the Tuileries to the west, the Hôtel de Ville still burning, the stonework glowing brightly with the close of the day. She was drawn along by the crowd that streamed in thousands from the buildings and the courtyards to press her forward towards Châtelet, bearing her steadily south, over the river and through the Île de la Cité, the cathedral still intact but scarcely visible through the circling smoke, its towers disappearing into the troubled air. Finding herself at last alone, face blackened, hands smeared with incriminating blood, alone again in the empty streets, feeling her way down the long walled avenues of locked doors and closed shutters towards the final welcome sanctuary of the avenue de Tourville.

Unlike any river that was ever known, this river made of blood and molten lead, the barges moving steadily through the flood, the helmsmen moving in the red light of fire above and fire below . . .

There was also an older woman. Moving through the smoking streets, searching for this ward gone missing, at last turning back, against all the horrors of the streets, the falling walls and corpses strung on railings, the dying. Turning at last into the avenue, away from the crowds, the smoke and fighting, and into a street suddenly gone quiet. The shutters closed. All other windows boarded up. And where her apartment had once been, a stream of broken masonry, a building gutted, the walls collapsed, the furniture, curtains, clothing strewn across the street.

Within each boat, the doomed souls sang, each barge lined with its naked choir that held aloft a smoking poem, all singing in a wild cacophony 'Kyrie, Kyrie' as they rolled beneath the toppled bridges and past the falling stone of courts, palaces, cathedrals . . .

She was not alone. Despite the stillness, the sudden silence. A hundred yards before her rose a small tableau, a row of blue coats and a flash of red. She was now able to see them more clearly as the smoke drifted. Five or six soldiers. Waiting. Two standing with their rifles raised, the heavy Chassepots of the Versaillais. Three kneeling or squatting behind some heavy object, now emerging from the smoke, a *mitrailleuse* on its tripod pointed in her direction, with them looking at her, and she, now motionless as well, looking back at them, encircled by the toppled walls, the street lightly strewn with other presences, with what had looked like clumps of clothing but now were bodies spread and flattened as though by some crude obliterating force. Near the silent soldiers, a horse was lying on its side and struggling to get up, the silence broken for a moment in a listless whinnying, the horse arching its neck, its rear legs lifting and moving, but for no more than a moment.

> *The soldiers watching the doomed along the burning river, watching the barges pass below the broken bridges, inverting their arms and all submitting to the beautiful cacophonous music of the doomed souls as they pass, the city all about them toppling, the stones slipping into the burning river of blood and boiling mercury . . .*

With Tante Agathe now addressing herself at last to the fires that had broken out across the city, to the presence of these new forms of ugliness about her, to the rude opening of the apartment on the avenue de Tourville, the scattering of its secret inner spaces to the half-light of the street. Clipped branches like welcoming palm fronds lay about her on the paving stones. Cinders, fragments of paper wafted past her in the heated air. Such peace she had not known for weeks, such serenity as reigned there in that moment in the avenue de Tourville. The faces of the men behind the weapons were still indistinct, but with each of them now starting to move, their movements slow and laboured as though impeded by the smoke and heavy air, but with even the movement of the young soldier behind the *mitrailleuse* now visible through the dense smoke that coiled about him. With the trembling hand of Tante Agathe rising towards her throat. Opening just one button on her dress. To the loud sounds, and to the silence.

Seven

MILLY-LA-FORÊT IS NOT far from Saint-Germain-sur-École. I went down again, just two days later. Curious to do as Colette bid, to speak with Monsieur Jalabert. Eager to follow the hints, the suggestion of some revelation that Monsieur Jalabert managed to imply, in our short time together at Saint-Germain-sur-École.

I stopped at the old house on the way. It was a sunny morning, and at Colette's suggestion, we took another stroll in what was left of the garden, around the last of the flowerbeds that had not been overtaken by the shrubs and brambles and cages, making our way towards the high stone wall that ran along the front of the house. I told her of Lucien, and of our visit to Père-Lachaise. She greatly enjoyed my tales of the *clochard*, her laughter ringing like silver out across the garden at how his shoes flapped their way up along the rue de la Roquette, how he scraped such detailed memories from somewhere deep within his hair.

She took my arm. She seemed pleased that I was on my way, so quickly, to Milly-la-Forêt. I assisted her as we made our way down the pathways cautiously, through the weeds and fallen branches to the same iron bench where we had sat before.

—Here. Sit with me here. In the sun. It is not often that I have the opportunity.

She walked with great difficulty, leaning upon her stick, but when she sat down she sat erect, her back not touching, as it never seemed to touch the back of any chair. I worked for a time with a pair of ancient secateurs that were lying on the bench, cutting back the branches which reached across the driveway, and hauling out some of the weeds and bushes that had invaded the gravel.

Colette watched me in silence.

At length, I slumped beside her, perspiring with the unfamiliar effort. She then did something strange, something unexpected. She turned to me and placed her hand on my forehead. Feeling the sweat with her hand, letting it run between her fingers, and then wiping her fingers on her handkerchief.

—The sweat, *Nicolas*. My father. The only moisture

we ever saw up at Deception, as he would say. You remind me of my father, in so many ways.

The smile. The smile was surely for her father. It seemed a question might at last be welcome.

—What sort of man was he, Tante Colette? My great-grandfather? What was he really like?

She did not speak for a time. I watched the expression on her face, which seemed to change, as though she were balancing the good and the bad in stages, and wondering which to tell. I watched her as she looked to the sun and the wilderness of stooping branches, to the brightness glittering on the leaves. As though deciding, as always, what information should stay with her, and what should be passed on.

—You remind me of him. So much. The air of distraction. Your thoughts are not always with us.

—What really happened to him, Tante Colette?

—Prison. And deportation. Do you know about the deportations? The hasty trials? The thousands that were sent?

She looked me in the eye and smiled.

—This much, I'm sure you already know. It is well known. It is no disgrace. About this, it is again with our friend Monsieur Jalabert that you must speak. Monsieur Jalabert knows so much that we have ourselves forgotten. The dates, the trial, the sentence. All the legal matters. He has seen the records.

She smiled, but I noted that her hand was tense, gripping and releasing the ball of her stick. She began to look around the garden, as though searching for some distraction, some new line of conversation. Behind us, I could hear Clémentine talking to her parrots, seeking to catch them and move them from cage to cage, I imagined.

—He was of course not shot, *Nicolas*, like so many thousands of others in the courtyards and parks and gardens of the city, in the abbatoirs of the Luxembourg Gardens, the Parc Monceau, the Buttes-Chaumont. I too have read the histories. He was wounded. He was hidden by friends and not discovered until some days later, when the random killings had stopped. His lucky wound, he always called it. Even much later, at Deception, when the pain would return, he called it his lucky wound.

—There was much suffering to follow. He was led out three times to be shot on the plain at Satory, and each time was reprieved and flung back in prison. He was sent at last to a prison island that lay off the coast. He lived in squalor with hundreds of others in the old naval dungeons for more than a year, and then was sent away, condemned to a life of forced labour. Exile. The deportations.

One day, she said, she would tell more. Of how terrible it had been, not because of single acts of cruelty, but because of the breaking, the exile, the thousands of young lives that were destroyed, interrupted, wounded in ways that never could be healed.

—A heavy price, they paid. A price that those to follow, too, were to pay in other, unseen ways. Our mother. Perhaps my sisters and I, in our own ways.

She had struggled to her feet, as though this conversation was now over.

—The deportations. So very cruel. For all who were deported. For all those linked to those who were deported. The exiles' time on the island, and the famous escape. These things are well enough known. These are facts, indeed. You may find them in the history books. I told you, when we first spoke, that he was the Emperor's soldier. This was the truth, when there was still an emperor to serve. You will read harsh things about those who fought for Paris. But most were simply patriots. Men and women who resented the defeat. Disbanded soldiers with nowhere else to go, who believed that they could, at least for a time, hold Paris, and the nation's pride, against the enemy.

—You ask what he was like, my father? He was never easy, *Nicolas*. This I admit to you. Our mother told us much of our father, in those later years when he would not come home. Of how misfortune came heavily upon us, long before we left Deception, our mother always wanting to leave, and our father thinking always that by staying on, by just one long and limitless effort of will, the earth would break open and let the grass through, that the sky would cloud over and the rains would come. It was my mother's view, and something that even as a child I could observe—that in every situation, there was for our father an ideal form, some special shape, our mother would often say, that was more the shape of dreaming than the shape that things could ever take, in the world that lay around us. Perhaps especially up at Deception. Above all, at Mount Deception.

She peered at me more closely, her eyes carefully measuring my response.

—My father was a difficult man. A broken man, perhaps. He could never bow to circumstance.

She touched my face again. Her father.

Monsieur Jalabert, I was told, had the best suite of rooms in a hostel for the aged. I was met in the foyer, gleaming, disinfected, and taken to his rooms by a nun, a Daughter of Charity in full rosaried flight who clicked and billowed through a maze of paths and outbuildings, until we reached his rooms, off a shaded garden court.

Monsieur Jalabert was formally dressed as he came unsteadily to the door, in blue suit and waistcoat, handkerchief and dark silk tie, as though ready for a full day of legal affairs.

He showed no surprise that I had come so soon. He invited me into his rooms. Monsieur Jalabert was indeed well established, with three rooms of his own: a bedroom, a small salon, and a larger, well-lit room that was furnished as a library or an office. The walls were lined with books, mostly old books bound in leather, with long rows of statutes and cases similarly bound. In the middle of the room was a large desk, a splendid inlaid piece topped with leather with rich mouldings in ormolu and green-shaded reading lamps. Monsieur Jalabert shuffled his way behind these and sat down, bidding me to sit in a leather chair on the far side of the desk, as though we met in some form of professional consultation.

With the green desk lamps before him and the light behind, I could read little in the expression of Monsieur Jalabert. I watched the movement of his wrinkled hands, his gestures measured and elegant even with the awkward hesitancy of age. So very, very old. Older even than Colette, so stooped and shrunken, and seeming more so in the harsh brightness that flooded through the thin curtains than in the darkness of Colette's room. I thought for a moment, in that momentary haze of brightness, the distortions of the light, of a young man in this same suit, same collar, same handkerchief. An awkward and unattractive youth. Accommodating and punctilious. Arriving with his papers at the house on any kind of pretext. Following, with his oppressive and detailed attentions, a tall and distant young woman with her mind much on other matters.

A lifetime spent in waiting?

Monsieur Jalabert placed his elbows on the desk, and clasped his fingers in a judicious pyramid, a posture of long and cautious patience. Of a meticulous discretion.

—You are keen, Monsieur, to know more of the story of your family. Mademoiselle Colette does seem to think that I might be able to help.

—I have come a long way, Monsieur Jalabert.

—To find out all that happened? In Nouméa, and later at your Mount Deception? I can tell you what the histories say.

—I have read the histories, Monsieur Jalabert. The public events. There are gaps. They don't tell the full story.

—Indeed, they do not. And neither—as you may now have discovered—does Mademoiselle Colette.

He smiled. Not at me, particularly. He looked over at his cabinets, his books.

—Why did they leave Australia, Monsieur Jalabert? Why did they all—almost all of them—come home? So suddenly?

He turned his chair towards the light. Focusing now on something in the garden.

—It was sixty years ago that I first asked myself the same questions. The questions you are no doubt now asking yourself. Perhaps it was seventy years. At a time when there were others still alive who could have given me the answers I felt I needed. Which, like you, I felt I needed, at that time.

Monsieur Jalabert seemed to want to stay with the mystery. He sat back in his chair. He clasped his hands, and looked at me. He said nothing for a time. Then he spoke, this time in English, and with slow precision, speaking as though reading from a book, an English that was slow and stilted, an English more from ancient grammars than an English that was ever spoken, his careful measure of words seeming to touch on wider meanings, each sentence framed by an aura of other words withheld.

—My father always knew more than he told me. My father's papers contained much that Madame Duvernois had told him, that Colette herself did not know. About New Caledonia, but also about Mount Deception. Letters, papers, documents. But how far should I take the matter? How far should I trouble her? And if I happened to find out more than I needed to know—if I were, for example, to bring a trove of new and telling documents to light—would that have made her more, or less my friend?

The light was behind him. I could not read his expression.

—I will tell you what I know of these people. Of your family. It is strange. Mademoiselle Colette wishes me to tell you what I know. Yet there is much, still, that she will not tell me. So be it. I am their lawyer. I like to work more with what is proven than with what has and has not been told. You too, I am told, are a lawyer, though not yet in practice. I have my instructions. Like good lawyers, let us take things step by step. Let us talk first of the trial. Of imprisonment, and exile, and the famous escape. And then, perhaps, we will talk of Deception, and all that happened there. Of all who came to Mount Deception. All of them. Of those who left. And those who stayed behind.

Step by step. As with Colette. I hadn't come, though, for further uncertain stories. I tried to see beyond the spectacles of Monsieur Jalabert, beyond the guarded smile and clasped hands and what seemed like long and cautious preparation; this Monsieur Jalabert, who seemed to give with one hand—a hint, a gesture, a comment to be half-heard, perhaps mistaken—and then to draw back with the other. I decided to opt for frank questions, if only to watch for signs of frank evasion.

—I do think she tells me lies, Monsieur. Not exactly lies, perhaps. Half-truths, at least. The love affair in Paris.

The emperor's soldier. The secret trysts. Stories taken out of novels.

—I know. Mademoiselle Colette has told me the same stories all my life.

—I know that they are not quite true. Or don't give the whole truth, at least. They are about things that didn't happen, or perhaps which did happen, but which meant something else. Something more than she is saying. There are gaps.

Monsieur Jalabert smiled and shook his head.

—She knows that I know that they are not full truths, as well. She has known, I do suspect, for almost seventy years. Yet still she tells me her stories. I do not disagree. Perhaps this is what friendship means?

—What should I do, Monsieur? Should I go? Should I just leave, and let them be?

—No. She does not want you to leave.

—Should I stop asking questions?

—No. She does not want you to stop asking your questions.

He held up a hand, as though to counsel a long tolerance.

—You must consider that there are perhaps things that she wants you to know. Things that she cannot say, because of her mother and her sisters, and because of all that has happened. The fact that such things have for so long been unsaid itself creates a burden. You say her stories contradict. Is it not possible, my young friend, that they contradict on purpose, so that you will continue to ask your questions?

The face of Monsieur Jalabert was distorted by the light. With an expression that still looked like a smile, but which I now realised was not quite.

—Is it not what you do not know that brings you back, and back, to Saint-Germain-sur-École? Would you be here now if you had the knowledge that you sought?

—I think you know more, Monsieur Jalabert, than you are telling me.

—Of course. I am still their lawyer. Mademoiselle Colette and her sisters are my clients. My oldest clients. My last clients. My father was their mother's lawyer. But I can tell you, honestly, that I do not know all the answers you are seeking.

He looked at his books for a time. He turned his swivel chair to the window and the light, as though preparing to deliver some wider form of wisdom.

—I am their lawyer, and as a lawyer I have learned many things. Some of which I was told by my father, and others which I have learned from more than seventy years of practice. There are times when it is important that you should know more than anyone else. Times when it is important to be in command, to be in a position to surprise the world—suddenly, to surprise—with what the world does not expect you to know. I know, for example, that someone is helping you. That you are not putting this story together on your own. I know that you have a friend who also has an interest in this story. Someone about whom you cannot speak to Colette.

—But how can you know that?

He smiled shrewdly, but not unkindly.

—Because you have just told me. A mere speculation. Which you have just now confirmed to be the truth.

—A trap, Monsieur Jalabert?

—A trap? No, no. A stratagem, perhaps.

I thought of the papers. Did he perhaps know of them? Monsieur Jalabert had just said, 'If I were, for example, to bring a trove of new and telling documents to light'? Did he already have such documents, not yet brought to light? What kind of 'if' was this? Did he perhaps suspect that I had such a trove? I began to feel the burden of my rash promise of secrecy—now starting to seem obstructive, even foolish—to Julia. I felt the weight of the notes and translations of Sebastien Rouvel even now in my satchel.

He looked more closely at me, to ensure that his words were finding their mark. He leaned forward, unclasping his hands.

—But let me tell you, too, there are many times where

it is important to know less. Because then, you do not have to lie. I have known it since long ago. My friendship with these women has much to do with what I do not know. Many, many years ago, I decided that whatever happened there, in your country and even long before, however much Mademoiselle Colette seemed to want to tell it to me—her lies, as you call them, though indeed, they are never quite lies—it was important that I should not know.

He paused for a moment.

—If I could help you, of course, I perhaps would not. But the truth is, I simply cannot help.

—Then help me with advice, Monsieur Jalabert. Should I go? Should I say that I am satisfied, and thank her, and go home?

Monsieur Jalabert had retreated again to his position behind the desk, half hidden by the lamps. He shook his head.

—That would be unkind. That would be a cruelty. Crueller, I think, than you can imagine. They have waited so long for your visit. It is for your questions that their lives have, in a sense, been lived. Perhaps I am the only one who can tell you this. For years they have spoken of the person who would come. For years they have talked about how they would greet this person, when he came. Though for it to be someone as young as you, was, of course, beyond all our imagining.

This was, I now understood, Monsieur Jalabert's version of a joke. He dabbed gently at the corner of his mouth.

—There is something else you must consider. Something which I would have trouble expressing in my own language, and will perhaps express much worse in yours.

Monsieur Jalabert now spoke very slowly, choosing each word carefully for its purpose.

—It is not always easy, as a lawyer, to be kind. Have you read Balzac? The last page of his story, *Colonel Chabert*? The lawyer, Derville? 'Our offices are sewers which can never be cleansed . . . I have known wills burned; I have seen mothers robbing their children, wives killing their husbands, and working on the love they could inspire to make men idiotic or mad, that they might live in peace with a lover.' And so on. Read it, my young friend and perhaps you will choose for yourself another kind of career.

Was Monsieur Jalabert smiling? He cleared his throat, and moved closer.

—There is, just now, a happiness in that house. A pleasure taken in your visits. I say nothing against their mother. I do not question her intentions. But at last the long waiting, this life of shadows, has seemed to lead somewhere. I see a new kind of pleasure in their lives. Even Geneviève, I am told, is better than before. It is given to few of us, young *Nicolas*, to bring this kind of pleasure into other people's lives.

He silenced me with a gesture.

—Perhaps you should insist on being told more by Colette herself. You, who are now, it seems, the chosen future for these women. You should know how beautiful she was. Colette. Coming in at the end of the story does not necessarily give you the whole story—all that you need. Geneviève was the pretty one—as I'm sure you will hear but it was Colette who was the real beauty. Whose beauty just went on and on.

The beauty was there still. Monsieur Jalabert's hands were still clasped, lawyer-like. That beauty still a fact. Not just part of the history. Colette still had a power, a strength. Was this Monsieur Jalabert, this oldest friend, once upon a time—and still—in love with her? Was this another fact?

—Let me tell you something else; something that you may find more difficult to understand. Your visit has drawn out a purpose, a destination in their lives that might otherwise have slipped away. Strange lives, little changed from the time of their first arrival from your country seventy-five years ago. And always in a kind of exile, in a country that should have become their own.

—So you think I should continue? You think I should continue to visit Colette, listen to her stories?

—I think she wants to tell you. I do believe that she wants you, at least, to understand. Mademoiselle Colette has lived an odd kind of life. But she is not an odd kind of person. She thinks very clearly, and with wisdom; as clearly as anyone I have met, in a very long life. I see her affection for you. I see how she is now eager for your visits. She wants you to know, who have come in so very late upon this whole story. In her heart, I know that she wants you to see that there is a logic, a form of reason behind the strangeness that you see. I think she wants you, in particular, to understand.

Monsieur Jalabert smiled. His features were distorted by the green glow from the lamp, his eyes still searching carefully for my response.

—Your purpose in all this, you see, my young antipodean friend, is to bring these secrets to a close. We are all close to death. We have all lived for far too long with half-understandings and half-truths. I say 'we', you may notice. Mademoiselle Colette and her sisters and me. Be it for better or for worse, I do believe the purpose of your coming is to bring this long and sad performance that has been our lives to some kind of ending.

To bring things to an ending. I had promised Colette that I would call in after seeing Monsieur Jalabert, to tell her of my conversation with this oldest friend. We would take advantage, she said, of the long evenings. She took me out into the garden again, to the same place. Speaking now more closely, more intimately, as the raw hues of late sunlight began to fade.

—You will be our support, *Nicolas*. We have decided. For all of us. The custodian of the things I tell you. It is you, dear *Nicolas*, who will make the choice. Of what is to be the past, and what the future. Of what to pass on, and of what will die with us. And with this house. We will tell you all, so that you will know not just what you see, now, at the end of it, but also something of the living and the dying that brought it about. You will sift. You will decide. How to leave us all, yourself and your children, with a visitable past?

She smiled secretively. A visitable past. As though the phrase had been long rehearsed, perhaps practised on her sisters.

And it is true, she said. They did not marry. None of them. As though I had asked. It was something, she said, that I must surely have wondered about. Something that my own children might ask one day? They did not marry. Nor was this something that happened in a moment. You did not become unmarried at any point in time, in ways that anyone could grasp at and quickly seek to change. The years passed. They became older. That was all.

There were times, she said, when marriage seemed

possible to them all. There were young men, from good families. It was Geneviève who was the pretty one—the one, perhaps, who seemed most normal to them, the young men who would come to visit, in those days. But time simply passed. And yet, she said, the time did not pass simply. There was always something that made it difficult for visitors, difficult for young men to approach the house, through that tall gate and up that driveway, with their mother always kind, always gracious and kind and welcoming, but always anxious, too concerned, always wanting to protect.

And all that time, their lives were becoming stranger. They were, in the beginning, robbed by all around them. It did not seem so at the time. The jolly gardener, who seemed to obtain things at such reasonable prices, the *agent de biens* who sold off the estate, who could always find people, a friend here, a business associate there, who wished to assist them by buying the property in bits and pieces. It was only much later that she came to understand how far they had been robbed in this way. It was the elder Monsieur Jalabert, then just a kindly neighbour, who explained what was taking place. She herself, still very young, was the one who could see it most clearly, what was happening, what had already happened to them all. Not in such sadness, like Geneviève, or like Clémentine, who seemed somehow adapted to it all.

She spoke of the gates and the same long driveway, of those four unusual women to be met if anyone would finally brave the house, the biggest, saddest house in the whole country around, of how hard it must have been for any young man to walk down that driveway, to be received in this way at the door. These four women, their mother lost in the manners of another age, in conventions that she had perhaps herself broken and who now lived with some more oppressing sense of obligation, some strict adherence to ancient proprieties as the price they had to pay, all four of them fussing around any visitor that came because they did not know how to receive in any other way. Their nervousness, their awkwardness, running from one to the other and transmitting itself to their unfortunate guest, who would fidget and stammer and clatter his teacup in his saucer, with weak and frantic glances at Geneviève.

There he would sit with his saucer and his cake, just wishing to be gone, with Clémentine twittering to fill the silences and Geneviève silent and awkward, knowing that this thing that was happening to her was called her death, dying in those moments to the sound of Clémentine's chatter and her mother's clatter with the teacups and her pained glances, straining always to be kind but looking at him as if he were intending to make them suffer, to rob and plunder and be gone. One after another, the young men who came to see Geneviève—always, she said, it was for Geneviève—would sit with their tea balanced on their knee until at last the time arrived when they could leave without impoliteness, make the long walk down the driveway, and not be seen again. Such awkward, awkward moments. As Monsieur Jalabert could tell. Their dear friend Monsieur Jalabert, the one of all those young men who always would come back.

They should, she said, have sold the house. They should have gone to Paris, as Geneviève once tried to do, or even just to Fontainebleau, where they would have been less lost to themselves. It was their mother who would not hear of leaving, who could not bear the thought of living elsewhere, the thought of others living in this place. It was as though she thought they could not be unhappy, not really unhappy, as long as they stayed on in this house where she had known happiness in her childhood. That whatever it might cost in other ways, there was, in their staying here together, some kind of protection; that whatever sadness the house might bring was less than what might come to them with nervous smiles and politeness from outside. Until it was too late to seek to change her thoughts, to bring her to see that the threat might come more from within these walls than from what lay beyond.

***

As I left, the evening falling, I glanced up at the window to the room of Geneviève, watched the breeze lifting a faded lace curtain, and heard the faint sound of a voice within the room, that of Clémentine perhaps. Geneviève, the pretty one, for whom the young men came. For whom the house was so oppressive, who spoke the things that others dared not say. The one who had grieved, Colette now hinted, who had railed openly against her mother, against all the unspoken things, the secrets, the shadows that had kept them there. Who lay upstairs, talking to no-one, seeing no-one except her sisters.

What did I know of Geneviève? One faded photograph from her youth, her face shaded deep within a heavy cloche, half hidden by the cluster of her sisters. Beyond that, nothing other than what I had been told, the whole life of this woman no more than downcast eyes and whispers, all now looking after Geneviève, her protests now lost in silence, for years now the visits of Monsieur Jalabert perhaps the sole respite in the long ritual of looking to the slow decline in comfort of the second sister, Geneviève.

You have not met her, Colette said, and said again on each of my visits.

—She is better. Better this week than she has been for many months. Soon you will meet her. It is to be hoped.

The house now showed, Colette had said, the sadness

it had seen. In knowing this, I would come to understand why they had let it slip away: why they lived here still in a kind of loving amid the memories it holds. That what they dreaded most, now that they were old and weak, was that this new violence, this new disruption in the streets of Paris, would flow into their lives one more time; that it would open doors, attitudes, and provide, in the way of all such violence in the past, a passage and an entry to their lives.

Looking up at Geneviève's window, I thought of those young men who braved the gate and driveway and the approach to the big house. I thought too of all the young men who might but did not come, who started down that driveway but did not finish, the sound of the gravel too loud beneath their feet, the silence of the large house at the end of the driveway too menacing, hoping to meet Geneviève along the way before they arrived at the house, hoping even to see Clémentine attending to her birds, but worried always that they might meet the mother and perhaps even this severe older sister. Worried that they might suffer the mother's strangely anxious looks, bear the burden of her formalities and then all the women together, these three strange and perhaps unearthly-seeming women and the mother moving in their old-fashioned clothes between those already sour and dark and musty rooms. Worried that all might crowd in upon them with some unspoken need and secret anxiousness, each seeming in their awkwardness to say, yes, we know that this is not as it should be, we know that this is not how it should be done but we do not know how it should be done, and need to be saved from what it is that we are becoming. With Geneviève in tears within herself, already drawing back into her coffin, Clémentine already drifting off into her world of confusion and Colette carrying the burden of it all upon her shoulders: Colette, already beginning her long waiting, as I now suspected, for someone like myself to walk down that driveway and look her in the eye, and say to her, Your mother, Colette, why did she leave? Why did she come back? Colette, already learning now her rôle, already practising to look me in the eye and to pass on her mother's apprehension in rich disguise, some part of it a lie and some part of it also an invitation to return for further lies, when I would ask, Why was it that she left, that windy day?

I thought of the funeral soon to come; a dark wooden box and ropes, the coffin slowly let into the earth. I thought of the few mourners to attend, the old *curé* and the sisters and perhaps Monsieur Jalabert, the remaining sisters finding him a chair so he could sit beside and peer into the open grave; they being told that in that box was Geneviève, as they had been told for so long that Geneviève was in the room above, the old *curé* weaving from ancient and well-used words some kind of living for Geneviève, some kind of virtuous and exemplary life out of the emptiness and blown curtains and cautious whispers; that Geneviève had been this splendid thing and that, and then the box lowered, gently, there being nothing left but more whispers and murmured phrases of regret by one or two kind neighbours thinking, Well that's over and only two more to go, the two ancient sisters standing beside the grave with nothing but odd and uncertain memories and that sad decayed calamity of a house.

Eight

—THE WHOLE THING FALLS naturally into four sections, Nicholas. It just needed rearranging. A bit of sifting. I've set it in proper order, I think. The way Rouvel meant it to be.

Julia drew me into her apartment. After further days of silence. Useless days. Days that saw only a steady growth in longing. You have to keep your end up. I wanted to impress. I arrived with bold tales of new files and newspapers and dossiers. Of new contacts and interviews and assignations. Of deep researches, thoroughly pursued.

Julia just brushed it all aside, in a warm but flustered greeting. She appeared to have risen from sleep. She was wearing a rumpled bathrobe, her hair in great disorder. I took it as a compliment. She gestured at the increasing clutter in the apartment with an amused wave of her hand, a smile that was childlike, helpless, as though it was the first time she herself had seen it. There were signs of intense concentration everywhere, half-eaten tins of food, abandoned coffees and ashtrays full of half-smoked cigarettes, with rejected pages of typescript scattered in balls across the floor.

The cat rubbed itself against my legs, mewing hungrily.

—It's almost ready, Nicholas. It's only a plan at this stage, of course, but it's more or less readable. Most of it. Here!

She thrust a bundle of papers into my hands.

—Read it! Dear Nicholas. Do sit and read. You'll see why I've been so busy. Why I haven't rung.

I threw open a window. The air in the apartment was thick and stale. Julia's eyes were still glazed with deep fatigue. I suggested that she take a shower while I looked over what she'd written.

She had not, she laughed, been properly dressed for days.

Her typescript had a title. *Les Codicilles du Diable*. The Devil's Codicils.

—Do you like it, Nicholas? Anne Thieulle likes it. My editor. Editions Grandet think it will work. It's named after one of the sections. One of the key poems. It fits with his death. His testament.

—It's strong, Julia. Provocative.

—It's very strong. Once I called it *Les Codicilles*, the whole thing just started to fall into place. It more or less began to write itself. I'll take a shower. Be quick, Nicholas. Please tell me what you think.

—But Julia, there must be fifty pages here. A plan, you say?

My words were lost in the flushing of the toilet and the flow of water from the shower. I looked for something for the cat, and then sat with her papers on the bed.

The typescript was neat, a little core of order amid her vast profusion of handwritten notes and gaping reference books, the rejected and crumpled pages, the dirty cups swimming in saucers of spilt coffee and browning banana skins.

Julia stuck her head out of the bathroom, swathed in a turban of wet towels.

—Just find yourself a comfortable spot. I'll get you a coffee in a few minutes. I'll go out and get us something to eat. It seems like days—I don't know how many—since I've slept or eaten properly.

In minutes, she pushed her head out again.

—What do you think, Nicholas? Or is it still too soon to tell? I really must know what you think.

The book was to be in two parts. There was a long introduction, divided into four sections. 'Childhood and

Education', 'The Siege and the Commune', 'The Deportation' and 'The Aftermath'. The second part was to be a transcript of *Les Codicilles du Diable*, with an extended commentary, still incomplete. The *Codicilles* were to be set out in a neat and numbered order, with each longer section now given its own name: 'The Chateau of Rocks', 'The Cell of Banded Light', 'Tales of the Anvil', 'The Leviathan', 'The City of Stone', 'The Prophets of the Desert', 'The Salamander', 'The Palace of Justice'. In each instance, her commentary would run to about three times the length of the original poem, or *codicille*, as they must now be called.

Julia emerged in a cloud of steam and soapy perfume, wrapped in a bath towel, rubbing vigorously at her hair.

—Tell me, Nicholas. What do you make of it?

—Do you think Sebastien Rouvel meant it to be read in any sort of order? Did he really mean it all to fit into any kind of pattern like this?

—The pattern is clear enough. It's quite obvious, if you just look a bit deeper. It's all sort of *emerging*. When you look closely enough.

Julia went to the open window, shaking her hair out over the wrought iron, towards the crowds milling about in the place Monge.

—You have to realise, Nicholas, that he didn't have time to finish it. Some terrible thing prevented him from putting it all together, something that sent him off into the desert, the last stage of his pilgrimage, leaving his papers unfinished. It's up to me—it's up to us, Nicholas—to put them in their proper order. The order that he intended.

—I've called the sections 'Fire', 'Water', 'Earth' and 'Air'. I know it's not very original, but it fits. You can get some idea of when they were written. Where they fit. The bits that were written in Paris—or about Paris and the Commune, at least—are mostly about fire, and burning. The bits that must have been written in New Caledonia, about the deportation—perhaps on the *Danae*—that's the water phase. Then there are poems that seem to be mostly about dry places and the desert, and I've put them all together. They were probably the bits he wrote in your country up near the desert. Earth. 'The Castle of Rocks', 'The Harvest of Stones'.

—But shouldn't they be the last bits then? If they were the bits that were written in the desert? And what about 'Air'?

—There is a whole group of bits about some kind of resolution. Some kind of peace. A drawing together. A transcendence. I haven't read it all yet. Something he had been working his way towards, in hints and flashes, all the way through. Most of the fragments—you've seen bits of them—are very dark. Very obscure. Almost cynical, despairing. But there is a whole group that offer some sense of redemption, some kind of spiritual resurrection and life and hope. Like 'The Salamander'. As though he'd worked his way through it all, Nicholas. Paris and deportation and all, and had finally reached some kind of inner resolution. I've put all of those together, because I'm sure he meant them as some kind of unity. They all fit, somehow.

She moved some files and folders from the desk. Rouvel's writings now sat in four neat piles. Julia flopped down, exhausted but happy, on a chair piled with papers. She ran her fingers through her wet hair, gazing out the window at the place, its canvas awnings and busy market stalls.

I must have frowned, as I skimmed the papers. Julia suddenly dropped to her knees, taking my wrists in her hands.

—Nicholas. You will help me in this, won't you? Please? I've had such trouble. Such opposition. Humiliation, even. It's very, very important to me!

I was startled. There was a dark glint in her eyes. I had seen it before. It showed a kind of anger, but also an excitement of the kind that comes with the thought of winning, of the promise of victory. She shook my wrists, and then smiled. An easy, appeasing smile.

—It's all about a new kind of sensuality, Nicholas. An ennobled kind of feeling. That's why it's so important.

Leading towards spiritual fulfilment. The late poems—the ones I've managed to look at so far—look on to another kind of future. They move against the darkness of most of what he wrote before. There's one about swimmers in the lost Atlantis, mating beneath the waves. In soft embrace. Bodies linked and drowning, or growing like vines together. Lots about fresh tendrils, and breasts and milk in the desert. It all fits. It's there, complete! A wonderful order, a whole political order, a whole spiritual *system*, Nicholas, once you've worked it out.

We sat and read in silence, as the day drifted into night. I sat in the space Julia had created for me on the bed. She sat on the floor before me, wedged between my knees, turning the pages, moving them from one pile to another. I stopped reading and looked down at her, so deeply absorbed in silent but profound excitement. I watched the straying hair that ran out from her clasp, the thin strands that crept up from the base of her neck. So oddly at ease, she seemed, nestling there between my knees. So intent, so utterly absorbed. The cat had settled in her lap. Below the window, from over near the bottle depot in the place Monge, I could hear the sound of glass breaking.

She read on into the darkness, turning the pages around and around to follow the coil of writing. Now and then she would turn her head and smile up at me.

At last, she moved up onto the bed and propped herself beside me, against a pile of pillows and box files. Her green eyes, behind the spectacles, were still lost in dazed reverie over her crumbling pages, the draft of her plan, her fingers still flicking from page to page, too excited, too distracted by the wealth of the whole bundle to concentrate properly on any part. Still grateful, it seemed, and to excess. Stroking my shoulder absent-mindedly with one hand as she supported the manuscript with the other. An invitation to touch, to some more intimate caress? But always with her eyes running back to the yellowing pages, to the manuscript in her hands, to the pages fanned out across the floor, and piled in crumbling leaves across the bed.

Her hair was still creeping from its clasp. Steadily, almost mysteriously. She reached around and released it distractedly, so that it fell about her shoulders, her head now bowed before me as she bent again over the papers, her hair falling in rich brown coils about her neck. Her shoulders bent towards her papers, her pullover bagging loosely from her body, the air of her apartment an odd mixture of perfume, the warmth of her body, the stale smells of work. She looked up from her papers now and then, and smiled, touching my hand, or pointing out a passage, a striking phrase, from the page. Leaning over to look at what I was reading.

—I'm so glad you are here, Nicholas. That you've come.

She murmured softly, into my shoulder, her eyes still on the papers.

—I'm so glad we have found each other. That I now have someone to talk to. Someone who understands. I've been so alone with this story, Nicholas. So alone with my Rouvel. Somehow speaking to him, but with him never speaking back. So much has changed. So very quickly. Because of you, dear Nicholas.

She nestled deeper against me. I gave up, finally, my pretence of reading. Gave up being the scholar. The translator. I took the papers from her hand, and placed them on the floor.

So, we made love, Julia and I. Moving at last from the reading. Drawing ourselves from the past. Separating ourselves from the future. Grasping, from the midst of it, a fragile fleeting present. With the lights turned down, the curtains open to the unsteady light that ran in from the place, we burrowed recklessly amid the scatter of papers, the toppling files, the boxes and plates and wrappers. Seeking the deep assent of touch, and silence. To the odd uneven beat of breaking glass. To the broken light and unsteady motion of a whole troubled city, the sounds of anger and resistance and violent contest in the street.

Not speaking. Letting the words, with all their betraying links and furrows, gently slip away. Letting our thoughts, the wild pendulum of dreads and hopes that sweeps back and forth across each present moment, quite lose itself in passion, pleasure, the deep closet of desire. With our bodies for that moment gone opaque, substantial; bridges now to nowhere, passages to no other place, but only back to ourselves. In that shifting half-darkness and the unsteady moving light. Across that mad carpet of falling papers. With the two of us not looking beyond each other or forwards or backwards for that space in time, but only to this place, this shape, this moment.

Julia drew away and raised herself on one elbow. She caressed my face. Tracing my mood, my thoughts, in the fragile shifting light.

—Dear Nicholas. I do forget. I do forget my best self, my real self, so badly. I do get so lost, Nicholas, in all these things we talk about.

Through seeking to know too much, perhaps? More than the fragile body will allow? I said nothing. I sealed her lips with a finger. With words, it all comes creeping back. The world of fragments. With words come punctuation, divisions, tenses. A world of was, and will be, of the need for sleep, of tasks set for tomorrow. With words, the separation recommences, lured from ourselves again and from these surest forms of understanding and towards some knowledge yet to come, the prospect of richer stories lying in the shadows beyond, stories ripe in mystery and exotic promise, too tangled with our dreams and our fragile entry to the lives of others. Julia's story. A city in flames, a poet lost to history. My story. A cruel leaving, and a death in the desert. But still, in my hopes at least, with some small sense that Julia and I might now be at the edge of some new, some stronger story of our own?

I woke deep in the night, to the sounds of violence somewhere in the streets that lay beyond the place Monge. Not far away, just over the rue Mouffetard, I could hear renewed shouting, the sound of sirens and the breaking of glass. Light fell through the gap in the curtains, the streetlamps in the place Monge still blazing brightly but this time with a new and unsteady glow, a mix of red light and moving shadows from the fires now burning through the city, beyond the rue Mouffetard and through the troubled streets of the Latin Quarter.

Julia lay beside me on the floor, the two of us sprawled naked among the twisted sheets and scattered papers. 'Like a wet rag,' she said before she pulled at last away and fell into a deep sleep. Like a wet rag, wrung out with the excitement, the intimacy, the revelations and the mysteries that rose from the papers, the dossiers and all the airless closeness of her tiny apartment in the rue de la Clef.

Outside was the city, friendless and forbidding, the streets beginning again to be disturbed. I thought of poor Lucien, lying on an iron bench somewhere, or perhaps stretched out over a metro grille to catch the last warmth of the day. I thought of the dank, half closed-up house down at Saint-Germain-sur-École; of the weedy driveway, the branches reaching out across the gravel. I thought of my cheerless attic room in the Grand Hôtel Jeanne d'Arc, over by the Marché Sainte Catherine, where there was nothing but my own trove of papers, similarly spread out under a low and sloping ceiling, a sagging bed, a basin and perilous enamel bidet on an unsteady iron stand.

In time, it grew quiet. The welcome space between the last revellers, now rioters, and the first early morning trucks, the sound of the market stallholders in the place Monge. I watched Julia as she moved and some of the papers moved with her, clinging to the sweat of her bare skin. I watched the filtered streetlight mould the contours of her body as she slept amid the wreckage of her room. Locked in with Sebastien Rouvel's wild deranging scrawl. Exotic, fantastic and obscene.

I watched her, stretched out in the half-light. Naked in the slow heat of the night. Her body still taut, though, like a spring. Her mind elusive still, still remote, tenacious and forbidding, still racked with awkward yearning, or so it did seem as I watched her, even in the deeps of sleep. I ran my hand across her shoulders, gently, not to wake her. Wanting only to touch her, to get closer. Wanting to soothe her deep into her body again, to ease her restless sleep. Seeking to take in the best, the finest of this present moment: the filtered light, the precious touch of silence, the breeze moving the curtains, and the sleeping form of Julia, the light moving on her body, stirring occasionally and speaking to herself, dreaming amid her papers.

Mumbling, now and then, but indistinctly.

I looked over at the main pile of Rouvel's manuscript, a dark shape in the dim light of the room. Wondering, in those moments, if when she woke we might begin as a world beginning, and not just as a tail end? That if we could know ourselves and one another better, we might be wiser, perhaps even safer, where we touched the lives of others? Nicholas Lethbridge. Julia Dussol. For most of the night, I simply sat watching Julia as she slept and turned, smoking Julia's cigarettes and watching the Rouvel papers, almost luminous in the soft light that came in from the place, the top sheets moving lightly, lifting gently in the breeze.

Nine

IT WAS, LUCIEN HAD told me, the last library in Paris to throw him out. The Bibliothèque Arsenal, down by the river, not far from the place de la Bastille. It was one of the oldest libraries in Paris, a place of musty smells and creaking floors, of ageing wooden panelling and ancient cabinets, the books and manuscripts catalogued in elegant handwritten entries in gigantic leather tomes. The woman who looked after the slips for ordering books wept, apparently, when she told Lucien that he could no longer work there. She told him that too many of the readers were complaining, that Monsieur le Directeur himself had asked her to break the word to him as gently as she could, that the staff in the library were sincerely sorry, and that if he would agree to wash . . .?

It was a library, though, to which he referred with great affection. Perhaps because of the librarian's tears. Lucien insisted that we meet there. Outside, of course. He had something important to tell me. Something I should know. Something about Duvernois.

—He was led out to be shot.

Lucien pounced on me as soon as I appeared. Shouting, about the shooting, across the square. Bouncing towards me across the gravel, his rags streaming, as though he had been waiting half the night.

—He was led out to be shot. It's in the diaries. That's why I thought he had been shot. In the Bibliothèque Arsenal. The diaries, the letters they sent home. That's where you'll find the truth. Not in the newspapers of the time. Not in the official records.

He was flushed, heaving and puffing with the effort, stumbling over his words. There were family stories about these mock executions. Now, it seemed, to be confirmed.

—They shot him. Almost. Lined him up with a number of his friends, and even shot two or three of them. That's what I most remember about your Duvernois. That's why I thought he had been shot. While they were still up at Versailles. Duvernois wore an officer's uniform. That was what protected him. They kept many of the officers aside, you see, for some great legal massacre, on a grander scale. But then it settled down. There were only a score of executions once the first butchery stopped. It was only the small fish that got slaughtered in the streets.

It was a damp and muggy morning. We sat on one of the iron benches, and Lucien recovered his breath. I handed him a coffee I had brought him from a nearby café.

—So many of the important Communards managed to get away. To other countries, on forged passports. To Switzerland and Belgium and especially London. Longuet, Pilotell, Eudes, Vallès—the list went on and on. You stood a better chance if you had carried some responsibility. The less significant you were, the greater the likelihood of a quick shot to the head.

The diary he spoke of was kept by a prisoner called Lalande. Charles Lalande. It was written when Lalande was imprisoned on the Isle of Pines, off the New Caledonian coast. Lalande had also been a captain in the National Guard. He was a lawyer, caught up in the Commune in protest at the humiliations of the war. He quickly found his way into a position of command. It was this that led him to the stake, on the plain of Satory.

Lalande told mostly of his own feelings, recalled in great vividness and long after the event; of how, after all that he had seen on the streets, it was this, preparing for death and then his unexpected preservation, that broke him. How he had begun to weep as he listened to the dying moans of those on either side. They were allowed no blindfold. He and Duvernois and one other were left tethered to their posts, unharmed by the blast, to watch the others die. It was then that he broke down and wept. That he confessed to everything that he was ever asked to confess to. That he betrayed self, friend, anyone he was asked to betray. The saddest part of it, Lucien said, was poor Lalande's conviction that his life had ended at the stake. After that, he lived a kind of living death in the prisons and on the transport ships and on the Isle of Pines, where there was nothing to distract him from these thoughts.

—What happened to him then?

—Nothing. Nothing whatsoever. That was the tragedy. He died there, like a lot of others. Not of his wounds, though he had been wounded. Not of disease, or old age. He just died of heartsickness. Of not wanting to go on living. You can read of it, in their diaries and letters. Badoux, Bauer, Ballière, Jourde, Paschal Grousset. So many died of the nothingness. They died of the rumours of amnesty that came and went. Poor Lalande had a dread of the amnesty, of what life beyond the amnesty might mean. His real death—his second death, his body's death—came as a relief. The diary was brought back by a friend.

—But what did he write about Paul? About Duvernois?

—Almost nothing. Just that he was tied to a bloody stake as well, and got ready to die, in the same way. And that he was not shot.

Lucien was silent again, scratching at his head, dredging into his vast archive.

—He did say one other thing about that time. I remember now. About your great-grandfather. You can read it yourself. You are sure he left no diary? No letters, himself?

—No diary, Lucien. No letters that have survived. Scarcely any memories, even among his children.

—When they were taken back inside, he and the other prisoners who were spared were crazed, weeping, begging. They were all wounded; their wounds were largely untreated, and they had been kept in darkness and with little food for weeks. They were made to stand for hours during some farce of a trial, and then were led to the stake. Duvernois was younger. Much younger than the other two. But after they came back inside, Duvernois had said nothing, while Lalande wept and the other survivor raved into the night. That's what he wrote. I remember it now. Duvernois just spoke to no-one. Not in the prisons, not through the deportations that were to follow. Scarcely ever spoke to anyone, again.

Deportation. I had been to New Caledonia. The Pacific's Devil's Island. A rowdy, fruitless French class visit, organised from my boarding school in Adelaide. Nouméa. There was a long flight out from Sydney in a bucketing DC3, a small airport and a truck with drums on the back, drawn up for refuelling. Three weeks we passed in that green and hot and sluggish place of rich, fleshly vegetation, of coconut palms and banana trees and vast sleepy banyans, their roots hanging in thick curtains from the branches, prising apart the stones, the bricks, the rickety buildings that lined the drowsy streets.

I could recall the nights, the plagues of flying ants attracted to the hostel lights. I remembered how they crept through the slats of the shutters, through every tiny crack and crevice, how even their mosquito nets, the long and ghostly pyramid shapes lined up along the dormitory, offered no protection as they flew in and dropped their wings, creeping and probing until they found a way to the damp of a perspiring limb, with hordes of mosquitos keening late about the nets, their high insistent rhythms winding deep into the night.

I remembered the avenue de la Victoire with its long lines of palm trees, and the wide streets of the town, an odd mix of concrete-slab-sided buildings and battered wooden structures, ancient houses or houses that looked old before their time, surrounded by coconut palms and the thick leaves of banana trees, standing tall but fragile upon their foundations, perched up on the hillsides that ringed the central part of town, built high to catch the breezes and bring some respite from the heat. At the end of a long street of wide verandahs, the rue de Sebastopol, there was the place des Cocotiers, where the Kanaks sat with their dogs in the dust beneath the trees, the tall *flamboyants* which blazed in green and red and not a coconut palm in sight, and the old music kiosk at the northern end, with our teacher's stories of the prison musicians who were brought over from the penitentiary on the Île Nou and who played there on Sundays each week for years, and of the convict murderer who once conducted the orchestra; a man, we were told, who had served up to his wife her lover's heart in a *ragout*.

We were taken on a tour of the prison ruins over on the Île Nou, where, with the others, I ran and threw stones and clambered over the toppled walls and along the stone jetties that the convicts had built out into the bay. We were told of the floggings and the beatings, and how the groans of those being punished carried across the waters each Wednesday evening like the stroke of a well-wound clock, towards those in the town, or towards the political exiles on the bleak slopes of the Ducos Peninsula that lay out to the west.

I remembered leaving for a moment the noisy games

of the others and standing on a stone jetty at Nouville to look out across the harbour, the Grande Rade of Nouméa, at the dark slopes of the Ducos Peninsula and beyond Ducos to the razor-backed mountain range that ran along the centre of the island. I recall looking out to the cloudy peaks, the distant ridges biting into the soft and misty clouds, the green of the nearer hills and the sharp blue of the sea. It was for just a minute, a brief pause in a holiday lost in pillow fights and throwing rocks at seagulls and football on the beaches, with no knowing until Agnes told me much later that any fragment of myself had ever known that sea, those barren slopes and those sad sounds on the wind.

We stayed in an old wooden hostel, walled in broken *persiennes*, long shutters that encased the wide wooden verandahs where my class was assigned to sleep. Beyond, there was a garden, with strange fleshy plants that twisted and interleaved with one another, plaiting themselves together in thick ladders across the walls, and in and out of the wreckage of a pavilion to the rear; a garden where there was no further space for growth of any kind, where even the air itself seemed thick, green, lush and overripe.

Lying awake in bed long after the others had gone to sleep, I would turn over and over in the night, looking along the ghostly shapes of the other mosquito nets and listening to the sound of the crickets outside, beating against the thick and heavy air. Each day I woke to see the scurrying cockroaches, the teacher complaining loudly and the sullen fellow with the moist insistent cough who brought us bread and bowls of chocolate, shrugging and pretending with each morning not to understand. I could still see his beaded sweat and mottled skin and filthy singlet—a being scarcely human, more like the tangled vegetation in the walled garden to the rear, his skin like old bark and his body like a mouldering trunk, his long and horny fingers groping about like swaying tendrils, his rich flow of phlegm and weeping bloodhound eyes still the strongest of my memories of all the listless sadness of that place.

—I've been there, Lucien.

I bought him another coffee. I braced myself against the richer stench he gave off on mornings like this, where the layers of coats combined to ripen his rich mould of filth and sweat. Lucien clasped his mittens around the paper cup, to keep it warm, and ran his nose across it, drinking in the fumes.

—I went there once. I was very young.

—To Ducos? To the Isle of Pines?

I told him how we had walked all over the old prisons, how we explored every nook and cranny of what was left of the prisons on the Île Nou, and the ruins over on the Isle of Pines. Swallowed up by the jungle. Just bits of walls and steps and things like that, but with the forest growing up through it all. Of how we swam and climbed the walls, and were scolded by the unfortunate teacher who came with us.

—What about Ducos? Did you really see Ducos? The *enceinte fortifiée*?

I vaguely remembered Ducos. Just to the west of Nouméa, framing the whole western side of the harbour. A long line of steep, dark, ominous-looking hills, covered in low vegetation and with few houses. The group had left someone behind, and we had to return, almost all the way back from Nouméa, to pick him up, a hot and snivelling boy waiting in a panic in the wind. I recalled some kind of cactus, like giant yucca plants, offering to spike anyone who ventured off the narrow tracks that wandered up and down the slopes through the coarse dry grass. We battled our way through it to get to the top of one of the ridges, for a view back to Nouméa, to the east.

—If Ducos is where I think it is, then there's nothing there. It was just a bare neck of land, with a couple of industrial sites of some sort on it, or perhaps marine wrecker's yards. Lots of old drums and rusting hulks. Nothing else.

Lucien then spoke of the islands as though he had been there too. He told of the diaries of the *déportés*, the letters of those who had been sentenced, some like Paul to an *enceinte fortifiée,* a fortified place, and others, including the women, to *déportation simple* on the Isle of Pines. Not that they would have stayed there long. Within weeks of the arrival of the first female *déportées*, there were complaints, on the part of the commandant, Boutin, about the moral dangers of the female presence. The dangers for his soldiers. No-one spoke of the dangers for the women. There was an incident—not recorded in any official way, but because of it all the women were removed, quickly brought back to Nouméa or, in the case of the worst of them, sent on to Ducos.

I asked about the diaries.

—There is lots of writing about the prisons. From the prisons, I should say. There was Achille Ballière, for example, who escaped with your great-grandfather. Like your great-grandfather, he was an architect—or was it engineer? He helped on the barricades, and was sent to rot on the Isle of Pines. He was plucked off the island, just as he seemed to be getting used to it, and sent to Nouméa. Spent his time writing. Sad writing, about boredom and the perils of being bored, and about friends dying of boredom. Blue seas, blue skies, white sands. They died like flies.

—Does he mention my great-grandfather? Did anyone else write about Duvernois?

Lucien's attention had drifted to the far side of the world, to things that happened a hundred years ago. He began to scratch, and scrape at his hair, his coffee spilling as he writhed upon the bench.

—I'm going there, you know.

He sniffed his coffee, bathing his face in the rising fumes.

—I'm going. To Ducos. And to the Isle of Pines. That's where I want to go.

—There's not much there, Lucien. A few overgrown ruins. The forest has covered everything.

—I need to go there. To know. For my files.

He was not discouraged. He stared across the blue expanses of water and shining white sands, the Pic N'Ga, Kunaméra Beach, Ouro and the Pic Meunier. We simply sat, as Lucien's coffee cooled, thinking of Ducos and the Isle of Pines, of all that we had read, of the long hours of nothingness, the sudden afternoon rains, the endless rumours of general amnesty, the unbroken space of sea and sky, of sickness and desperation in a seasonless listless idyll in the unrelenting sun.

It was Monsieur Jalabert, Colette had said, who knew about the escape. I decided to go down again, the very next day, to Milly-la-Forêt, to talk first of the escape, and then perhaps of other things. Determined to probe further the secret smiles, the dropped hints, the strict but armed discretion of this Monsieur Jalabert. But determined, too, not to be drawn into defeating games of lawyer's cat and mouse.

I arrived unannounced—I thought that Lucien's account of my great-grandfather from Lalande's diary might provide some kind of pretext for the visit, if one were needed—but he was waiting in his study. Composed. Some books set out before him. As though prepared for just such a visit. And as neatly dressed as ever.

The escape.

Monsieur Jalabert gestured to his books. To the shelves that lined the walls.

—This, even your great-aunt would be happy to talk to you about. Your great-grandfather's escape, in late April 1873. With the great Marquis de Rochefort. You ask for facts. Here, I can give you facts. The escape was famous. Books were written about it. Manet painted it, Henri Rochefort and the escapees, making their way across the Grande Rade in Nouméa. I can lend you a book. Many books. Everything that is in the books, I can tell you. And perhaps more than this?

I told him that I already knew a little about the escape. About Nouméa. I told him about my boarding school, and our visit. It was, I knew, one of the few successful escapes from New Caledonia. One of the very few escapes by Communards. There were many wild stories at the time—tales of beautiful heiresses bringing schoon0 ers to the rescue, anchoring just beyond the coast but few real escapes. I knew that my great-grandfather's escape had nearly failed. The boat had been carefully arranged, an Australian collier from Newcastle. The escapees rowed out from Ducos in the dead of night, in a boat that my great-grandfather had brought across from the place where he worked, on some officially sanctioned form of release, in Nouméa. I knew that the escapees had climbed into the wrong boat; climbed aboard, and then overheard French being spoken, and climbed out again. That they found at last their Australian boat. That their departure was delayed, because the captain was ashore, and drunk.

Monsieur Jalabert took up the story.

—Their escape was better organised than most. By Rochefort. On credit. On the mere strength of his name. An orderly escape, fit for a gentleman. You must know something already of this Rochefort. The most famous Communard and *déporté* of all, even though he fled the country before the slaughter began, and was never really a participant. His real genius was for self-promotion. Flaubert once said that it was dangerous *not* to say that Rochefort was the greatest writer of the age. More famous then than Hugo, and now largely forgotten.

Monsieur Jalabert struggled to his feet and crossed over to his shelves, placing his hand on another large leather-bound volume. He passed it to me. *Retour de la Nouvelle-Calédonie*, by Henri Rochefort. It was heavily illustrated with engravings of Australia and the islands, and signed by the author.

—Rochefort had his own version of events. Colourful lies, much of it. You'll find your great-grandfather mentioned a number of times. Something too, about his time in Sydney. His decision to stay behind when the others left for Europe. Poor Duvernois—as reserved, always as closed up to himself, as Rochefort was extravagant, full of his own importance. His comments on poor Duvernois, I should warn you, are not always kind.

Monsieur Jalabert put the book down in front of me, and stood behind me for a time as I turned the pages, the maps, his hand resting on my shoulder.

—The details are well known. It is all described in Rochefort's own book, and in the books that were written by the others who escaped. By Paschal Grousset. And François Jourde. By Olivier Pain and Achille Ballière. The only one without a book was your great-grandfather, Duvernois. And he was perhaps the best writer of them all.

The escape, he said, was Rochefort's own idea. He had the contacts, the influence that was necessary. He had already tried, from the prisons on the Île d'Oléron, and Île de Ré. Before leaving France, he made contact with sympathetic parties, all Freemasons like himself, in Sydney. Already, he had fixed upon the idea of an Australian boat of some kind, moored in the harbour, the Grande Rade, as the best means of escape.

Paul had written for his journal once or twice, *Le Mot d'Ordre*. They knew each other a little. As soon as Rochefort arrived on Ducos, he began to ask by which door they would be leaving. At this time, contact with the mainland was easy. Many *déportés* were licensed to work over in Nouméa, and some, like Paul, went backwards and forwards between Nouméa and Numbo, the only township on Ducos, on various forms of work. Paul, released on licence, worked for a grocer, a Monsieur Dusser, on the rue de Sebastopol, ferrying supplies across to the peninsula.

Rochefort saw that they would need a boat, to cross the harbour. Paul could now supply it. It was in this way that he became involved. He stole the boat of his employer, the unfortunate Monsieur Dusser, on the night of the escape. It was Paul, by some accounts, who negotiated the terms of their passage with the Australian captain of the PCE, at anchor in the Rade. As the least known of all the escapees, he was in the best position to help, to move about without being noticed.

The plan was that those on Ducos would swim to a small rock at the end of a small island or peninsula that jutted out into the Grande Rade, just to the north of the settlement at Numbo, to await Paul and his boat, and those who lived in Nouméa. From there, Captain Law of the PCE would take them to Australia, his ten thousand francs to be paid on their safe arrival.

—So the plan was executed. It was not without its complications. But it worked.

Monsieur Jalabert shuffled over to his shelves again, and came back with a reproduction of a painting. Mostly water, with a small boat. A dark figure in what looked like a bowler hat. A tiny darkness, in a wide and unfriendly ocean. Edouard Manet.

—And Marie-Josèphe? Madame Duvernois? Did she know of the plan?

He sat behind his desk, again, his hands clasped, again, in a judicial cautiousness.

—I know a little from Mademoiselle Colette, who told me of her father's time in Nouméa, and a little told by your great-grandmother herself—Madame Duvernois, I should rather say—when I was very young, when first I became curious, as you are now curious, about what had happened there. She did not tell me much. Enough to satisfy a young boy. A mere adventure story.

—But how much did she know of his time in Noumea? Were there letters of any kind? Were they in contact through this time? Did she expect him to return to her in France?

Monsieur Jalabert paused. As though making up his mind, or waiting for some comment, or a question. He raised an inquiring eyebrow.

Did he know less? Did he know more?

He smiled, and went on.

—What did she think, at the time of his escape? We do know that she thought of herself as his fiancée at this time. Did she know that he was leaving with the others? This was something I could of course never quite ask, not of Madame Duvernois herself, nor of Mademoiselle Colette, without opening up questions about subjects which we had long agreed, without words, never to speak. About which we are still in agreement, I might add, never to speak.

—And yet, Monsieur Jalabert, you speak to me. You ask me not to go. You ask me to ask my questions.

Monsieur Jalabert rose awkwardly, and gestured to the door.

—There are some papers, as I said. Some letters, from my father's files. In time, you may see them. There are things that you perhaps should know. Others that can happily die away with the passing of time. I will think carefully about this. About what knowledge I am bound to keep, and what knowledge I am bound to destroy.

Monsieur Jalabert peered closely into my eyes as we shook hands. I wondered again if that look was a sign that Monsieur Jalabert knew more than he was saying, or just wanted to know more. Another stratagem.

—Above all, it may depend on what strange and misguided versions of the past I may feel in conscience bound to prevent!

Ducos. Had I seen it, without knowing, the rocky outcrop from which they crept? Was the place that I did now remember, that I thought of as most likely, the place that they left from? Or would my vision of their leaving, my version even of the famous escape, be just another of Monsieur Jalabert's misguided versions of the past? So much—about this at least—had been written. First-person accounts, so very vivid, of how they waited at the harbour's edge, the last lights of the Île Nou still glowing to the east, and on the far side of the Grande Rade bursts of light flashed from Nouméa, from the lamplight on the jetties pushing out into the sea.

They told of how they crouched, half-naked in the darkness and the steady falling rain, on the thin neck of rocks that thrust out from the northern flank of the Baie Numbo, the lights of the camps of the soldiers still burning in the distance, throwing moving yellow shadows against the canvas of their tents. Of how they listened to the faint sounds of the conversations of the guards, laughing and joking with each other as they patrolled the Numbo beach, the sounds carrying across the water, the rain now masking them in darkness as they moved out onto the rocks, masking also the vast tracts of the harbour and the boats that waited there.

They watched the fires along the jetties on the Île Nou, the blazing prison gaslights moving with the wind, and to the south, a solitary lamp burning at the end of the soldier's jetty at Numbo. They peered out into the blackness of the harbour for the Australian collier, with the rain still falling, a steady unrelenting drizzle all about them, adding keenness to the cold and to the wind, waiting for the small boat from Nouméa, for Monsieur Dusser's stolen cutter approaching slowly through the darkness and moving in dangerous closeness to the rocks, its sail dropped in concealment, the only sounds the patter of rain on the water, the beating of the waves masking in merciful rhythms the soft slap of the oars.

They rowed out across the harbour, moving steadily through the rain towards the gaslights on the jetties of the Île Nou, towards the place where Rochefort had seen, from the hillsides of Ducos that afternoon, the sturdy PCE moored and waiting, creeping from one boat to another until they came at last on the collier, anchored perilously close to the Île Nou, only to be confronted by an uncomprehending watch, the captain himself being nowhere to be found, there being no-one on board with any knowledge of the Marquis de Rochefort, or any plans of escape.

That night they spent in anguish, the captain long delayed on shore, with further delays to follow with the wind falling away, with the sun beginning to rise and the PCE still unable to leave the harbour, moving at last in painful slowness through the rising light of dawn along the shores of the Île Nou, moving in slow steps out of the Grande Rade, the escapees expecting at any moment a cutter packed with soldiers to set out from the Île Nou, or a siren suddenly to sound from Numbo, or a steam chaloupe to break out from Nouméa to catch and board them before they struck the open sea. They edged out of the harbour, inch by inch, and were soon beyond the range of any boat that might follow, the heavy PCE slowly turning at last beyond the long sheltering arm of the Île Nou, and out towards the open sea. The escapees were able to come on deck, to congratulate themselves on their escape, to look boldly out to sea and to their future. To their return to France. But with my great-grandfather, less jubilant perhaps, keeping as always to himself, now looking back towards the shore, to the last glinting of the sun on the sheds and rooftops of Nouméa, to the sun that shone on the hills that rose so steeply beyond the Vallée des Colons. Wondering, perhaps, about the next phase. The next country. About a young woman, by now a stranger, far away?

Ten

JULIA AND I WENT to the Palace of Versailles. It was at my insistence. To visit the sacred sites of 1871. To look at the Orangerie, where so many of the prisoners were first kept, and to search for the sites at Satory, tracing the stories of hundreds of prisoners exposed in a vast open and muddy yard, with holes cut in the walls and the barrels of a dozen *mitrailleuses* pushed through, ready to cut a swathe through anything that moved.

I had great hopes for Versailles. Hopes more fixed on Julia Dussol, it might be said, than Rouvel and Duvernois.

It was the first time I would see her since our night together in the rue de la Clef. Days I had spent in the streets, the cafés, the libraries and the archives, but with little on my mind, I soon came to realise, other than Julia Dussol. I felt the onset of a familiar anguish. The frantic imaginings. The mind starting to glow, to turn in on itself, to go over what had been and might be to come, with visions of ecstasy and of the cruellest deprivation, toppling over each other in unsteady and obsessive succession. Julia Dussol. The rue de la Clef. The fire, the shouting, and the sound of breaking glass.

Versailles, though, was a mistake. Julia was clearly reluctant. This time, I was the one who rang. Who made the arrangements. Who insisted that we go. Julia arrived late at the station. Flustered, more than a bit distracted by some task she'd had to leave. She suggested we just have a coffee instead. At length, and again at my insistence, we finally took the train.

On the way, we talked of the route the prisoners took, trudging out to Versailles in long lines of thousands, some roped together in batches and others falling in exhaustion by the side of the road, with tales of quick dispatchings with a bullet to the head, with accounts of violent and abusive crowds lining the route, of pelted filth and beatings and even lynchings along the way as the guilty and the innocent were marched in starving herds together, as the notorious cleansing, the pious Expiation, took its course.

Versailles itself, though, was disappointing. As Julia

had maintained it would be. There was very little left to see. There were no remnants at Satory, no open plain, no walled prison, no bloodied stakes or killing ground, and no public access anyway. The Orangerie at Versailles had long been returned to its old purpose, and was now just one more part of the Château tourist circus.

Julia hung back grumpily.

—Really, Nicholas, what did you expect to see? Chains and manacles, and filthy straw still on the floor? Prisoners still straining at the leash?

She was restless and cantankerous. She had seen the Orangerie many times as a child. There were no reports, indeed, of Sebastien Rouvel ever having been there, or in the muddy discomfort of Satory. She was yearning for her desk, her notes, her folders back in Paris.

—But was he ever actually in the fighting, Julia? Did Sebastien Rouvel bear arms?

It was a mean question. I did not expect an answer. It was meant purely to annoy. Better a decent argument than this close and testy silence.

Julia was unabashed.

—That was not his rôle, Nicholas. You know that. He was an organiser. A leader. Charismatic. I know it may sound odd, but it's obvious he would have been wasted on a barricade. No-one else had his knowledge, his view of the whole.

I did wonder, indeed, at Julia's own detachment. How she too moved through the smoke and barricades without any of it touching. These were, after all, her streets, her cause, her generation.

—And what about you, Julia? And what is happening in the streets?

I took some weak refuge, some excuse, in my foreignness, my own confusion about what was happening. Julia, though, did seem distracted in some deeper sense. As someone not to be wasted, either, on a barricade?

At any rate, she chose simply to ignore my question.

—He'd been collecting, Nicholas, from back in his days in a dusty corner of the Préfecture. He knew the systems, the way the city worked, better than anyone. He had his collection of dossiers, too, on half the city. On important people, from both sides. On the members of the Assembly, now fled here to Versailles, and on most of the members of the new Commune. He was needed. No-one else knew so much. That's why it was so important that he escape, that he try to join the others in London.

I thought again of the place where the prisoners were kept. The little I had seen of it. Here, in the Orangerie. With Paul-Auguste Duvernois, badly wounded, kept at Satory, and then in a naval dungeon somewhere over on the coast.

—Not everyone understands this, Nicholas. It's part of what my book is about. It's not just about Sebastien Rouvel. Not anymore. It's about the difference between gifted people, people with a sense of destiny, and the others. The mass. The special kinds of choices that special people have to make. The hard decisions. Do you think you can afford to have people like Rouvel just standing around behind the barricades, waiting to be shot?

It sounded less convincing, spoken in this way, to me, to the open air, to the tourist crowds milling about us, than it had amid the books and papers in her apartment in the rue de la Clef.

We stood for a time outside the Orangerie. We could not go in without paying for a further ticket, on top of the general entry.

Julia was becoming hot, prickly, exasperated.

—What did you actually think you were going to find, Nicholas? I just don't know why we're here.

She strode off. I struggled to keep up. With a growing sense of panic, a feeling that things were, already, slipping from my grasp.

—I'm sorry, Julia.

—It's fine, Nicholas. I do understand. It's just that our time would be better spent elsewhere, that's all. With the papers. There's so much to do. We can come to these places later. Afterwards. You just won't find anything there. These people are very good at getting rid of history. All you need is a new coat of plaster. A broom and a bit of soap. That's why the journal is so important. It's something that slipped through. Something that's come back to us, almost from the grave.

She smiled at last.

—Through you, Nicholas. I do appreciate it. I really do.

She squeezed my hand. Not entirely with conviction.

—Come, Nicholas. We really are wasting time.

We wandered back to the streets of Versailles itself, and sat for a coffee. Our conversation flagged. Perhaps we were both tired. It was hot. I was annoyed, as well. Bright sunlight. Fresh air. Stout boots. Somehow, we seemed to have slipped back to a place that was less than where we began. We tried to talk of books, dates, papers. Of Sebastien Rouvel. Of anything that might placate, absorb, engage.

—You just don't understand the difficulties I've had, Nicholas. The opposition. No-one wants the real truth. It's always been easy for the Right. Rouvel was a thug, a mass murderer. But the Left—you'd think they'd understand! Instead, they seem to want to unload all the bad things that happened—the execution of the Archbishop, the slaughter of the Dominicans—onto his shoulders. So that the cause itself remains pure and clean.

—And what about my people? What about Paul Duvernois?

—It's a very interesting story, Nicholas, but there's no deadline on it, is there? The truth is that most of the Rouvel story can be told without a mention of any of them.

—So, my story is just a diversion? A footnote to yours?

—I'm not saying that, Nicholas. It's just a question of priorities. It's a matter of the difference between real history, public history, and an interesting private story, that's all.

I played with my coffee spoon.

—I need to tell it, Nicholas. Rouvel. And soon. In spite of everything.

In English, Julia had little accent. Enough, though, to mark out each word distinctly.

In spite of everything.

The phrase sat before us, exposed. In spite of Nicholas Lethbridge? I felt an urgent need for further credit. I took a deep breath.

—There is something else, Julia. Something I haven't yet told you. Something I should perhaps have told you.

She raised a tired eyebrow.

—You recall the sisters? 'Unknown at this address'? Well, they're still alive, still there. I've met them. Two of them, at least. And they've seen him, Julia. Sebastien Rouvel. They've listened to him. They've actually spoken to him.

She sat up abruptly. She reached for another cigarette.

—Why didn't you tell me this before?

Why hadn't I told her? I couldn't rightly say. Private story, or public story? I wasn't quite sure where it should fit. Perhaps it was Colette's caution that made me wary. That made me feel I had something or someone to protect.

—This is so important, Nicholas. They might just hold the key to everything. You should have told me.

—You wanted the papers to be kept a secret. They—the oldest, Colette, at least—doesn't seem to want to talk about him, or not directly at least. Not yet. They probably have secrets of their own. I guess it's a matter of finding the proper moment.

—And you've decided that now is the proper moment to tell me?

—I just think there's more in my side of the story than you want to take into account.

—When can we see them? I need to talk to them. As soon as possible. Surely you can see that?

—I'll arrange it, Julia. As soon as I can.

—The 'proper moment', I presume?

—The proper moment, Julia. It's delicate. I think.

She began to drum her fingers on the table. The cigarette was stubbed out almost as soon as it was lit.

—Look, Nicholas, I think it's best if I just go back. You stay. See the things you need to see. It's really not a problem. It's wonderful, Nicholas. Having you here. Working with you. We're just at different stages. We'll work together when it helps, and when it doesn't, we'll just go our own ways. Isn't it better that way?

She rose, and bent to kiss me. It was clumsy. We fumbled, as I tried to rise. She pressed me back into my seat. Managing to turn a decent shove into something like a caress.

—I'll call, Nicholas. Very soon. I've got some news for you, too. There are some questions. Some really, really interesting new questions. Some more proper moments. For your story and for mine.

Versailles had been awkward. Julia did not ring. It was several days before I felt I could do so. I wanted to recover lost ground without really knowing, indeed, what it was that we had lost. I eventually rang her and fumbled with an apology, which was cheerily dismissed. Within hours I was back in her apartment in the rue de la Clef as though nothing had happened. As though we had simply never set foot in Versailles.

She greeted me at the door with all her old enthusiasm. It was mid-afternoon, unpleasantly stuffy in the closed air of her room. I opened the window and sat back on the bed, invited to read the piece that she was holding, reading over her shoulder as she sat cross-legged amid the notes and the detritus of a heavy day of work.

She leaned back against the bed. Her old position. Nestled between my knees. I worked through a clutch of papers. Much of the time, though, I simply looked at her. Feeling the intensity of her presence. Observing the soft slope of her back and shoulders. Thinking of her thoughts. Seeking to think my way, deep, deep, into Julia Dussol.

I could tell, though, that she was also distracted. That her busyness with the papers was only part of the story. She was hovering, manoeuvring, choosing at last her point of access.

—You know, Nicholas, your big problem is that you want too little. That's your real problem.

Julia turned and looked up at me, to see how I would respond.

—You say you want to know, but in the end, you have just too narrow an idea of what you want to know. It's too vague. It's too personal. You're too easily deflected. Someone hints that something might be 'delicate', and you just back off. You can't write history like that. That's your problem, Nicholas.

She put aside her papers. As though attending to the cat, which rubbed against her, seeking her attention. I could see, though, that she was wanting to talk of something else. Something carefully considered. Something that had been carefully rehearsed.

—You are not really being very courageous. You came here looking for some kind of personal reassurance. But we're now looking at the history of an era. Not just one or two people. This is the point about Sebastien Rouvel. He's an emblem. A sort of representative. Epochal, somehow. There is very little that was personal about him. That's why his writing is so difficult. And so important.

She leaned back against the bed, against my knees again. I could still feel the pressure of some new intent.

—What is it, Julia? What are you wanting to say?

—It's just that there are more questions, Nicholas. Bigger questions. Indelicate ones. I told you that my early work was on the London exiles. Everyone thought that Rouvel should have gone there, with Brunel and Eudes and Vallès and the others. Why he stayed on in Australia is one of the great mysteries I'm going to solve. Even greater, now that we have these.

She shook a handful of the papers at me.

—There's something I've been wanting to ask you. Something else. Something really important. There's some 'she' that is everywhere here, on almost every page. Especially in this section. What do you make of that?

She turned to look at me, rising to her knees.

—Do you think there's any chance, Nicholas, that this 'she' could be your great-grandmother? This Marie-Josèphe Coignard?

She had already separated out a small pile of pages. She sat back, and read one short passage after another; 'the red sap running in caressing rivulets across her quivering breasts', her 'soft tongue stroking in tenderness the dry, hard scales of those stone fish that sing beneath the boiling sands'.

Watching me closely.

—Well?

—I don't know what it means, Julia.

—It's just that this 'she' does come back and back, Nicholas. It's here, and everywhere. Like an obsession.

—It's just some kind of symbol, Julia. It's about a desert. You can't say that it's about any kind of real woman.

She is locked amid the rocks and the baked desert sands, her head only to be seen above the cracked tablets of stone. Far out in the desert he hears her voice singing these bitter songs of childhood. Her hair is spread like rivers which course the desert sands, her breasts like mountains far below the earth. Her mouth is an open chasm, the most perilous crevasse to hide amid the broken hills . . .

She read the section, over and over, in French and then in English. She looked at me again, peering over the rims of her spectacles.

—What was he doing there? Why did he die out there, so far from anything? Of all the places in the world he could have chosen.

She raised an eyebrow. I felt my skin starting to prickle, and something like a run of perspiration down my back.

—Nicholas, if you really want to know the truth of what happened, then what you find out might not always be pleasing. You have to ask all the questions. You have to keep on asking. Even the ones you don't want to ask.

—But Julia, all you've got here is a 'she' of some sort, and lots of mists and mountains and nonsense about worms and veils and singing in the desert. It could be anywhere. Anyone. Most likely no-one. Perhaps you're looking for the wrong kind of meanings.

—The wrong kind?

—It's just very general, that's all. It could be about anyone. These are not real people. They're just ideas. Images. Probably symbols of some kind. Not real things, Julia. Their strength lies in how they make you feel. Not in what they tell you about anything.

She took up another passage from the pile of typescript. She was still troubled. She spoke slowly, with precision. Smiling, caressing my knee, but only cautiously.

—I want you to come with me to Vincennes, Nicholas, to the Château. The military archives. We'll go soon. Tomorrow, even. I have something to show you. I'm almost certain. Something you'll find interesting. Something we can then take with us when we arrive at the 'proper moment' to talk to your Tante Colette. To assist her memory a little, perhaps?

She nestled back between my legs again. Her pullover had slipped to one side, exposing her neck and shoulder. I desperately wanted to lean forward and caress her. To stroke her face. To massage her neck. To soften her intent. To draw her away from the papers, across the papers, as we had done before. To have her think once more through the body. Through the living, in that same fragile space we had uncovered on my precious visit, as much as through the dead.

She drew her pullover back up to cover her shoulder, but did turn and smile at me again.

—We'll work on it, Nicholas. Keep our minds open to every kind of possibility. We'll see what we can find. Together. Out at Vincennes.

Night after night the children would creep down to watch him writing, Agnes and the smaller children watching in silence through the coarse weave of the hessian, as Sebastien Rouvel sat amid the moths and the heat in his cottage, down by the sheepyards, the cottage little more than a pile of rock, stones that were left over from the building of the house, with an iron roof and a canvas bag for water hanging outside in the shade of a pepper tree with its flaky bark and faded red berries and dusty pungent leaves. There he would sit at a table their father had found for him, bent over in the soft yellow light of his lamp, working through the piles of papers he had brought with him in his filthy bag, and always working—or so it seemed—on the same pieces of paper, writing over them and around the sides and between the lines and over and over again. Writing as though he had come there, to a place of such desolation, to fill the absences about him. Writing as though against some urgent and certain ending, soon to come.

Agnes could tell how they would go down in the evenings to watch him, moving barefoot through the thistles in the half-light of the late summer evenings, watching always in fascination as he wrote, always with the curtains drawn—the curtains no more than old chaff bags hung over the holes in the walls—because the cottage felt cooler that way, closed up against the infernal heat which seemed to beat even in the darkness on the flat and creaking iron of the roof. They would watch him as he sat, squinting at the page through his broken spectacles and now and then seeming almost to stab at it with his pen, mumbling strange things under his breath and sometimes words that they could hear. Nonsense, most of it had seemed. About things that were impossible, or could only be, in books. About things they all knew, in and around Deception, but in new and outrageous combinations. About so many strange things, all mixed in together, and no story that any of them could follow, no tale that did not seem hopelessly mixed up with another, and that other tale yet untold.

She told of how sometimes in the very depths of the night, when it was hot and they could not sleep, they looked out their window and saw him working there. How once or twice she and Colette had stolen together to his hut at night, and watched him through the open windows, because sometimes very late at night he would at last draw back the curtains to let whatever moving air there might be flow into the shack. How they hid and watched through the window, and how sometimes he would read aloud, read from his writing to himself, reading with the page held close to the soft glow of the kerosene lamp, struggling to read through his one good lens. They saw him more than once do something strange, saw him curse and tear his papers and screw them up into a ball and then sit back with his head in his hands, under the light of the lamp, surrounded by a ring of light and fluttering moths. And then they saw him straighten out the paper again, press the paper flat on the table and then begin again with his writing, his stabbing at the paper with his pen, writing as though he knew that this was the last of it, and that the writing, good or bad, must now soon reach its end.

Eleven

COLETTE SEEMED EAGER, AT last, to talk more about Deception. It was on my next visit to Saint-Germain, a sunny Sunday afternoon. We sat outdoors again, within the range of Clémentine's cheerful singing. Her stories started, as before, with my attempts to clear away some of the debris and to clear the driveway. There was something in the brightness of the sunshine, the clear air, the smell of labour, perhaps, that brought on the memory, the wider telling.

There must, she said, be thousands of such stories in my country, of a man travelling alone to mark out his land and then a woman arriving some time after to find the raw beginnings of a house. Stories of the first small rooms thrust up against the emptiness, in a place that seemed in some way to resent their intrusion and fling it back at them in the daily form of flies and snakes and beetles and a thousand other creeping things, as well as the more resounding strokes of fire and disease and drought and flood. Like some biblical tale of retribution it did seem, up at Deception, with plagues released in cruel and measured sequence, as though her father had been seeking in that vast labour of clearing and ploughing the evasion of some measured punishment. As though he was seeking by sweat alone to bypass a destiny that was set fast in the abbatoir of Père-Lachaise, watched over by the peculiar God that ruled those barren reaches, perched on the hills that ringed Deception, mocking him like one of those accursed birds that she could still remember, laughing from the distant trees.

What she most recalled was the silence, her father coming home at the fall of light each day almost blackened by the sun and nursing hand or foot or shoulder from some injury. He scarcely spoke to their mother, or to any of them except perhaps in exchange of prattle with his favourite, Clémentine. She recalled his body reeking of dried sweat and some richer odour of determination that drove him out day after day, their mother trying always to break through the crust of resolution with which he protected these shrinking dreams, putting to him always the idea of another place, the return to this house in France.

—My parents' marriage, *Nicolas*, was not a happy one. I do not disguise the fact. After so much difficulty, so much separation, so much pain, in the end it brought them little happiness. Too much had come between them. There was too much misguided obligation. If either party had been less dutiful, less determined to act honourably towards the other, both might have been happier.

Already by the time of her most clear memory, the house at Deception was almost a ruin, the iron stripped in places from the roof, with the walls, flung up too quickly in the days of gross expansion now showing signs of buckling, so that the children were forbidden to go near. As though their father had known that this house that rose from rage and guilt and humiliation, from grandly flawed ideas bred in the fetid air of dungeons and the slaughteryards of Paris, could not last; that it was the gesture, not the endurance, that was what mattered most of all.

And so she and her sisters had lived and grown within the boundaries of a design half realised and still half mere idea, a set of near-sacred sketchings marked out by stakes and stones, as in the high-walled garden that was marked out to the front, largely unwalled to the very end but with its brief moment of trellises and arbours, rose bushes and oleanders. By the time of their leaving it had shrunk to a small vegetable patch with a few dogged palms and thick and knotty-stemmed rose bushes hanging on, with some of the roses still blooming briefly before the full heat of the summer, and with only the large pepper trees growing and flourishing and destroying all around them but providing the thing they came to know as more needful than the scent of roses: precious deep green shade.

She could remember how they would ride out or walk across a broken country that was now more like a graveyard than a landscape, their father's property soon taking in the unroofed ruins of a dozen others, their childhood studded with toppled cottages and sheds abandoned by others who had given it up and slipped back towards the south. She could remember the northern settlers' wagons creaking past the house along the road back down to Quorn and Port Augusta, with everything they owned piled high, their children walking beside them in the dust and her own mother's eyes following them with a kind of envy however wretched their condition.

What made it different in their father's case, Colette insisted, was the idea. Even their mother, whose life the idea was principally meant to serve, whose life had withered with its flourishing, would admit that it was this richer resolution in their father and this determination not to see, that both gave dignity and ensured failure in almost equal measure. Even their mother had said as much, years afterwards, when word came through about their father's death and the flooded creek that ran like bitter irony through the dryness of Deception: that the thing which gave their father dignity in all his misguided struggle and determination was the dimensions of the idea by which he was impelled. Even then, their mother told them, and long before they could hope to understand her meaning, that it was the idea of what he did that gave it dignity. That the true tragedy was not the loss of family and property and finally of life, but rather it was the shrinking of the idea, the idea of Deception, once and for all.

Agnes's stories had been different. They were mostly of the house. Deception. A large house, spread low to the ground, with scattered sheds and outhouses, the kitchen separate from the rest and almost like a large house on its own, lying at the southern side of a cobbled courtyard with storerooms and coolrooms and its own cellar. A house, she said, that was always dark, with thick stone walls that were wider at the bottom than the top, with tiny windows that were placed high and shaded always by the wide verandahs. Many of the central rooms, the living rooms and parlours, had no windows at all, with the whole house built like a bastion against the heat, a fortress against the light, with shutters on the few windows to bring to the burning day the relief of darkness, if not the cool of night.

It was a house where sometimes at the height of summer when the heat was at its worst the children would drag their mattresses down into the cellars and deep into the coolness of the earth where, amid the boxes and the barrels of food, they would lie down and try to sleep, terrifying each other with tales of lizards and beetles and spiders until Clémentine or perhaps Geneviève would panic and go back upstairs. A house where at night everything would be opened, the doors and all the windows, to risk the intrusive insects in the hope of a cool breeze into the house, to release the heat of airless rooms and the dusty smells that came up from the baking flags and floors of bare and polished stone.

For a time it flourished. Agnes had some old photographs showing prosperous men and women with blank unfeatured faces within the shadow of huge hats and proud to be guests at such a place, moving in dark and heavy clothing in a well-furnished garden with benches and arbours and trellises. Those gardens and wide corridors and fine rooms and capacious outhouses soon seemed, though, like some kind of outrage, some crude presumption against a nature where the sole things permitted to stand tall were the rocks and jagged ranges that circled to the west and to the south. As though any mortal house standing erect and breaking the rhythm of the flat Willochra Plain was a crime for which there had to be atonement, in furniture sold off and chandeliers shipped back to the south, the unroofing of the outhouses and the iron sold off in stages to pay for seeds or stock and to forestay some further debt. As though, in slow stages, all had to be beaten back into the earth and rock from which it was impertinently wrenched, each stone now looking to take its revenge and toppling in slow stages in a place where it seemed nothing was ever meant to grow, where the only things meant to survive were native to that place, the lizards and the emus, grey and withered as the trees.

Agnes never thought in terms of gesture and retribution, of crime or punishment. She just told of wild dogs, of thistles and cracking iron, and of the rains that did not come. The last of Deception, after Marie-Josèphe's leaving and the death of Paul, was handed down to Agnes and her new family, who stripped it before her wedding of every last bolt and hinge, every door and nail and window frame. They left it to the wild straying sheep and abandoned cattle to wander among the stones. It was some half-conscious act of exorcism of language, place and people, a rite of desecration wrought by hammer, rope and crowbar, some mute unthought determination on the part of Agnes's new family to ensure her virgin purification from all that went before, so that the next phase of her life and of the lives of her line to follow not be trammelled by this raw incaution to the north. Ensuring that no-one further would be tempted, that there should be no thing left standing at Deception to meet with those traces in the blood; that no further run of prosperous seasons should tempt someone of their own lineage to move back to Deception, to try like Paul to mark out his redemption across that bleak domain of blasted grass and rocks and stunted trees.

—You want me to speak of Agnes.

Colette smiled at me, and took my arm more firmly.

—You have a right to know, and perhaps you know already.

As though the reassuring closeness of my body might brace her better for the task.

—Agnes's story is a complicated one, *Nicolas*. It is a story, though, that will be told. In proper stages, as I have said. And at this proper time.

She stroked my hand as though I needed, in advance, some kind of reassurance.

—Her life, we came to know, has been very different from ours. It was for this—in part, and I say this not as an excuse, not for our mother or my sisters—that we felt it better to break the connection. To let the life of Agnes take its own direction. This was, to us, her nature from the first. Her destiny, to look forward and not backward. This is perhaps not easy for you to understand.

She knew, she said, that her father had worked for years in Sydney while waiting for her mother; staying on in Sydney after those he had escaped with left for home, the confinements and humiliations of Ducos now tempting him to turn the wreckage into some grander undertaking. Her father, through those years of labour on the wharves, became intent on some new form of recklessness from which he could not be dissuaded. As though all the cruelty he had known could at last be overshadowed by some new and splendid gesture requiring even richer suffering and even grander sacrifice.

—You should already know, *Nicolas*, by simple calculation, that my mother was not your own great-grandmother. That Agnes was only half our sister. No doubt, you have already established this. No doubt this is what you wish to hear?

It was not.

—Agnes was born in Sydney. After our father left to take up Deception. This much, you must surely know?

I did not. Such tricks the mind, our close affections, play. Those elusive frames that shape our ways of knowing. That open up so many blind alleys, but stand so steadily between us and what lies before our eyes.

Did even Agnes know? She certainly never spoke of it. Nor did my parents. Where had the knowledge ended? The fact had never been denied, as it had never been asserted. Did Monsieur Jalabert tell me, in his way, in speaking of Marie-Josèphe only and more distantly as Madame Duvernois? My thoughts had just never run in that direction. Had never been permitted, by myself or by others, to run in that direction. Perhaps I had some vague and unqueried notion that Marie-Josèphe had arrived in Australia, in Sydney, much earlier than Paul's first journey to Deception. More likely, I'd just never thought of it at all.

Colette did not look at me as she spoke, but continued to touch my hand.

—You should also know that our mother loved Agnes. She loved Agnes like a first child, and bore neither her nor her father any reproach that we could see. She brought up Agnes in our family and our language. The only moment that was different was on that day when we left, where she took Agnes apart and told her to stay. That someone must tell Papa. That she must wait with Papa, until he too should agree to come home.

Of Agnes's real mother, they knew very little. Only that she was born in Vienna, and that she came to New South Wales with her family after some untold disaster. That her story was one of great musical talent, of kind ladies in splendid dresses who complimented her and entertained her and her parents for a time in harbourside gardens, of a father who drank and a mother who ended in a hospital for the insane. These things had not been talked about—not the Voyagers' Hotel in Sydney, which was owned by her father, nor the sad affair of passion with Paul Duvernois, nor Agnes's birth nor the death of her mother soon after. Their own silence and that of their mother on all these matters, Colette insisted, was a testament of their true affection for Agnes, the restraint of curiosity perhaps the deepest form of loving they could show.

Agnes had arrived at Deception towards the end of 1878, brought across from Sydney by Marie-Josèphe. They arrived to meet six months of blistering heat, suffocating even in the darkness of a rambling half-completed mansion drawn together from the surrounding rocks and already cluttered, her mother later told Colette, with unpacked furniture and crates of objects that were still being delivered when there was no longer any money to pay for them. Almost from the time of her first coming their father had been forced to go away, droving his sheep or cattle along the roads far to the south or carting grain for others on the roads between Hawker and Quorn or Port Augusta, leaving Marie-Josèphe with her babies in the half-completed shell of the house. There, her mother had lived in a kind of exile, their few neighbours shrinking off into their own misery as the years drew on, and she unable to speak to them in their own language anyway, imprisoned within her foreignness and all within the broken ruin of her husband's vast imprudent dream.

—Was this a betrayal? His daughter, the house, and all that was to follow?

Colette let the words hang in the air.

—Perhaps it should have been seen so. Perhaps our mother should have made the simple accusation. Instead, *Nicolas*, each of them erected a vast wall around themselves, writing in vast letters 'I owe', 'I ought', 'I must'. If each had spoken more frankly to the other, if our father had just once let 'I am' or 'we are' come in place of those high-minded notions of what he thought ought to be, then we would not all have been drawn into the vacancy of his blindness. This lack of knowledge of each other might not have created so many ample spaces into which others could intrude.

Ample spaces. The fact that I had not known about Agnes was evident. Colette still touched my hand.

—Try to think kindly of these people, *Nicolas*. All of them. Of us, as well. I can see you find this difficult, that you did not know. Their lives, their choices were constrained. So important it is that you proceed with kindness as you come to understand.

***

Those who understand cannot judge. It's an undercover legal maxim. The rules of evidence are there for many reasons. Partly, at least, to keep you at a distance. To keep you 'uninvolved'. See too much of the story—the inner world of those who did it, as well as of those to whom it was done—and real judgment must get harder. Empathy might just cloud decision. Affection bend the facts. I thought then of Paul, and of his years spent labouring in Sydney. The Rocks. Staying at the Voyagers' Hotel. Of how his eyes must have followed her as she came from the smoking kitchen, nudging her way gently through the throng that gathered in the early evening. I thought of how he looked for her on his return from the wharves, stepping up the uneven footing of the rough stone stairs that led away from the harbour and cruel labour of Walsh Bay, from the oat stacks and barked orders and the dark cavernous holds, to where the Voyagers' usual crowd of stranded Germans, Italians, English, Russians and French drank and argued in the smoke and bustle of the crowded bar.

While scarcely knowing it himself, he began perhaps to seek her in those moments when he pushed his way through the crush of drinkers, the rich odour of sweat and spilled beer, to look for a coffee and some bread. Watching her each time as she sought to pin back the hair that strayed about her as she moved through the crowded rooms, ignoring without rudeness the comments of the drinkers, smiling at each request and bowing now and then as though mechanically to some harsh command from the old man in filthy flannel who ruled her from the bar. This girl with the deep blue eyes and the delicate olive skin flushed always an ugly red with the heat of the kitchens and the coarse labour of the bar, her long blonde hair caught up in a loose and straggling chignon, her simple dress carrying the odour of beer and kitchen smells, her face streaked always with sweat and grime as she pushed her hair out of her eyes with the back of a perspiring hand.

Did she enter his room, his rough shelter of packing crates and corrugated iron, to replace a towel perhaps or to fetch soiled clothing with a half-smile of greeting and no further exchange? Was she the first to speak? Was it perhaps her music, so faintly heard from below, that had drawn him to that place? Sitting on an iron bench far down the terraces, looking out across the harbour, watching the seagulls duck and weave and the bright summer light catching the vast stretch of water that led off to the east. Did he then hear her music?

The Rocks. Home to so many who had arrived in Sydney in body but not in spirit, to so many of those who needed to cling to the water's edge. To emigrants who had missed their ship, or sailors who were drunk or had gambled the last of their earnings and were left stranded on the shore. To the hangers-on and misfits, the whores and touts and sharpers and anyone who could feed on the misery of others in a maze of hotels and bars and worse; this nation made up of all the world's detritus, of ageing forty-eighters from all parts of the world, of old Mazzinis still calling for bloody union and tattered followers of Kossuth and Ledru-Rollin.

Was she the first to speak? To enter his room and say, here everything is broken. All is consumed. As though speaking to the air itself. Not looking at him. It being difficult, through her falling hair, to tell to whom she spoke, her hair showing gold in the light that ran in from the bar. But speaking with strength, as if speaking of something she had long thought, had long needed to say. Looking up, and smiling wanly, and making as if to leave.

With Paul then asking about her music. And she consenting to sit with him for a moment, her hand rising to push into place one of the strands of wet hair that fell about her face. Sitting erect on the bed, suddenly aware of the ugliness of her reddened hands, wrapping them in the towel she was holding, but all the while watching Paul steadily, the steadiness of her gaze telling him in that moment that she too had long been watching him, that she now knew him perhaps better than he knew himself, that he and she were equal strangers in this place, strangers in the midst of their own lives. Sitting in silence, with he then touching perhaps her hand, raising his hand to stroke her perspiring cheek, far softer than the coarse jute of the Walsh Bay wheat sacks, the flaking bark and harsh rocks of Ducos, and she leaning towards the pressure of his hand, letting him mould his hand about her cheek as though it was the only caress she had ever known, bending towards him, bending down so that he could reach forward and further caress her face. Stooping, so that he could see in the dim light of the suffocating iron room the tears that formed in her eyes and caught for a glistening moment the low glow of his lamp, her eyes now looking deeply into his, her lids heavy with a weight of fatigue and a dangerous unhappiness from which even new forms of unhappiness might seem to bring relief.

Twelve

The Château de Vincennes. So much in Julia's conversation. Where she so often worked. It was at Vincennes that the records of the Conseil de Guerre were kept, the notorious military dossiers of the alleged Communards. Those that survived. Hidden for generations, piled up in boxes in cellars around the city. Thousands of records, she explained, had been lost to rats and to the damp. Thousands were stolen and destroyed.

—It's high time you saw it, Nicholas. The national archives. The nation's greatest shame.

We drove out to Vincennes in the early morning. The heat was already rising. Paris heat. Lifting in waves from the bitumen, the concrete, and blowing past us in grey gritty clouds of dust. Tempers on the road, amid the congested traffic, were fraying. Julia was cheerful, though, in rich anticipation, tapping her fingers on the dashboard with excitement.

I told her, warily, about what Colette had said. Of Agnes and her mother, of Paul's time in Sydney, and The Rocks. Not wanting to bring on demands for a visit, an interview of her own.

Julia, though, was intent on her own mission. She merely nodded knowingly. As though this was no more than confirmation.

—Just wait, Nicholas. You'll see. Oh, you'll be amazed at what you're going to see.

She gave nothing more away. She just smiled and teased. She seemed fresher, more relaxed, more vibrant and friendly than she had been on our last meeting. We concentrated our attention on the traffic and her battered *Plan de Paris*, finding our way around through back routes and along narrow one-way streets, evading the blockages and barricades and reroutings of the inner city, but moving steadily eastward, towards the Château de Vincennes.

The Château was a gloomy place, lost in the Parisian outskirts. The largest medieval keep in France, a place that had seen more than its share of slaughter in peacetime and in revolution, but now turned to sleepy bureaucratic uses, its ancient structures endlessly adapted and remodelled, now serving mainly as a disorderly military archive, housing millions of records of the bloodshed that had been, a musty repository of ancient crimes and betrayals. The Château's archives were open to the public, but, as Julia had already warned, were always guarded by some cranky *fonctionnaire,* some superannuated soldier whose task was to insult and obstruct in the hope that scholars would leave off their inquiries, or take them elsewhere.

We threaded through the Château's vast open courtyards and past the keep, the famous crumbling *donjon*, to an outbuilding of later date. We climbed a wide staircase, past ancient swords and helmets in ornate configurations, past banners and pikes and standards, towards the heavy doors of the military archive. The obstruction was in place when we arrived. This time, a woman of uncertain age with steel-rimmed spectacles, groomed in severity. She was positioned behind a peeling desk between us and the doors. She sat leafing through a huge pile of pink official-looking forms with a great show of intense concentration, administering now and then a very slow and judicious tick.

We stood in front of her for a time. There seemed to be no-one else in the building. We waited quietly, patiently. Then foolishly, as time slipped by.

Julia's voice suddenly cracked like a whip.

—*Madame!*

The woman started in shock from her seat, the forms in disarray. Julia's voice echoed up and down the draughty halls. Down the corridor, one or two doors opened, and curious heads poked out.

—Madame. Excuse me!

She then apologised in a lower tone before the startled woman could respond. Our credentials were quickly inspected and the usual forms produced, one, two and three, to be filled in, elaborate details on who we were, why we were there, the *but de recherche,* the object of the research. More forms than usual; more even than at the Bibliothèque Nationale. This too, Julia had explained. There was still much in the files of the Château de Vincennes to which many patriotic Frenchmen would love to set a match. That there was no collection of dossiers more discrediting, no greater national embarrassment, than the dossiers that recorded the judicial processes that followed the fall of the Commune.

We were sent into a musty reading room, a room of old files, cardboard and dust.

The dossiers were brought in boxes. In each was a mixture of folders, some leather and some cardboard. The contents were written in a variety of hands. Many contained just official forms—*formule no 6*, they were called—printed out for the mass trial and mass condemnation, the spaces quickly filled in by hand. Some were more extensive, with long submissions by witnesses, or extended prosecution testimony, variously addressed to the *Sixième*, the *Huitième*, or the *Dixième Conseil de Guerre.* There had once been more than forty-thousand dossiers, Julia explained, but half of them had simply rotted away.

The room was unbearably hot. The boxes were heavy, thick with dust. Our shirts were soon wet with perspiration, the ancient papers sticking to our hands.

The files were often telling in their sheer brevity. The haste, the carelessness of the procedures, were reflected in the official lists, the densely printed forms that permitted a simple, one-sentence recording of whom, when and where: *Nom, Date de la Condemnation, Peine*; name, date, decision and punishment.

Paul's dossier had survived. The entries were simple, squeezed into the modest spaces. Name: Paul-Auguste Duvernois. Date of condemnation: 26 January 1872. Punishment: Deportation to a Fortified Enclosure. That was all. Paul had been fortunate, Julia explained. His trial was held in January, many months after the fall of the Commune, when the process had settled into more reputable procedures. The sentences were lighter. The dossier showed he had been imprisoned, in the old naval forts on the western coast, at Cherbourg and Brest and

La Rochelle. The trial and passing of the sentence must almost have been a relief.

An attached document, in a brittle paper which almost fell apart in my hands, stated that he was the son of Jean François and Hermine Justine, and that he was born in 1845 at Caen, in the department of Calvados; that he was an architect, and that he was serving in the 173rd battalion as a captain at the time of his capture. Witnesses testified that he was seen bearing weapons, and that he had directed the construction of barricades in various named parts of the city.

Julia glanced at his papers briefly, explained some details, and then left me with his dossier to work among some papers of her own. In the judgment of the court, Paul had participated 'in an attack, the object of which was to bring massacre, pillage and devastation to the region of Paris'. Under sections 87, 88, 91 and 97 of the *Code Penal*, he was sentenced to imprisonment for life in an *enceinte fortifiée*. There was no reference to a sentence of death, in the way Agnes had told. Some of the papers may have been lost. There were no depositions from witnesses, as in many of the other files. Perhaps some of the documents had been stolen, or suppressed.

—Here. Here it is, Nicholas. I knew it!

Julia suddenly called me to the desk where she was working, sifting through a box of files.

—This is what I wanted you to see. This is the one.

There was a sheet of paper, separated from the others, on her desk.

She held it up.

Coignard. Marie-Josèphe Hélène. *Massacre, pillage, dévastation*.

There it was, set out in an awkward scrawl. The name, the crime, the date, the decision, the punishment. *Déportation simple*. Less severe than Paul's sentence, but deportation sure enough. To the Isle of Pines. Then, a year later, in another hand, another ink, a commutation listed, to domestic service in Nouméa. The name Dufour. *Procureur-Général*.

We drove back to the city. Trapped in the furnace of the Renault, Julia fanning herself with pages from the *Codicilles*. It was easy to avoid talking. Heat rose from the bitumen, the long lines of cars and buses. The traffic was dense, the streets obstructed, the CRS and traffic police out in heavy force, with roadblocks along the route in from Vincennes.

Julia seemed amused. She caressed my neck, teasingly, as though I was a truculent child, needing to be coaxed to a better humour.

—Oh, come on, Nicholas. It's not so bad. Really. It makes her practically a national hero, these days. I'm surprised there's not more about her in the histories. *Massacre, pillage, dévastation*. It's quite an achievement at her age. A mere slip of a girl!

As we drove, I thought of Tante Colette. Who must always have known. Who had almost told me, when I thought about it. *She followed him to the Ends of the Earth. She followed him to the Ends of the Earth.* The pain, to all, of deportation. Tante Colette, who preferred to tell her gentle and romantic stories, but who left these small cracks, small hints and fissures in all her stories—as though hoping I would see, and probe again?

Marie-Josèphe had been pardoned early. *Amnistié, 1877*. Three years before the General Amnesty. It was the last note in her file. So why didn't she return home? Why did she stay in Nouméa all those years? Why was her dossier so sparse? And why did no-one ever speak of it?

As we crossed the *périphérique* and drew closer to the centre, the signs of unrest were increasing, with large crowds of shouting protesters carrying banners, pouring from the metros and moving along the streets, spilling out across the roads.

—When did you see this, Julia? How long have you known?

—I'd never seen it. I guessed it, though, almost straight away. And there was something in Rouvel's journal. Just hints. One idea led to another. I guessed. I assumed. Informed hypothesis, Nicholas. Why else would she have been there, in your part of the world? So far away, at such a time? Following your great-grandfather? It seemed most unlikely. A young woman of her background—it just would not have happened.

Beyond that one simple sheet of paper with its hurried handwriting, there had been no detail. There was the date of the trial. November 1871. The sentence, *déportation simple*. There were no appended documents. No mention of family, not even the names of parents. No mention of birthplace. Nothing except the sentence, and her name and label: *concubine*. There were no testimonials, no denunications by interfering neighbours of the kind that were attached to so many of the files. Just the record of name and trial date and sentence.

And that bleak word. Concubine.

Julia put her hand on my shoulder.

—Don't worry, Nicholas. I know what's troubling you. It means nothing. It was a policy. If a woman was married, the husband was identified. If not, she was described as a concubine. All it means is that she was a young woman with no husband who was found somewhere she shouldn't have been. That's really all it means. Be kind to your great-grandmother. To this Marie-Josèphe, rather. All I'm saying is that the whole story—the real story—is a bit more complicated than you think. Or than your Tante Colette wants you to know.

I was silent. Looking to the street ahead. Annoyed. At Julia? At Marie-Josèphe Coignard? At myself?

—The miracle is that she wasn't simply shot. As a *petroleuse,* or some such thing. Others were not so lucky. Poor wretches, with not a shred of evidence against any of them.

I had heard of the *petroleuses*. Lucien had spoken of them. That was the wildest fiction of all; the idea that the streets were thronging with young women carrying bottles of petrol to set fire to the homes of decent law-abiding Parisian citizens. Simply to be in the streets, he explained, was cause enough to be rounded up and shot or, at best, packed off on the long march up to the prisons at Versailles. Thousands were sentenced.

Not so many women, though, and few *bourgeoises* like her. And almost no women of her age.

—So few women were deported, Julia. That I know. Only thirty were sentenced to deportation. Just twenty or so were sent. Almost all with strings of earlier convictions. Why her? There seemed to be no charge. Just the general *pillage* noted on her file. Where was her family?

—It was disappointing, Nicholas. Disappointing. That I'll admit. I thought that we'd find more. You can see that some of the dossiers are quite elaborate. So many records were destroyed. Families using their influence. Think of the thousands, just like your Tante Colette, doing all they could to wipe the record clean.

—But Julia, a young woman, not yet twenty years old, being sent away to the other side of the world?

—The scale of the thing was enormous, Nicholas. No-one knows how many thousands were killed. What was the life of one young girl in all that? It is strange. It is exceptional. I'll grant you that. She was a *bourgeoise*. It would have been conspicuous. And she was very young. Why the family didn't try—how they didn't manage to extract her from the Conseil de Guerre, we'll simply never know.

She shrugged her shoulders.

—Maybe they never knew. Maybe she never told them. Perhaps she was humiliated, ashamed. In the same way that your Tante Colette is still ashamed. But now, at last, you can really talk to your aunt. I shouldn't have teased you with this. I know I've been cruel. I just thought you needed your nose rubbed in a few hard facts. These were hard times, Nicholas. Such bitter times. It's important that you know.

We passed a long line of armoured police vans parked in the shadows of a long line of elms. We watched the long lines of armed CRS officers, stroking their batons, shifting from foot to foot, waiting for a sign.

—No-one has forgotten it, Nicholas. No-one.

I thought about what Lucien had told me. I thought of Sebastien Rouvel, whose own light sentence was the scandal of the age, who got leave from the *enceinte fortifiée* on Ducos to work across the Grande Rade in Nouméa within a month or so of his arrival—in stateroom-style, if all reports were true—on the dreaded floating cage, the notorious *Danae*. The worst transport of all. How he was set up within months in a comfortable house on Mount Coffyn with half a dozen of his former allies working for him as assigned servants.

As we drew closer to the river we found ourselves in the midst of new turmoil, trapped in a narrow street with thousands of shouting students coming towards us, some rocking the car as they passed, some waving their fists and chanting slogans, but others laughing and joking, their leaders now waving burning brands. We crept our way back along the rue du Faubourg-Saint-Antoine and on towards the Hôtel de Ville and across the river, with the crowd still moving around us, the heat of the day seeming still to rise, even as the light began to die away. Despite the lights, the braziers and the fires of refuse that were blazing in the streets, I felt the darkness of the city closing in. Despite the thousands of excited, wide-eyed students, milling behind their banners, the raging fires, the overturned cars, the smell of tear gas hanging in the air. Despite the presence of Julia, her hand still on my shoulder, but now looking beyond me and out into the turmoil and off into some remote dreamworld of her own.

It took us hours to get back to the rue de la Clef. Exhausted as we were, Julia insisted that we get straight to work, though it was now late in the evening. The apartment was close, stuffy. Opening the windows just seemed to let in more heat from the street. Julia had a feverish glint in her eye. As though we had now crossed a threshold. She cleared a space on the floor, in the centre of the room. We must now go over the whole of the Rouvel papers, she declared, to review them against what we had just seen. *Massacre, pillage, dévastation*. A real *déportée*. A genuine Communard! Who else, she teased, could boast of such a great-grandmother? A new Louise Michel. Younger, more beautiful. Rising from the depths of history. The *Codicilles* would need to be reworked. From the beginning. The whole thing.

For hours we worked, with Julia transcribing from Rouvel's writings and jotting notes into the margins. Taking down everything that I knew. All that Agnes had told. All that Monsieur Jalabert could tell of life on Ducos and in Nouméa, and of Rochefort's escape. All that I knew of Paul, of his time in Sydney. Of his journey to the west, his waiting there for years for the arrival of Marie-Josèphe. All that we now knew of Marie-Josèphe. *Massacre. Pillage. Dévastation.*

At last, she took another cigarette and pushed the papers aside. She slumped back exhausted in her chair. Still elated, still in a state of high excitement, but with the exhaustion starting to show. I was taking notes from a tangled page of Rouvel's papers. One where he had written a full page, but then another, upside down and between the lines. Upside down, but with each upended second line, as far as we could establish, running on from the one before. Julia watched my contortions with the page. She laughed as I tipped it back and forth and turned it round and round in my hands.

Her laughter broke like fresh air, like sunshine, across the dark, close atmosphere of the apartment.

I stopped. For just a precious moment, we seemed to see each other. Julia, laughing with real warmth, with a teasing affection in her eyes. For me. Not just for the papers in my hand. It was something we had lost, in our headlong pursuit through the folders, the dossiers and boxes. Something we had scarcely known since that first greedy tumble through the files and sticking papers. With the Editions Grandet deadline pressing. With all of troubled Paris, all of posterity waiting for the voice of Rouvel. Something we had touched on just once or twice, the first time that we met, looking across the papers and at each other in the place de la Bastille, and again, in greater intimacy, in those moments on the bed and across the floor and through the clinging papers in the rue de la Clef.

We stopped, for just a precious moment. When one of us might have spoken once again and as though for the first time. Of Nick Lethbridge, or of Julia Dussol. Not of Sebastien Rouvel, or Paul-Auguste Duvernois, and not the *deportée* Coignard. Of who we were, and not just what we wanted. Of what was happening in the present, and all around us in the streets. Not just of what had happened, or what might have happened, or of what it all might mean. The chance, perhaps—or was it just the heat, or fatigue, and my exhausted imagination—to climb out of the sink of other people's lives, and back into our own?

Julia smiled. Again, the teasing raised eyebrow. There was the shouting, the movement of light from the fires, still burning in the streets. Something concrete, something fleshly and stout-booted, seemed suddenly to join us in the room. She made as though to stand, as though to come to me, not to the papers, by the bed.

She had forgotten, though, a small sheaf of papers that had been resting on her lap, which now scattered to the floor. She stooped to gather them. Her eye was caught by something on a page. She knelt, moving quickly to the next page and the next. Reaching for her spectacles.

It was some time before she spoke. Her voice again sharp, and steady. She held a new piece of paper in her hand.

—You do realise, Nicholas, that at the very centre of this, there is something else? Something very important.

—There's something that you and I are still just circling around. Something that you don't seem to want to know. Even to think about.

I said nothing. I watched her adjust her spectacles. She lit a cigarette.

—Do you think he was really so very friendly with your great-grandfather, Nicholas? Do you think it was some bond between them that drew him to the desert? Did they have so very much in common?

It was a conversation that we both knew was coming. Though perhaps not just at this moment.

—Don't you think it's time that we were a little more frank with each other? Did Marie-Josèphe genuinely like Sebastien Rouvel? Did they perhaps see each other in Nouméa? Did she perhaps organise her life so that she could see him again? There are things—hints, in the papers. In the poems. Things that are consistent. We have to hypothesise, Nicholas. To speculate.

I looked at my papers. To the window. Anywhere but Julia.

—It all adds up, Nicholas. There's a strong sense here—it's not quite clear yet, but I'm working through it—that these two were drawn to each other. Some form of gravitation. Paris? Nouméa? Mount Deception? The first two could be chance. Mere bad luck, if you like. The third, never. Why else would he have travelled all that way? Out to the middle of the desert?

—He'd lost all his money, Julia. All his power. He was ill, and needed care. He had nowhere else to go.

—There's more to it than that, Nicholas. There has to be. You have to think about what is probable. About how most people would act. About how you would have acted. That's the best kind of guide.

She drew deeply on her cigarette.

—She was lonely, and a long way from home. You have evidence—your own aunt has told you—that things were never easy between her and her husband after the first flush of romance. That there was always some barrier. Some obstruction. Despite what your family may have said, Nicholas, there is plenty of evidence that he, Rouvel, was an attractive man. You have to at least entertain the idea that there might have been some kind of contact on the island. Perhaps even in Paris, years before. We just don't know enough about them. That's all I'm saying, Nicholas.

I thought of what Lucien had said. About the right stinker that he was.

Julia saw that I was floundering. She put down her cigarette and came to sit beside me on the bed, ruffling my hair and laughing.

—I'm not thinking details, Nicholas. I'm talking about some deeper thing. Some shared obsession. Long separations. Denials. Threats. Resolutions. But always drawn towards each other again by this richer thing they shared. It's here, in the papers. Not named, perhaps, but described in other ways. I only have his side of it, and I admit, it's very, very strange. Obscure. Perhaps he scarcely knew himself. You have to read closely. Very closely.

—And Paul? Did he have any say in this?

—Paul?

She went back to her desk.

—You always think of Paul as lofty. As noble in spirit. I'm beginning to think that he was a bit of a nuisance, tramping around in other people's lives with his misguided ideals. Even your Tante Colette seems to say as much. You've got to listen, Nicholas. You've got to hear what is being said. You have to trust the writing, to follow the evidence. That's all I'm saying. The writing, Nicholas. You've got to think a bit more about what was possible, Nicholas. Not just what you'd like to hear.

The writing. The old photographs. The written word.

I think we look for refuge in these things, in remote gentility, grand gestures, formal postures of elegance. For all that's lost to us, in the sweat and mess of present daily life. On this, Lucien had strong views, expressed when we were sweating up the rue de la Roquette. It's the lower functions, Lucien insisted, that contain the higher truths of history. Ignore the costumes, he said; just trust the kinship of the body with the bodies of the past. My best knowledge of my great-grandfather would come through sweat and pain and straining muscle. Struggling up to Père-Lachaise. Of Marie-Josèphe Duvernois, *née* Coignard, through my own senses, through touch and sight and smell. I should think about Sebastien Rouvel through the way the pince-nez might have tightened on his nose. Or through how his feet moved and blistered within his boots on the track up to Deception. How the papers would have clung to his skin in the heat, and lifted as he raised the turkey quill. The best truths of history. More in what the body feels than what the mind records.

Was this another proper moment? The proper time to tell Julia more about Paul's time in Sydney? About the Voyagers' Hotel and the birth of Agnes? I could see how it would feed her thesis. How little chance of a fair hearing Marie-Josèphe would stand in that particular court. I decided to wait and see how far she would get without it.

I thought of Monsieur Jalabert behind his lamps. And of deception, spreading about us, creeping outwards in all directions like some thick and darkening pool.

Julia yawned, at last, and stretched. She wrapped her arms about herself, as though against a slight chill in the air.

—My feeling, Nicholas, is that your version of all this is going to look pretty foolish when the papers come together. There are going to be a lot of questions still unanswered. I'm really beginning to see a new kind of order. Something just below the surface. Something that goes beyond what either of us imagines. Forget about your feelings, Nicholas. Trust the evidence. Are you serious about this? You have to make a choice.

She looked back at her desk, at the pile of papers still to be worked over, to be translated. She sighed, smiled wanly to me, half buried in my own pile of papers, and bent herself to the task.

I woke deep in the murky tracts of night to noises from the streets that lay beyond the place Monge. Again, I could hear the faint sound of sirens, and the crash of breaking glass. I had fallen asleep on the floor. Julia slept, half-clothed, amid the papers on the bed. Her lamp was still alight. She had fallen asleep while working, a pen and clutch of paper still in her hands. I watched her sleeping, though hardly peacefully. I took the papers from her hand and drew a cover over her, turning off the lamp. Light filtered in from the streetlamps, those that had not been broken, in the place.

So many questions, still unanswered. You have to make a choice. I found myself thinking of a restaurant. A cheap restaurant, just beyond the square Louvois. Always very crowded, always extremely noisy, the tables squeezed together, the lunchtime patrons coming and going in quick jostling succession. I found myself thinking of the single waitress, the poor wretched sweating waitress, and the swinging door that led into the kitchens. I would hear her being scolded as she swept through to the kitchens. I would hear her being scolded as she swept back to the patrons. With the door itself just swinging happily, part muffling the angry sounds from either side. I risked a kind word. She responded angrily. '*Quoi*?' I did not go back again.

I sat on the bed and lit one of Julia's cigarettes, and thought of the last passage we had translated—one that Sebastien Rouvel had written in the islands, Julia was convinced—about banded light and the moon filtering through the tall shutters; a passage which told of the sounds of insects in the night and the strands of light that fell, the rich erotic tremor from that intermittence of dark and light, the seeing and then not seeing, the knowing and then not knowing; with Rouvel as the seer of the poem, watching the fall of light and shadow, teased by these alternations, of mystery and revelation and deeper mystery to follow.

I watched Julia as she sighed and moved in her sleep, burrowing deeper among the papers on the bed. Julia Dussol. This most intimate of strangers, less known to me each time I saw her, amid the strangeness of this room, these papers, these toppling folders, these forbidding, taunting photographs. I wanted to wake her. I wanted to take her in my arms, to hold her still and captive. To talk more, perhaps even for the last time, of Julia Dussol. Of Nicholas Lethbridge. Of people, places, happenings that swam free from the dangerous vortex that these stories had become. We'd talked so little of ourselves, it seemed; so very much of others. So little of the present, so intensely of the past. So little of the living, so intently of the dead.

I wanted to wake her, and talk more of the dangers. That perhaps this retreat into the mists of history was just a deeper plunge into isolation, a deep retreat into ourselves? A deluding form of refuge, that brought us only closer to all we sought to evade? That perhaps all attempts at telling, all our tales of distant times and places are mere disguise and costumery, just another form of theatre for our more troubling fantasies? That all our versions of the past—even these closer family stories, and perhaps these especially so—must end up like some kind of overcoat, coming to us fresh and stiff and unrumpled and with the promise of a fine shape of their own, while soon being moulded to the sad shape of the naked body, taking on the wearer's familiar outline quickly bending to the dictates of local sinew, bone and muscle?

I wanted to wake her and tell her that we should put aside the writing. That we should throw away the maps and files and yellowed pages, push back the walls of her apartment, and level the buildings up and down the rue de la Clef, and open out the place Monge so that it might run, flat, red and featureless, further than the eye could see. So that she would understand the emptiness. So that she would search not just for the meanings, for the ready, quick solutions, but for just a little longer, for the scale and for the richness of the mystery. I wanted to take her hand and make her see what I had seen, to trace for her the fallen walls, the faint line of the verandah and the track leading over the creek bed to the north and to the west. I wanted to tell her again what Agnes had told, and what Agnes had failed to tell; to give her the heat, the dust, that last day at Deception with all its cracks and its confusion, so that she too could peer with me into the crevices, pause with me in the realm of what was silent, dry, unmeaning. To start, at least, with some small knowledge of that vast repeating, defeating emptiness that Sebastien Rouvel had come to at the end.

The night is more than just lack of light. I stood by the window looking out at the lights reflected in puddles of water in the place Monge. The night is so much more than just the daytime world cast into darkness. The night is the time of dreams, the time when all the memories and imaginings grow too rich upon you, and good and bad and love and dread can grow to mighty forms. I was sorely tempted in those moments to pick up Sebastien Rouvel's writings, and to move off through the night. To leave with this last image of Julia, spread out again amid her papers, still perspiring, her body glistening warmly in the streetlight from the Place. To let her wake alone, with the feeling that this had been some kind of dream, some foolish scholar's fantasy, some aberration bred out of too much coffee, late nights, and lack of sleep. To vanish into the disturbance, the faceless hubbub of the city, and to go back to the Ends of the Earth. To stand on the peak of Mount Deception, and scatter the papers to the winds and desert ranges, as Agnes had once hinted I should do.

Thirteen

I WENT BACK TO the hospice at Milly-la-Forêt. One more time. Drawn back by the vague promise of further papers. Drawn also by the half-speech, half-silence of this Monsieur Jalabert. I arrived to the same unsurprised and orderly welcome. I was shown into his rooms, as though by precise appointment, to be greeted with the same smile, the same air that suggested we were in some way partners in this matter.

Partnership—and if so, would I be a true partner to Colette? Or further, to Julia Dussol? I thought again of my wretched harried waitress, and of the swinging door.

He pointed me to a chair and took up his own chair behind the desk. As though in consultation. His hands clasped in expectation. Monsieur Jalabert. Was he indeed the true custodian? Was he indeed the Oldest Friend? He placed himself behind the lamps, again. To prevent me from reading his real intent, from reconstructing, across the marks of age, the youthful face that looked at the young woman with freckles and with auburn hair?

—Tell me, Monsieur Jalabert, about Rouvel. You did mention, at Saint-Germain-sur-École, Sebastien Rouvel.

He looked at his papers. Arranging them in a neater order. He looked up and smiled.

—Rouvel. Always, it does creep back to Sebastien Rouvel. The story of your family, so quickly it becomes the story of Sebastien Rouvel. I am surprised you did not speak of him earlier. Of Rouvel, before the time of Mount Deception. Before the deportations began. Perhaps even before the end of the war, and the fall of the Commune?

Monsieur Jalabert raised an eyebrow. Turning, as always, a statement into a further question? Seeming to know more than he did in order to elicit what he did not know?

—We do know that he came to Deception. That his life ended at Deception. The life of our friend Rouvel did take many strange turns in the years following his deportation. This I can tell you. This was well known, but has since been much ignored.

Monsieur Jalabert smiled and held up a hand, as

though these things must now have an order, one thing to follow another in the way he had determined.

—Many strange turns. Not long after the escape of Rochefort. Something that is not in the histories. Especially not now. When suddenly the whole world seems to be seeking some new Sebastien Rouvel. To feed the disturbances in the streets. Someone to lead, to instruct.

He paused to look at me closely, as though with some unspoken question, as though creating a space for me to talk about the writings of Rouvel. As though he knew of its existence? Was this another of his stratagems? I was silent.

At length, Monsieur Jalabert spoke on.

—Sebastien Rouvel went into business. The *enragé,* the scourge of the *bourgeoisie,* soon became a *bon bourgeois* himself. Quite prosperous, and in a remarkably short time. And do you know how?

Monsieur Jalabert waited, watching with amusement my curiosity grow.

—Slave trading.

—Slaves?

—In effect. Of course, it had another name. These were enlightened times. Enlightened words were used. The demand for cheap labour was huge in that part of the world, for the sugar plantations in Queensland and in Fiji. There were plenty of able-bodied men and women around the islands who could easily be duped. Slave trading. Blackbirding, I believe your people called it. With contracts, of course. With regulations about repatriation and the like.

—Is this generally known?

—It is generally known, and it is generally forgotten with regard to our friend Sebastien Rouvel. To the extent that anyone has ever cared about what Rouvel did in his later years. It is in the records, though; the newspapers, the documents. It's there for all to see. Rouvel quickly made large amounts of money from the trade. It was not called slave trading by anyone except, perhaps, by the British, who patrolled the islands. It was a scandal, even so. A British naval officer was killed by the traders. Missionaries, even a bishop, were slaughtered by the islanders. There were threats of yardarm hangings for anyone involved.

But it was through this, Monsieur Jalabert said, that Sebastien Rouvel was caught up in the trade. An Australian captain had a cargo of Eromangans, riddled with disease, that he had picked up from the Île de Maré. He was followed by a British corvette, and found his way into the Grande Rade at Nouméa, where the British could not follow. Rouvel, it seems, had some knowledge of English, picked up during his days at the Lycée Louis-le-Grand. He bled the man first of his knowledge, and then, at a scandalous price, of his ailing shipment. He took the Maréans off his hands and fattened them up in sheds on the wharf in Nouméa, and resold their contracts to the next trader in port. In the space of a few weeks, Rouvel had established himself as a trader, without much capital or even much knowledge of the trade.

—How do you know this, Monsieur Jalabert, when it is not in the histories?

—Some of them know it. But it makes a poor ending to a tale of revolution, does it not? A sad conclusion for our gifted *enragé*? If your friends in Paris know anything of Sebastien Rouvel, they will know this. It is not that the historians tell outright lies. It is more that they have chosen to end their story sooner rather than later, while it still has a moral shape, some chance of an improving message. Run it on a little longer, and it starts to come apart.

—And you?

—I had a purpose, at one time, to know. You may have guessed it. I have no wish to discuss it. As you, now, have a purpose. I, too, had friends with knowledge, as you now have friends. When I was your age, there were many still living who could help me in my quest. Many people I could talk to, who knew Monsieur Sebastien Rouvel.

I told him the little I knew of Paul's time in Sydney. About Agnes, and the Voyagers' Hotel.

—Rouvel's work took him to Sydney. Many times. While Mademoiselle Colette's father was there. That is all I can rightly say.

—Monsieur Jalabert, I have to ask you. Did you know that Colette's mother was herself a *déportée*?

—You have been to the Château de Vincennes?

—I have.

—And so have I. Then you know almost as much as I do. Certainly more than Colette thinks either of us knows. Almost as much as I do. But not quite. I did tell you of more papers? Letters? Just a few.

—Did her mother know him in Nouméa? After the escape?

—There are indications that she did.

—Monsieur Jalabert, who was Sebastien Rouvel, really, to these people?

Monsieur Jalabert smiled again, but only to himself.

—That is what you may one day ask Colette. That is what you may, one day, be brought to ask. He lost his money. That is certain. But not, it is possible, before he had helped others. Before he put others in his debt. Within his power?

Monsieur Jalabert made an open gesture with his hands.

—Of this I have no proof. I know enough to raise the question. Anecdotes. Inference from anecdotes. That is all. Novelists and poets may deal, my young friend, in what is merely possible. We lawyers must try to stay in the world of what is real. Within the balance of probabilities, at least, as your Anglo-Saxon colleagues would have it? Beyond reasonable doubt? That is perhaps too much to hope for. It is possible that there was some more extensive contact. Of some kind. With Madame Duvernois, even. So much is possible. Merely possible. But one thing I can tell you—one thing I must tell you—is that he could be generous. Not everyone thinks of Sebastien Rouvel as your family does. Not everyone sees him as they saw him. When you inquire—and you must understand, I have spoken to some who knew him—you will find that he was bright, witty, full of charm. A natural leader. Many liked him. He was known to be kind—liberal, even. From this, as much as from cruelty, he gained much power.

—But Monsieur Jalabert, why was he poor? In the end, up at Deception? Agnes told me he was in rags. Sick, poor and alone. Why was he there?

—There, I cannot help you. He lost his money. A nickel scandal in the late 1880s. Thereafter, he vanished from Nouméa. From the documents, the newspapers, even from private letters. Even from conversation, it would seem. Rouvel had many business acquaintances. Many admirers. But few friends.

Monsieur Jalabert slumped back in his chair, shrank

back into his collar, his ancient suit. He was suddenly tired. He ran his hands over his papers in a dismissive gesture, spreading them across his desk.

—Do be careful, my friend. Because of all the gaps, and things we know nothing about. You'll be drawn in. Dragged back into the past, and one day you'll be old like me and like your aunts, and your whole life will have passed in thinking about the past. I've seen so much of it. Old houses, housing nothing but the past in steep decay. Old people still living backwards, living their lives through what happened in the lives of others. There are better ways, Monsieur *Nicolas*, so much better. You should listen to me. Do you know what I would really like to do, even this late in the piece? I should destroy it all; destroy all the letters, empty out all my files, burn down that old house, and drag your poor aunts out into the light of day. Send them down to spend the last of their days in a beautiful, light, airy apartment overlooking the beach at Nice or Saint Tropez. That's what I'd really like to do.

We sat without speaking for a time. Looking at each other. Monsieur Jalabert seemd wryly amused at being inspected and assessed in this way. He gently wiped the corner of his mouth.

Suddenly, he pulled open the drawer of his desk.

—My young friend, I have just made a decision. One that runs against much of what I have just said.

He drew out a small bundle of papers.

—I had thought to destroy these. Except that I have come to think that they might one day be needed. Needed to prevent those bad histories from being told. Needed to prevent graver pain. These are letters from Marie-Josèphe to Paul. From Nouméa.

He spread them across the desk.

—They came to me, passed on with my father's files, mixed up in some other papers. It seems he chose never to give them to Colette. And nor have I. They are all from the house of a family Marie-Josèphe stayed with in Nouméa. It seems she worked there as a kind of governess.

There were just three or four letters, in a beautiful cursive hand. They had been bound together tightly at one time, the paper compressed and breaking where the pressure of the ribbon was too firm. I handled them with great care, setting out the pages on the stone, noting date and place, and setting them in careful order.

—I'll read some to you. In a kind of English. In French, it is very beautifully, very carefully written. And probably rewritten many times. Just listen.

So I am finally permitted to receive your letters. Four, all at once! You have probably heard that most here in Nouméa and even those on the island have suffered as a result of your escape, though me no more than the others. For this, I have Monsieur Dufour to thank. I am told that Rochefort and the others are on their way to Europe to fight for the amnesty. May he succeed! To date, he has done us all more harm than good.

Yes—many things are greatly changed in this place, and I do not know what form of letter I should write. To write of my affection would be cruel, and a punishment for both of us. I will not tell you, Paul, that I love you and find life here intolerable without you, for I can—dying a little—tolerate it. I will not tell you that I love you, because that could be read as if I need you, and I find that, again, dying a little, I do not. If you do not love me, Paul, I ask you to forget all about me and go back to Europe, like the others. It is foolish to have escaped so far, and then to be imprisoned yet again. Your best intentions are the most dangerous. Please believe that.

I reached for the letter. Monsieur Jalabert held up a cautionary hand.

—People often write to set up blocks and barriers. On purpose. Especially when they write such careful letters as these. Each word so carefully chosen. It may be that the more we read, the less we seem to know . . .

It is only months since you left, but so much has happened to me in that time—and not just your leaving—that has changed everything. I am not what I was. I cannot afford to be. I am learning, without bitterness, to take my pleasure from things that cannot bring me pain: the Dufour children, and my several good friends in this place—those who were not sent back to the island after your escape.

I try to see all these things, even my own life, from some distance, as someone like Madame Dufour perhaps would see them, and I beg you to do the same. All promises, all undertakings between us are at an end. That was the choice you made. We have been the victim of too much cruelty from others to be cruel to one another; and now, it would be cruelty indeed to write of affection, or to make further promises.

—It is a strange letter. Intimate, but also cold and distant. Perhaps this was how people wrote to each other, in those days. She is telling him to go away, to forget. While keeping the door open.

But do promise me one last thing. That as I reproach you for nothing, you will do the same. Not for this letter (because I know it is not kind), nor for any harsh thing that you will hear of me from others.

—These are troubled letters. There is affection, but also a lot of pain. What is the reproach she speaks of? What is the cruelty she writes about? Do you know what it means?

Monsieur Jalabert began to fold the letters, carefully, in the way they had been tied.

—There are others. Others, more intimate, more dangerous perhaps. Take them away and read them. They touch more closely on the things you want to know. That you perhaps now need to know about, if there is any chance of the truth being told. They are for your eyes only, unless, and here I must emphasise this, unless you think that by showing them—to this friend, for example, who most certainly led you to Vincennes—you might be able to prevent bad histories, further pain. On this condition only can you show these letters.

He passed them over.

—Monsieur Jalabert, just one last thing. You must believe that I do not want to hurt these women.

—I know. Which does not mean, of course, that neither you nor I will not hurt them.

—You speak of tragedy. You speak of pain. Tell me about yourself, Monsieur Jalabert.

—Yes. I did think that you might ask. But have you not had enough of stories? Lies, concealments, tales from romantic novels?

—There's little here, I begin to think, that I will find in novels. Will you lie to me as well?

—No. But neither will I tell you all that is true. I have known Colette since I was fourteen years old. Fourteen. Our lives have been closely linked. They might have been linked more closely indeed—and here you are perhaps permitted to think a little of your novels—except that there was always something else, some special closeness between her and her mother, which prevented, which obstructed. There was no place to stand between them. And time passed. Decades. That is the simplest way to put it. That in our ordinary routines, time passed. In friendship, and later, after my father's death, as the family's lawyer. My pain? It is not there. It is, at least, no longer there. There may be passion in the things that have happened. But there can also be a passion in those that have not. And I have known friendship. Passionate friendship. For seventy-five years. Can you, at your age, believe in such a thing? That's some consolation, surely?

—Have you spoken to her of this, Monsieur Jalabert?

He smiled and drew away from the light.

—In more than seventy years, I have not. Even seventy-five years. Like you, I wanted, first, to know. The lawyer. To have the facts. To see the whole picture, as you might say. Wherever there was a gap, I named it a mystery, calling to be solved. This is often a mistake.

Monsieur Jalabert closed the book that was in front of him. He looked to the door.

A cry. A broken wineglass. The stain of red wine on the young woman's muslin blouse and the sudden awful silence in the room. I thought of Madame Dufour sitting on the bed in the little pavilion deep within the garden, mingling her troubled thoughts with the rich disorder of her plants, listening to the sounds of her *institutrice* taking the children through their lessons before the full heat of the day and despite all that had happened the evening before, the gentle repetitions of arithmetic, the declensions and the conjugations, the *mensa mensae, mensam* and *amo, amas, amat* ringing quietly but reassuringly once again through the house, the children now immersed in a slow and familiar world of grammars and additions and ink stains, all happening strictly as before. Madame Dufour, long in urgent need of a teacher for her children, agreeing to the presence of an educated *déportée* only on condition that she be banished to this small pavilion at the furthest end of the garden, that there be clear rules about the access that such a woman could have to the house.

The dinner would have been good, with Madame Dufour's own unease perhaps unnerving the servants a little, but despite a certain awkwardness—a sprinkling of red wine across Monsieur Rouvel's cuff, and one or two *haricots verts* finding their way into Marie-Josèphe's lap—as hostess she could commend herself on putting together, against all the assaults of climate and distance, a tolerable elegance. The young woman being placed next to their guest, despite her protests; foolish protests, though able to be interpreted, as Madame Dufour at first chose to interpret them, as an excess of modesty. The fact that he too was a *déporté*, that he had by some reports narrowly escaped the stake at Satory, was left behind in the few short months in which he had been on the *Grande Terre*.

This was a complicated world, a world upside down, in which you could not expect things to happen as they had in the world in which she was raised. Had their dinner guest, this unkempt, reserved, insinuating man, shot the Archbishop? There were those who said it was he who signed the papers, that he ought in justice to have been the first to be shot and still deserved no better. But Monsieur Dufour was insistent that the man had been defamed and vilified—and that he had since paid for whatever indiscretions were his, and was now emerging as a significant citizen in the new Pacific territory. That he was a model, indeed, of the whole spirit in which the colony was conceived.

For a time the conversation kept to innocent and

guarded subjects, on which the girl would enter as well as any of the others, all the while being quietly courteous to their uncertain guest, who entertained and graced and even charmed, who took a lively and extended interest in the plans for the education of the young Olivier, and in Monsieur Dufour's attempts to raise a decent aubergine.

With the time arriving, though, for the Dufours to leave the room, with foolish excuses and looks of true concern cast in the direction of Marie-Josèphe, whose frantic gazes left Madame Dufour with a deep sense of treachery. Yes—it was for this that the evening had been planned, with Madame Dufour hovering awkwardly with her husband in the salon nearby, he smoking furiously and still unwilling to address in any way the strangeness of this circumstance in which they were excluded on convict instruction from their own dining room. Waiting in a neighbouring room, against all propriety and above all against the anxiety of the young woman's expression as they left, she rising to her feet and needing to be told to stay, with a short command barked at her by the retreating Monsieur Dufour.

A sudden noise. A broken wineglass. Red wine on the white muslin of her blouse when they returned. Her face turned away. The dinner guest, his dark eyes scarcely to be seen, his face wreathed in thick clouds of tobacco smoke, twirling his glass between his fingers. The Dufours re-entered the room, both grasping for some bland assistance, hoping their guest might at least offer some polite and superficial subterfuge, some cheerful banality which might cover for the sudden shouting and the sound of breaking glass. He sat in silence. With the girl as pale as a sheet, and in tears?

Madame Dufour then drifted from these troubling musings, her scarce-admitted imaginings of what might have happened and of what might have been said, these dangerous tendrils creeping from a world which lay so thick and raw about them and which could only partly be kept at bay by these stone walls and gentle repetitions, the *amamus, amatis, amant* that still sounded from the front rooms of the house, the young *déportée* having apparently learned, as Madame Dufour had not, how to reconvene her life no matter what had passed, in this house that was already smothered by a rich garden threatening to invade, its woodwork starting to merge with *bananiers* and *cocotiers*, the rich cascading bougainvillea and the penetrating vines.

Already, the white paint showed signs of blistering and peeling, the timber, still too moist for building, beginning to warp and move under the daily assault of heat and afternoon rains, the walls unable to exclude the heat, the moisture, the intrusive insects, the cockroaches and the lizards, the mosquitos and flies. There came upon Madame Dufour the same dreaming which came to her too often in that place as she lay upon the white bed in the kiosk, the little pavilion fitted out for the young *déportée*, in which she would fling off her white muslin and sticking corset and petticoats, and begin to live a life that ran within the logic of the place, away from the white of the buildings and the black of regulation towards the fleshly depths of her own garden, the stems of the hibiscus thrusting at her, the strands of bougainvillea pricking at her flesh and the soft wet darkness of decaying leaves trickling over her body and working its way between her legs, she moving like perfumed bath-waters the mould around her and over her body, sinking, sinking, and she soon lost to all other claims upon her in all that decaying softness and deep green. Watching a stick insect crawling along her arm. Thinking simple, green, moist thoughts.

Fourteen

I HEARD NOTHING FROM Julia for days. Almost a week. Eventually, there was a message, a summons, waiting for me at the Grand Hôtel Jeanne d'Arc. We would meet in the Jardin des Plantes. At two o'clock. Near the biggest summer house.

She greeted me warmly enough. There was the familiar cheerful smile, the arm quickly threaded into mine. With no apology for or discussion of the time that had elapsed, no questions about how I might have passed the week. It was all Rouvel. Immediately, Rouvel. Editions Grandet. The looming deadline. The precious final draft.

So much, so many bits and pieces still to fit in. I could have no idea, the effort it had been!

Julia flopped on a bench beside me and stretched

herself, closing her eyes for a moment, running her fingers through her hair. Letting the light, the warmth fall on her face. Her clothing was rumpled, slightly stale, her hair a greasy tangle, loosely tied. She brought no lunch. She shared my sandwich. It was some time since she had eaten. She was eager, she said, though in a distracted sort of way, to see these letters. The letters I had mentioned. That told so much more of Sebastien Rouvel. This mysterious Monsieur Jalabert I now spoke of, who now had found, it seemed, his proper moment. So many of these moments!

Julia played with the words. Near us, a man was playing with his son. A fat man. North African, I think. Playing hide-and-seek with his little boy, in and out of the box hedges, and even around our bench. The shrieks of joy made no impression, and Julia went on to talk about her week, her apartment, her writing.

I passed her part of Monsieur Jalabert's papers. I think I expected a reaction like her first response to the Rouvel papers. I was to be disappointed. She read them quietly. Listlessly, I thought. She seemed oddly uninterested in them or in Monsieur Jalabert.

When she had finished, she dropped them into her lap. As though the case was already closed.

—Well. One thing is clear, Nicholas. She thought that everything with your great-grandfather was over. Harsh things? She wanted it to be finished between them.

—Colette has told me, many times. Her parents were always like this. Never quite meeting. Each trying to protect the other, and causing more pain in doing so. The letters fit exactly what she said. They were dutiful, but not close.

—It's all so final, Nicholas. And at any rate, it confirms my thoughts exactly. It's not a matter of their not being 'close'. She's pleading with him to stay away. You can't dispute that.

I beg you, Paul, if you still have any affection for me, that you do exactly what I say and do not try to help me in the ways that you suggest. You can only do further harm and it is only because of the kindness of Monsieur Dufour that I have not been sent back to the Isle of Pines or even the Île Nou . . .

Paul, they have your letters, and Jeanette is now in trouble as well. I have told you, Paul, and now I tell you again, you can do nothing but harm if you try to help me. Please, please believe me. Let me repair my life in peace . . .

—It's clear, Nicholas. He probably had some stupid plan to rescue her. There are stories of such things. *Let me repair my life in peace.* She didn't want it. All had changed. Something else had happened. Someone else had come along. Just read the letter, Nicholas! Read it closely and you'll see.

She unfolded the third, by far the longest of the letters. This time, I could see the interest come upon her as she scanned the first page.

—He's here, Nicholas. She mentions him. Not by name. But it has to be him.

> *You say that he is there, in Sydney. But Paul, ask yourself, what reason would he have to help you, or me? If there is no advantage in it for him, what does he intend? Is he now trading in our flesh, as he does with that of others? Please, dear Paul, do try to see these things as they are, and not simply as you would like them to be! Again I find I see the dangers so much more quickly than you do and yet it is I who suffers most. There is more that I could and perhaps should tell you, Paul, but will not . . .*

There was little here for her to be pleased about. I said nothing, but Julia took up the gauntlet, anyway.

—It just doesn't mean very much, Nicholas. Again, there's almost nothing here. Just personal things.

—It has to mean something, one way or the other. It's hardly flattering. You can't just pretend that it was never written.

—You have to read the thing in context. She probably resented Rouvel's success. If it's really him she is talking about, Nicholas. Or perhaps it is just something she felt obliged to write to Paul. To mask what was really happening. To head off any rumours or stories he might hear.

—I do worry about this 'context', Julia. It seems to work always in Rouvel's favour, and for no-one else.

I wanted to question her about the trading in flesh, Rouvel's blackbirding. About his being sent so quickly from Ducos to Nouméa to live in comfort on Mount Coffyn. I decided not to raise it. I spoke only of the pardon, just months after his arrival—for Sebastien Rouvel, of all people?

—It's because he was not guilty, Nicholas. Or at least, he was not as guilty as was later made out. You say that Rouvel was a scoundrel, and then you find that he has been pardoned. You don't go back and rethink your first opinion. You just say, 'Oh, clearly he had influence.' Why can't you accept his pardon as evidence that he really wasn't guilty?

—There is real hatred in her writing. You can't deny that!

—Jealousy? Rage? Frustration? It could be any one of these things. Perhaps there is real hatred, as you say. But perhaps there is just a great show of hatred. For Paul's sake. In case he had heard those 'harsh things' she talks about. It all fits, Nicholas.

—It's ridiculous, Julia.

—It's hypothesis. Which has to include the ridiculous. And the unpalatable. We haven't even begun to talk about what Paul himself was doing—the harsh things that she might have heard about him, too—while this was going on. We haven't talked about this help that Sebastien Rouvel seemed to be offering. What help, Nicholas? What did he do for them? What was he offering? That's what really interests me!

She swept up the letters, and began to stuff them into her bag.

—I have to keep them, Julia. I promised. He said they were for my eyes only.

She glared at the letters and at me, thrust them back at me, and stood up to go.

—Julia, just tell me—what have I done wrong?

—Wrong?

She seemed surprised. Even slightly shocked. She came back to me and stroked my cheek with her hand. Her surprise was genuine, sincere.

—You've done nothing wrong, Nicholas. Nothing at all. It's just that things have moved on. The story. The history. You've been dragging your feet. You don't always seem to be able to see things clearly. That's all.

—But what about us, Julia? You and me?

She swung her bag over her shoulder.

—We're very different, Nicholas. Sometimes I don't think you understand the seriousness of what we are doing here, with your 'family thing' and all. You're sacrificing real history for your own feelings. For your family. That's all that's wrong.

She smiled at me, though, with a touch of the old intimacy, the first friendliness, and squeezed my hand.

—It's all beginning to fit together, Nicholas. With or without your precious letters. They don't really tell us anything much that I hadn't thought of already. I'm starting to see the whole picture. What really happened. What he was trying to say.

—I thought perhaps there was more to this. More than just these people from the past.

—Of course there is. It's only for a time, dear Nicholas. Only until the deadline. Then there'll be time for lots of other things. For us to get to know each other. I promise.

The child ran between us, the apologetic father in close pursuit. We exchanged a kiss, made more awkward as we stepped out of their way.

—I'll call. As soon as the work is ready. I promise. As soon as it's done. You'll be the first reader. The very first. And please, do bring the letters. Your great-grandmother's precious letters. Your former great-grandmother, perhaps I should now say. I do need to take some notes. I'm almost finished. Then we'll really talk, Nicholas.

She set off, but I called after her.

—Julia, just one thing. I've meant to ask: do you remember Lucien? The tramp from around the Bibliothèque Nationale, the one who knows so much?

—Lucien? Poh! How could I forget! Everyone knows poor Lucien.

—Did you ever ask him about all this? About the deportations, about Nouméa, and Sebastien Rouvel?

—He knows nothing. Absolutely nothing, Nicholas. If you're talking to him, you are wasting your time. It's all catching up with him. Names, places, dates; I can tell you, they're all starting to slide together in his head. And the smell! I had to have a word to the librarians. In the Arsenal, and the other libraries as well. Underneath all those stinking rags, there's a truly nasty mind at work. Don't you be fooled, Nicholas. I did everyone a favour, I can tell you.

The call from Julia came the next day. For me to come to her place, that very evening. The day was hot. The metro down to the place Monge was close, oppressive, smelling of stress and overheated bodies. When I arrived, the door of her apartment was wide open. Even so, the air was stale. I thrust my head in and called to her. She answered from her desk. Without looking up. Without a greeting.

—I decided, Nicholas, that you probably should read what I've written so far. After our talk. It's only fair. I know you're worried. I know I've not been kind. But it's nearly all there.

The apartment was in an even deeper state of disorder, and I could smell the sweet odour of food beyond its time. The papers had spread further. I guessed there was a kind of filing system in the midst of it all, and was careful not to disturb the piles. Julia had clearly been working all night. Since the moment she had left me in the Jardin des Plantes. She was wearing the same clothes. Her air was feverish, extreme. I moved an empty tin of cat food from the bed.

—So the sister from La Villette hasn't been past recently?

—Did I tell you about Catherine? Dear Catherine, she just won't come anymore. Not until I finish, she says. She says I'm impossible. My friends all tell me I'm unbearable once I'm on the trail of something. You wouldn't agree with them, now, would you, Nicholas?

Julia offered a warm ironic smile. She yawned and stretched, and ran her fingers through her hair.

—I told them all to stay away. To wait. Just a little longer. I'm near the end. As you can see!

She laughed, and handed me a large bundle of papers.

—It's almost there, Nicholas. Do read. A coffee?

The papers were neatly typed. Contrasting with the confusion of the room. Julia clattered about in the kitchen while I looked over the first pages. I think I had expected a neat academic account, with footnotes and appendices, with citation of authorities and sources and apologies in those places where the information had run thin, or where there were gaps or large conjectural leaps. There was none of this. It was one wild piece of poetic conjecture from beginning to end, heavily seasoned with the ecstatic style of Sebastien Rouvel himself. The journal was quoted at length, but the spirit of the man—the provocative obscurity, the symbolic flights, the sudden shifts of mood—had soon crept beyond the long quotations and into Julia's own style.

The coffee, of course, never came.

I cleared a further space on the floor, pushing aside the papers and old food and coffee cups. I leaned back against a pile of reference books, shuffling from side to side until I was comfortable. Julia had vanished into the shower. I could hear her singing and splashing.

'The Aftermath'—it was the last part of her story—began with dramatic images of Sebastien Rouvel making his way north, out into the desert, circled by birds of prey and leaving a long line of footprints behind him, across a barren, sandy landscape ringed by gigantic dunes, making his way steadily towards what Julia called 'the centre'. On his luminous quest.

She came back into the room, in bathrobe and turban. She stood shivering by the window, rubbing her long hair, watching me read. As though holding her breath.

—Luminous, Julia? Rouvel's luminous quest?

—Just keep reading, Nicholas. You'll be surprised. Read it—do go on!

—Julia, these mists. There are no mists in this part of the world. Scarcely even in the depths of winter. And Rouvel and the *petite auberge* by the roadside near Deception?

—He had to eat and drink somewhere, Nicholas. We know from your aunt that he arrived sick and dazed. That doesn't mean that he had no money. And there are mists, Nicholas. In his poems. Even in the desert poems he talks of mists.

—Yes, but I don't think you would find many *petites auberges* in that part of the world. Mount Deception was miles from anywhere. He couldn't have walked there. It was too far. And in November, which is already hot.

—It's not the climate that's important, Nicholas. You know that. Just look at what he says. The story. The poetry. It's the poetry that matters.

I looked to Julia's four piles of pages, the larger *Codicilles*, neatly set out on her desk. The poetry.

—Did you think about what Rouvel might have intended, Julia, before you started shuffling? Before you rearranged them all?

I remembered my own childhood carelessness.

—There was no real order to them, Nicholas. It was just a pile of papers. More or less as he left them, when he died. You told me so, yourself.

—But even so, Julia, from what I can see, a lot of your 'late phase' material was written on the same paper as the 'early phase'. So much of the 'earth' section is written in the same ink as the 'fire' section. Doesn't that mean that they were written at the same time? Shouldn't those bits perhaps go together?

—He rewrote the earlier material again and again. He built up his ideas bit by bit, Nicholas. One idea led to another, sending him back to rewrite the earlier bits. Not proceeding from start to finish in a neat line. That was never his way. Always going back, reworking.

—Reworking for what purpose, Julia?

—Perhaps for publication. Perhaps he thought he would one day come home. He may have had some idea that he would finally finish his poem, and would then come back to France again. Once his pilgrimage was over.

—Pilgrimage? A *pilgrimage*, Julia?

—I have a theory, you see.

She sniffled. Still catching the cool breeze from the open window. She reached for a tissue.

—It's a theory you're not going to like, Nicholas. He knew that Marie-Josèphe could provide what he needed to finish the poem. It all points to it. Without her—her presence, her inspiration—the poem could never be finished. That's why it never ended, out there in the desert. That's why the whole poem was never finished.

—But Julia, he had no money. He was destitute. That's one thing Agnes did remember. He had only what he wore when he staggered in off the Hawker road. The only person he could think of who might possibly help him was Marie-Josèphe and her husband. It wasn't his spiritual needs that drew him there, Julia. It was poverty. The prospect of starvation. It was his need to find someone who would listen to his nonsense.

—Nicholas!

Julia came and knelt down beside me, tucking her bathrobe up around her. She took my face in her hands, looking into my eyes. Speaking slowly, gently, as to an idiot. Her wet hair falling in long strands between us.

—She was his mistress, Nicholas. His lover. She had been for years. Years before, at least. That's the key to the whole thing. That's the bit of information that you resist—that you just don't want to get your mind around. That's been sitting there, laughing at us, all this time! Your dear Tante Colette's mother. That's why she's so evasive. That's why nothing quite makes sense to you. Do you really expect her daughter to spell it out to you? The whole story?

The evidence was everywhere. I just needed help to see it. Julia spoke with frightening conviction.

—He came to find Marie-Josèphe. So that he could finish his poem. It's a magnificent story, Nicholas. I know it sounds far too easy, too neat, when I spell it out just like that. That's why I'm asking you to read what I've written. To read my commentaries on the journal. You owe me that much, at least.

She rested her wet head on my shoulder, her hair dripping over my arm. She was exhausted, but still alert in the sharp and febrile way that comes in short waves with the late stages of fatigue.

—I'm sorry. I'm being harsh, Nicholas. Cruel, even. I'm very, very tired. Let me tell you. Marie-Josèphe was totally abandoned by her family. As far as we can tell. She'd been surrounded by death and misery of a kind you and I can scarcely imagine. You've seen the letters. She was strong. She was an admirable woman, Nicholas. I mean it. A real survivor. My Marie-Josèphe is a far more interesting character than yours. You should grant me that, at least. Forget your fans and crinolines. That's how she could attract and hold the affections of a man like Sebastien Rouvel. That's why he wanted to see her, just one more time. That's why he needed her for his work. It's there, Nicholas. In the papers. You think you are protecting her in some way, but in fact it makes you underestimate her. Quite radically. As a person. As a woman.

I felt a sadness somewhere in the room. Julia seemed to feel it too. Her response was irritation.

—I really need to speak to Colette, Nicholas. Myself. You must let me talk to her.

I read on for some time, but only in a superficial way. A phrase here, a passage from there. The details were unclear. Julia's prose was almost as obscure and disordered as that of Sebastien Rouvel. My thoughts began to take a new direction, clouding the meanings, dragging me from the page. Thoughts about two kinds of history. A kind that invaded and uncovered, that asserted its rights against all forms of restraint. And another kind that conspired more gently with what had been. That assumed the kind of custody Colette spoke of, a gentler form of knowing that moved in Good Samaritan union with the past. Binding its wounds. Covering its nakedness. I wondered, too, if despite all the tough talk and the aggression, Julia's was not in fact the second kind. Covering gently, section by section, for her ancestor Rouvel.

I flicked through the pages, finishing none.

—Shouldn't we just wait, Julia? We'll only argue. I'll read it through, and then we'll talk. About the vision. About the details.

Julia was asleep. Her hair wet. On my shoulder.

'The Aftermath' was riddled with long quotations from the *Codicilles*, and increasingly infected with Sebastien Rouvel's own obscure ecstatic style. The most incoherent images, the oddest allusions that Julia and I had once puzzled over, were now conclusively decoded, but into even vaguer yearnings. Rouvel's 'dreams of angels which lay ground in dust and anguish amid the bitter rocks of forgetfulness', his tales of 'lizards of steel which tore their way free from within the breasts of starving children praying in their angry circles', and of all those who 'lived and moved beneath the sand, taking their shade from the three bright suns that traversed the darkness, amid the spreading roots of broken trees of crumbling stone'; all these were now just counters, phrases that gave direction to Julia's effusive epic of spiritual dreaming, her rich saga of grand passion pursued and grand passion unrequited. Her story of heroic spiritual transcendence, and the tragic price that had to be paid.

For Sebastien Rouvel had, in the years that followed his departure from New Caledonia, the years that passed in silence from 1878 to the last months of 1892, virtually vanished from the public world. The dull page of history, of recorded fact, tells us nothing of Rouvel in these years. We know that he stayed, while others returned, at the ends of the earth. Perhaps he was in Australia. Perhaps he was in Nouméa. Perhaps he was even in France, in Paris indeed, his beard shaven, unrecognisable after the rigours of exile to his friends or foes, walking again the streets of his fiery youth, the boulevard Saint-Michel or the rue Gay-Lussac, like some reproaching ghost, revisiting the shell of his former life, but moving through it now with soul transformed in the crucible of pain, defeat and exile.

Sebastien Rouvel had not vanished. Sebastien Rouvel was not dead. He lived, but in a new domain. We know that he was successful, in the external, the material world, through the later 1870s. Yet ten years later we find him alone and ill, dressed only in rags, perhaps, but luminous in vision. Luminous—described as such by those few privileged souls who caught a glimpse of Rouvel at this time, by those few who gained some passage to the inner life, so misrepresented in the shrinking outer form, the ragged shell of flesh and bone . . .

Julia slept on, on my shoulder. I thought of her, scarcely breathing, hunched over her typewriter, sifting through her papers in these closed and cluttered spaces. I thought of the closed curtains, the friends told to stay away. Of the hungry cat, the unwashed dishes, the ideas climbing one upon the other, one fevered word just breeding excess upon excess, and all taking on such vast and abominable strengths from distance, silence, unimaginable space.

What do we know, by now, of Sebastien Rouvel? That he was ill? Ill in body, but more than that, ill in the heart for all that passed in the years that went before, the collapse of ideals, the victory of bankrupt tradition, the return in triumph and oppressive cruelty of all those habits and ways of thinking against which he had striven with such distinction, so vigorously, from his youngest years.

What was left for him; to submit and die, oppressed and beaten? Or to engage in some new and mighty contest, to contend in some grander arena, the stakes no less than the recovery of the higher capabilities of the Human Spirit, the prize no less than the recovery of a richer collective human destiny, lost in the oppressions of habit and all the corrupting 'realities' projected by a social order that is lost in deep decay.

The light was starting to die. I looked across the files and papers. I thought of the wild mix of coffee and stress and lack of sleep that now coursed through these gleaming pages, on the life, the spiritual toil, the wild celestial dreamings of Sebastien Rouvel. I thought of the ferment in the streets below, the cars in flames, the paving-stone barricades, the vast processions, the posters and banners, the shouting and the bloodshed, the sense that all things that were known to us up to this time, that all solid and familiar shapes, were no more than a maze, a flimsy curtain, a cloudy screen of moving images disguising richer things beyond.

> *What we may trace in these last months of the life of Sebastien Rouvel is no less than a grand divesting. The image of a man taking on himself the whole burden of his species, forced step by step through war, through exile and despair, into the desert; beyond the fringe of the known, the established, the familiar, out into the desert sands where richer longings could go unimpeded, the only mark upon that vast immensity of blown sands and rocky turrets the courageous impress of desire and expectation.*

I thought too of Mount Deception, the new Deception that invaded Julia's thinking, its barren reaches now wrenched into depleted symbol, the resisting mountain ranges now the Château of Rocks, the vast trough at Wilpena just the Crucible of the Sun, with all the ruins, the heat, the flat expanses of Willochra Plain and all the arid lands beyond no more now than an algebra to match fantastic dreamings, with no concrete thing remaining, no stones to kick, no hard object still intruding to keep the reader to the earth.

It was growing very late. I let Julia slip gently to the floor, and covered her as best I could. I crept from the apartment, taking 'The Aftermath' back across the river towards the refuge of my room in the Grand Hôtel Jeanne d'Arc, circling across towards the Marais by a route that ran far to the east, beyond the range of barricades and patrolling vans and toppled cars, past the Gare d'Austerlitz.

I stopped on the bridge over the river. It was barricaded against the traffic. Fires were burning back towards the Île St-Louis, the glow rising steadily with the falling light. The buildings along the quays were still outlined against the sky. I listened to the late-night sounds of traffic, of horns tooting and of sirens sounding from each direction. I thought then of the desert, of those fields of baking rocks. Of the last pages I had read, that had brought Rouvel to the wilderness. Towards Deception. Towards his 'tragic immolation', as Julia now seemed to want to call it.

What, then, are the Codicilles? They are many things. The history of an era? They are this, in part, but not the narrative of dull fact. Rather, the Codicilles are the history of an inner struggle, between the world of matter and the world of spirit, the struggle to find, within the form of material things—The Jackal, The Leviathan, The Pillars in the Desert—fit emblems for a new realm of advanced understanding.

I stopped and drew the typescript from my bag, and checked the passage again under the light that fell from the lanterns on the bridge. The poetry, now deciphered, told the tale. Of Sebastien Rouvel pursuing his magnificent obsession from one hemisphere to the other. Blighted by the caprice of a fine but damaged woman, Marie-Josèphe Coignard, never releasing him, and never fully willing to answer to his desire. Incapable, indeed, of understanding the nature of his feeling, the richer political and spiritual contentions of which she was a part. Julia's 'Aftermath' portrayed her as gifted but finally insensitive; a woman who, through all the degradation of violence, imprisonment and exile, now carried within her the full psychological burden, the destructive inner reflection, of the slaughter and deportations of 1871.

Marie-Josèphe Coignard remained, in 'The Aftermath', a remote, symbolic figure. There was little personal detail, little embellishment. Julia had drawn on just a few of the brief portraits I had passed on from Agnes and Colette. Her Marie-Josèphe now 'distilled within herself, in hidden and unconscious ways, all the turmoil and the cruelty, all the destructive history of her time'. Exerting against all around her, in ways apparently unfathomable even to herself, the frightening power of the victim. Carrying, in all unconsciousness, the gravest wounds of her nation, passing them, like an infection, to the lives of others.

> *So he arrived at last, to the far place in the north, where she had waited; beyond the Château of Rocks and the Desert of the Prophets he came at last, after how many months or years of wandering in the desert we will never know, to that ill-fated place, Deception, where he imagined hope awaited.*

It was into this perilous sphere that Sebastien Rouvel, after many years, had finally returned. Attraction and resistance. Sensuality and release. These tensions, Julia asserted, were the very key to the *Codicilles*, to the richness of the mystery of Rouvel's later years, to any understanding of the real significance of his death in the desert. It was through this that his lifetime's pursuit of Marie-Josèphe Coignard, the most intimate domain of Sebastien Rouvel's experience, was in fact public, impersonal, epochal in its significance. It was this that made

Les Codicilles, on first reading, so obscure and so very private, so rich a public testament. So conclusively a spiritual history of the times.

> *Rouvel arrived, sick and exhausted, at the end of a long road that had led him ever northwards, driven onwards by the desire to see her yet again; drawn onwards too, we can be almost sure, by her own yearning, her sense of loss of that rich presence; her calling one last time in spirit to the one who had seen her through the long years of deportation, now longing to see him again.*

Even before his arrival in New Caledonia, that love, that irresistible attraction, had become the driving force in everything he did. Woven in with these flights of spiritual conjecture were claims of a more earthly kind. Rouvel had, of course, funded Mount Deception. Paul was in his debt. Not through any insidiousness on Rouvel's part, but from a disinterested desire on his part to assist Marie-Josèphe. To help her to retrieve some fragment of the world that she had lost, even if it must be bound up in the demented vision of the noble but misguided Paul-Auguste Duvernois, *au centre de l'Australie.*

> *But should we blame her for so much? It is the pain, the anguish, that has brought us the Codicilles.*

Written in uncertainty, in tentativeness, in painful groping towards some form of revelation. We can pity the writer, but appreciate the result, the rich toil which has brought to us this glorious testament.

Were they truly lovers? All hints of mere sexual union were, in Julia's 'Aftermath', quickly overridden by the far richer erotic dimension set out in *Les Codicilles*. Where Sebastien Rouvel's sensual longing for Marie-Josèphe Coignard was finally a bridge. A passage, charted in symbolic terms, towards the grander and more detached conceptions outlined in the obscure later pieces of writing. Between the desire that Marie-Josèphe evoked in the sensual world, and Rouvel's higher forms of longing.

This much, at least, perhaps we should forgive; if not what was to come, on that final day: the day Sebastien Rouvel left her world to ride off into the desert. This much we could pardon as the product of a savage time, were it not for what was to follow, as he, exhausted in soul but recovered enough in body to go on his way again, announced that he was leaving to go yet further on his quest, perhaps yet further to the north, seeking understanding in the sands and rocks and mirages of the deep interior. It was then that the final, the tragic act took place.

The whole *Codicilles du Diable* had become, in effect, a love poem. A love poem to, and finally beyond, the flawed Marie-Josèphe Coignard. Reaching towards her, and then, in its tragic final phase, through some cataclysmic shift in understanding, some deep change within Sebastien Rouvel himself, towards richer, less communicable realms beyond. The 'final, the tragic act' to crown it all still to come. It was the part yet to be written.

I thought of Julia's hand. Gentle against my face.

—I'll call you, Nicholas. I promise. As soon as the last bit is ready. You can tell me what you think. So we can have your thoughts, as well.

It was becoming cold on the bridge. The wind was beating up a chill from the dark waters below. To the west, the silhouette of Notre Dame rose eerily against the glow of fires that came on with the dying of the light. This ancient structure, surviving yet again. Watching, yet again, the passage of fire and blood. I saw the troubled motion of cars and pedestrians further along the river, of small groups in uncertain motion through the distant streets, the flight of an ambulance along the quays that led into the heart of the city. I looked down into the waters, at the reflections that rippled and ran through the darkness below. I stuffed 'The Aftermath' back in my bag and headed up, against the strengthening wind, towards the rue de Jarente.

Beware the sloping ceiling. Beware low ceilings that force you to bow, pressing low stooping thoughts upon you as you seek to cross the room. That was something that I came to understand in these last dark days spent all alone in Paris, all novelty long passed and the long and lonely nights beginning to tell, lying in my room in the Grand Hôtel Jeanne d'Arc with nothing in my hands but Julia's fevered manuscript, and scraps of our translations from the Rouvel papers. Receiving no further message from Julia, for days. Feeling unable any longer to go down to Saint-Germain-sur-École or even to see Monsieur Jalabert. Unable to find my friend Lucien, no longer sleeping in his usual place on the bench in the square Louvois, gone off on one of his obscure circuits around the city.

And so we lived in prison cells, amid the filtered darkness, the only light a stream that entered through the heavy bars of iron, the light entering from a window in a distant wall and moving then from cell to cell, each taking in the light left by its neighbour and then passing it along.

Most in the prison sought always to move closer to the light, through bribes and prayers and begging, moving closer to the light. But there are others who prefer the wisdom that comes from distance, who know that with each filtered passage of the light, each cell that comes between them and the light, it takes on further knowledge, further feeling, so that each cell, each set of bars between them brings greater understanding and access to power. He, the wisest of them all, moves stealthily in darkness, moving with knowledge and a concentrated wisdom at the far end of the cells . . .

During the day I tried to work in one of the libraries, the Bibliothèque Nationale or library of Sainte Geneviève, or any library that was still prepared to open its doors. After which I would face a lonely meal in a crowded restaurant amid the crush of other people's smoke and conversation. Or go to a cinema where I would sit again in silence, the smoke of those around me coiling and rising in thin aromatic strands before the silver figures moving on the screen. And then I would come back, at last, to the Grand Hôtel Jeanne d'Arc, up the winding staircase to my tiny room high up on the seventh floor, with its hot floral wall-paper roughly plastered over the weals and cracks, and noisy plumbing, above the movement up and down the creaking staircase, the late-night drunks and revellers in the Marché Sainte Catherine far below. To my room, where the roof fell so steeply towards the far end of the bed. Where to lie down, I had to climb in at the high end and shuffle down towards the low. Where, when I lay fully stretched out, my toes would brush the last fall of the ceiling. A place for rank unwholesome ideas, the worst thoughts of your own, the least welcome thoughts of others.

> *I am clad in vestments of power sewn from the salamander's skin and I have lived in the heart of fire, walking with limbs of iron and a soul of baked rock through the fire and across the burning coals, moving through the blaze that has consumed all others, watching their flesh blister and melt and fall away in bright steaming blood upon the fire: all walking on but as no more than ash and bones which break and fall away, while I fear nothing but only the dying of those yellow pitching flames, fearing only that moment when the flames would fall away and take all the brilliant lustre of my salamander coat . . .*

I would prop myself up on the bed in my tiny attic room, leafing through the last tracts of Julia's prose, scanning through page after page of typing, harried by violent corrections in red pen and changes and arrows and boxes that redirected matters up and down. All the while looking for hints as to the final act, to see what Julia would make of the dust storm, the children playing, the last sight of Sebastian Rouvel.

The life of Sebastien Rouvel. Yes, finally a tragedy, the tragedy of a soul too large for this world, too large for those on whom he squandered his celestial insight, too large even for that vast desert centre which claimed in the end its own. And in his death—not less than a form of martyrdom—we see the bitter irony. But now we have the papers, the magnificent testament of a fine soul's rich and tragic toil. Some relic at least of his profound contention, the soul struggling against its own elusive boundaries, its own finitude.

It seemed that Marie-Josèphe Coignard, now Marie-Josèphe Duvernois, would finally never match what was, in Julia's glowing words, 'the magnificent scale of the desire itself', which, in the frightening openness of the vast Australian desert, 'refined itself beyond such disappointments into a richer and purer impersonal sphere', a sphere of thinking and acting which even a poet of Sebastien Rouvel's stature could only hint at, could only 'pass back in such glowing fragments' as we find in the *Codicilles.*

I thought of Julia, exhausted and in deep fatigue, growing steadily colder in her towel, watching me read what she had written. I thought of the Rouvel papers, lifting and falling in the breeze that crossed her desk, the photograph of Sebastien Rouvel, still twisted on the wall.

The *Codicilles* had finally found its proper audience. Not in Marie-Josèphe, as Rouvel had perhaps intended, but only generations later, in Julia herself. Julia, now by implication Rouvel's Laura, his true Beatrice. Julia, standing hollow-eyed over me. Julia, lost to day and night and food and sleep, calling to me to read on.

Hours I spent just staring at the ceiling, at the bright floral wallpaper that lay over me like a thick and reeking blanket. Deciding, at last, to put my papers aside and crawl out and walk the streets. To risk the batons of the cruising CRS. To risk the fires and angry mobs, still coursing through the late-night streets. To share the restlessness of all those other stranded souls who trod the midnight streets amid the agitation, the shouting, the wail of sirens and the sounds of running feet. To walk away my darkest thinkings, and to tread, in long meandering voyages that ran east and west across the troubled city, my fears into the cobblestones. To return in the first morning light, in blessed thoughtlessness, to the Grand Hôtel Jeanne d'Arc.

Fifteen

Lucien, at last, reappeared. One morning, in the square Louvois. The Bibliothèque was closed, its gates defaced with posters. *De Gaulle: Assassin! Sois Jeune, Tais-Toi.* He and I sat on one of the metal benches, before the fountain. For a time, in simple silence. It was early morning. The streets were quieter than they had been for days.

—Tell me, Lucien. Do you know a Julia Dussol?

I thought he hadn't heard. But he turned to me, after a time. With a knowing glint in his eye.

—Dussol. Yes. I remember her. A tall girl—a student. With spectacles. She used to buy me coffee. For a time.

He thought for a while.

—She stank of soap.

—Did you know her well, Lucien? Did you talk to her about Sebastien Rouvel?

—She talked too much. She had heard that I knew things. She said she wanted to talk to me, but she talked too much herself. I listened to her nonsense. She asked me questions and then ignored most of what I had to say.

He ran a hand through his knotted hair.

—Like you, she was. Except that she talked too much. She told me she was related to Sebastien Rouvel. Maybe she was. Maybe she wasn't. She bought me coffee. I told her everything I knew. She bought me more coffee, and I told her a whole lot more that I didn't. I wasn't very interested, in the end. Nor was she. I told her what I thought of her history. She told me I was offensive.

I protested gallantly.

—She told me I was offensive. And so I told her a thing or two about her famous relation that she wouldn't have read anywhere.

—So you argued?

—She tried to tell me she was an historian. I told her she was not. She's a hagiographer. Do you know what a hagiographer is?

I did not.

—A hagiographer is a writer of saints' lives. Saint Sebastien Rouvel.

—Why is Julia not a real historian, Lucien?

—Because she's not pursuing open questions. She's made up her mind. She just wants to be fed her own answers.

—Lucien, I want to tell you something. About Sebastien Rouvel. Something no-one knows. Almost no-one.

He nodded distantly. His attention was to the sparrows, the footprints in the gravel. I reached into my bag and pulled out a couple of pages of the papers that I had managed to steal back from Julia's apartment.

—It's his writing, Lucien. There is lots of it, left behind when he died. I told you how he spent his last months in my great-grandfather's house. He left his things there.

Lucien took the pages, holding them up and at an awkward angle, peering at the flapping pages, fumbling with unsteady fingers.

—You say this is Rouvel? Really Sebastien Rouvel?

—It's his writing. I've had it checked. There are hundreds of pages of it. All written just like that, all over the page. And in strange images. It's poetic, you see.

—Why didn't you tell me this before?

—It's Julia, Lucien. Julia Dussol. She asked me not to.

—And you agreed?

—And I agreed.

I read him some short sections we had typed. I read

from the long piece Julia called 'The Estaminet of Grass'—which she thought must be about Ducos, or perhaps the Isle of Pines—of how he and his companions sat below the grass that frayed and parted in the wind and drank to all those who floated beneath the seas in cages of iron; how they sat upon the packing crates of slow despair and raised their glasses to the last of the blood that flowed, amid the crowds of insects that sang their misery to the barren hills.

I read to him from 'The Leviathan', one of the longest of the poems, which Julia insisted was a kind of key or coda, all about what she had started to call the 'tragic overconsciousness' of Sebastien Rouvel.

I am the Leviathan who trawls the deeps, who takes the compass of all minds, all knowledge that was ever known. On every day a thousand ships, all armed and with the cruellest of intent, set out to kill Leviathan and all his deep intolerable thought. From the depths I hear the singing keels that cut their way across the seas to find and kill Leviathan; all armed and with the cruellest of intent, yet fearing as they course the seas the least brush of his tail . . .

I pass sunken ships, passing slowly downward, their crews now accustomed to the darkness and the damp, the captains standing at the helm, their sails full set and all flags out and streaming in the currents, eyes wide with wonder as I course through these lower seas with no sound but the silent currents moving through their sails, the sound of one thought moving on another as I descend lower and lower towards the light that rises from the depths . . .

Lucien interrupted, raising a hand.

—It sounds familiar. I've read things like it.

He sniggered into his coffee.

—It's not actually very good. There were others who were doing this sort of thing. Much better than this.

—I don't care whether it's any good or not, Lucien. I want to know if it means anything.

—I'd say it can mean just about anything you want it to mean. Good material, here, for the do-it-yourself historian. And you say there's more?

—There's a mound of it. Hundreds of pages. What do you think?

Lucien mused for a time.

—Sebastien Rouvel. In Australia?

—In Sydney, we think. After his time in Nouméa. We think he worked there for a time, and perhaps in Queensland. And then, not long before he died, he travelled south, and to the west. We don't know how he lost all his money.

He arrived, sick and exhausted, at my great-grandparents' property in late 1892. Perhaps he hoped that they would look after him. And it was there that he died.

Lucien turned the papers awkwardly, fumbling with his fraying mittens, holding the pages close to his face.

—Sebastien Rouvel. A sort of poet?

He said it flatly, shaking his head.

—It's possible, it's possible.

We sat in silence. Lucien turned the pages around, peering into the writing, tracing the patterns with a filthy fingernail.

Lucien's bad smells told of deep and homely wisdom. We sat in silence, watching the birds peck in the gravel.

—And what about you, Lucien? In all of this, why do you help? Why do you care?

He grinned at me, and then thought long and hard. The stench of concentration thickened. He scraped at his hair. He looked around at the clean-limbed passers-by, moving quickly in gusts of soap and perfume, eyes glazed and intent upon some certain pointless destination. He waved a ragged mitten at the streetlamps, the passing buses, the high façade of the Bibliothèque Nationale.

—I am a *déporté*. From this place, from the whole world most of you people live in, the sorts of ideas you float around in, I think I am perhaps some kind of *déporté*!

The idea amused him. He coughed, writhing and shifting in his mound of rags. I wanted to ask more questions, but Lucien was preparing to go.

—Do you have a few *sous*?

I rummaged in my pocket and pulled out a handful of notes and change. Lucien took a few francs.

—We'll meet again. Later. We'll talk more about Duvernois. Now that I remember. I know things, many other things. I'll help you with your book.

—And what about me, Lucien? What am I doing?

He thought for a while.

—You've taken the wrong kind of holiday, *mon vieux*. That's what you've done. You've got a few mad dreams of your own, but they're not like that woman's dreams. These are broken lives you're chasing. They saw the worst that people can do to each other. There's knowledge there that ought to die with them. It's something you don't need to know about.

—Why do you help me then?

—Because you buy me coffee.

He winked. He shuffled and fidgeted, enjoying his joke.

—Because you don't talk too much.

He gathered his rags about him and stood up. He passed me back the pages.

—Be careful. Remember. It's just old. Old doesn't

mean it's true. Or even very good. Even if it's written by your precious Sebastien Rouvel.

A little closer to the gate, he turned again.

—And it's because you don't stink of soap.

We met again, much later in the day. The light was starting to fall. Lucien insisted that we walk down to the river. We sat alongside each other, our legs dangling above the yellow sweep of the Seine, our thoughts moving for a time in silence across the waters. Lucien munched a sandwich I had bought him, that he had thrust into his frightful pocket back in the Palais Royal. We looked out across the waters and towards the buildings and the movement and disturbance on the other side, the trees behind and the movement of the waters before us muffling the harsh sounds from the city.

He wanted to know more about the Rouvel papers. He asked me to read him some more sections. I read him the piece that Julia and I called 'L'Institutrice', about the teacher singing to children, with eyes gouged out and hands chopped off and all nodding in unison, and the much longer piece about the stake of execution, 'Le Peleton', the stake taking root within the blood and growing green tendrils and enveloping in thick green leaves the life of the condemned, the life of the condemned then growing with the new life of the stake.

Lucien began to scrape at his face as I read further, clawing at his hair in his distressed way and finally raising a hand as if to say that this must be enough.

—What does it mean, Lucien?

—Why do you think it must have a meaning? Just because it happens to be cruel does not say it has a meaning.

He concentrated on his sandwich for a time.

—It was written, as you say, in privacy. Perhaps in sickness. Or at a time when he was mad. Perhaps he never meant it to mean anything to anyone but himself. Have you thought of that?

—Julia's convinced that if we can find the key—if we can find out how to read this properly—we will understand all sorts of things. She says it's just a kind of code. She thinks it's real history. That we just need to work harder, work through the whole thing, and then we'll start to understand what each part means.

Lucien threw his paper wrapper into the water, and we watched it sail away.

—She thinks it means all sorts of things, Lucien. Things I don't think are true. What can I do?

He sat with his head in his hands, still scratching and scraping at his hair. Then he sat up straight, and stretched his arms, raising the scarecrow flaps of his rotting coat to the winds that swept up off the river and told me what he had come to think about these Deception papers, from the bits that I had read.

He said that they would all start to make sense if you worked over them for long enough, and especially if you tried to translate them into some other language. That bit by bit all those images which seemed to mean so much—or, rather, to carry some floating possibility of meaning—would start to attach themselves to things that you knew, or thought you knew, or indeed just wanted in your deepest heart to know. That the feelings of the writings would start to become your own feelings, and soon they would start to tell you exactly the kind of story that you wanted to hear, some fragment of a story that you wished someone would enable to be told, and that they would speak in words and feelings that ran far beyond your own capacity to tell. The more this Julia Dussol read it, too, the more it would seem to speak for her as well, especially for her, to draw out and nurse and speak at last these fragments of her own desire, and that neither version, neither her version nor my version, would need to bear much relation to each other, or to whatever it was that this Sebastien Rouvel may have thought that he was saying, all those years ago.

He stopped, and was silent for a time. I just sat in silence and amazement. He threw the last of his sandwich out across the water.

—You ask me what I think you should do. I think you should forget about your history. I think you should perhaps just write another poem, like Sebastien Rouvel's. One that does not contain a meaning but draws like a fishhook a meaning from the secret thoughts of others.

He gestured with contempt at Julia's papers, flapping precariously in their wrapper on the stone. But then touched them in a clumsy form of caress.

—This gives you too much freedom. By telling so little, it allows all things to have happened. All things that might be possible. A hundred years after, it still creates new meanings. Anything you might care to dream.

He slipped into an awkward, scratching silence, staring bleakly out into the water. Still looking at the river, he suddenly reached over and squeezed my arm, tightly, almost to the point of pain.

—Go and write yourself a poem. With me in it, if you need something that's real. Put someone in there to carry it all about. The knowledge. Someone who knows, even if the poem itself doesn't. That's what I want you to do.

Lucien was restless. He said that he had to go; that he had important things to do, somewhere to the north. He asked me again for some more money and I offered him a handful. He picked out what he needed. And it was then that he began at last to tell about the trip he made each month up to Montmartre, that pilgrimage the Canadian had laughed about in my first days in Paris.

—Every month, at least once a month, I go up there.

He leaned towards me, in reeking confidence.

—And do you know what I do?

Lucien's eyes were bright, expectant. I smiled and shook my head.

He chuckled and leaned even closer and whispered harshly in my ear.

—I shit in the place. In the basilica. In some dark and quiet corner. For years I have done this. I used to catch a bit of sleep there, you know. Just an hour or two. But then they caught me shitting in one of the side chapels. They now have someone who watches. Every day. Every day, they watch for me.

He wiped his mouth on his sleeve, and told of how it was usually in one of the side chapels, and often while the choir was practising. He told of how he would sit sometimes for hours secluded in the half-darkness and how he did it to the sounds of the most heavenly music, with Palestrina, Handel, Pergolesi all about him, feeling the whole place rise from the mountain and float towards heaven with the beauty of those sounds, knowing then that there could be no better place on earth to tell his small portion of truth. Thinking of how one day he would wander up there with everyone he knew, from all the parks and benches and ventilation grilles of the city, to wipe those high white walls with all their blood and shit, and force the whole city to think about what really happened. About what the 'deliverance' of the city really meant.

Lucien was becoming distressed as he talked. His odours thickened about him.

—Have you read *Mein Kampf*?

I had not.

—If you are going to tell a lie, make sure it's a big one. Or no-one will ever believe you.

Lucien searched my eyes for a response.

—That is the biggest lie in Paris.

He gestured vaguely towards the north. Towards Montmartre.

—Thank God it is over. And thank you, God, for letting us get away with it. That's what it says.

By now, Lucien was genuinely upset. The stench was becoming unbearable. It always did when he became excited in this way. After these spells of deep lucidity. He stood up to go. I stayed where I was, above the water.

—Do you think it's all just nonsense, Lucien? The journal? Do you think there's anything in it?

He scratched at his head again.

—I've already told you. It'll start as nonsense. And after you've worked long enough, it'll probably start to make sense. And you know why? Because it'll have turned everything in your head into nonsense as well. You know what I really think, about these poems of yours? I think that you have to choose. Life will make sense, or these words will make sense. You have to choose. That's why he went out into the desert. Some place where the nonsense could run without restraint. You just can't hope to put it all together.

Sixteen

Julia suggested, at last, that we meet again in the Jardin des Plantes. She was wearing the clothes she wore when we first met—restrained, classic, scholarly—but this time she was neat, clean, precise. The writing was finished. Almost complete. We kissed. In a way that was brisk, wary, even businesslike.

I passed the chapters of 'The Aftermath' back to her, without risking a comment. Even Julia seemed prepared to grant that we should speak, at least for a moment, of other things. Of one another. We made valiant efforts at light chatter; about the worsening conditions and the closure of the Bibliothèque Nationale, about the spreading strikes, and my need to return to England soon, for the coming term, and even, for a brief moment, my work on conventions and treaties.

Then she lit a purposeful cigarette.

—You must now let me talk to the old women, Nicholas. You must organise it. We've waited long enough. Editions Grandet want it now. I need to speak to your aunts. I need to talk to this Tante Colette. The one who seems to know.

—I can't do it, Julia. I have told you.

—You can't prevent me, Nicholas.

Her threat was carefully rehearsed.

—You should know what I think happened on that last day. It's only fair that you should know. It all fits together. If your grandmother's memory is correct, he stumbled from the house—you said yourself that he was stumbling, limping—and staggered off, and died somewhere in the desert, to the north.

She stooped down and drew another sheaf of papers from her bag.

—It's all here, Nicholas. The last pages of 'The Aftermath'. The bit you haven't read. You can read it now, or I can simply tell you what happened. What I'm now absolutely convinced really happened on that day. I agree that it's just conjecture, but it's a form of conjecture that takes in everything we know. Everything you've been told. Everything Rouvel wrote. Even the letters. Those letters of Marie-Josèphe.

She placed the papers on the table.

—Would you like me to show you? I'll find you the place. There's so little time.

It was simple enough. And much as I predicted. Sebastien Rouvel had decided to leave Deception, to travel further north. Driven by his poetry, his spiritual quest, his pilgrimage. Setting out to pursue some obscure mission beyond Deception, some form of heroic immolation in the vaster desert expanses.

—Really, Julia. I've no idea what you mean by this business about immolation. You just keep repeating it.

—Just finish it, Nicholas. It's really the next bit that matters.

Julia's capacity to describe his mission seemed to have long run out. The typescript drew on ever longer passages from Rouvel's own writings. Images of new forms of innocence, rebirth among the rocks and sandy reaches. Obscure intimations of another kind of childhood, a new freshness in wisdom, located somewhere to the north. Some cloudy vision of final transcendence, never quite defined.

Julia watched me closely, in some agitation, as I read.

Her portrait was now of a Marie-Josèphe Coignard in the last reaches of despair. What happened, she conceded, could only be conjecture, but a form of conjecture deeply supported by the key images, the most insistent themes of *Les Codicilles*. Marie-Josèphe demanded that he take her with him. She begged that he not disappear from her life again, leaving her in so desolate a place, Mount Deception, smothered by the broken dreams of a man she did not love.

I glanced up at Julia. She looked away, just blowing impatient smoke out across the lawns, the gravel beds, the flowers.

Marie-Josèphe took the pistol, the same pistol that Agnes had taken inside when she returned with the horse, and threatened Rouvel with it. Julia's version was now a clumsy collage of all that I had ever told, of Agnes's stories, of Colette's cautious memories, now taking on more strongly the colour of cheap tragic romance, the characters toppling quickly into dismal caricature, the plot stumbling awkwardly from one weary cliché to the next.

I hardly needed to read the pages that followed. I'd somehow seen it, many times before. In a dozen old movies. It was crude, flat and badly plotted. Rouvel tried to take the gun, to calm her. In the ensuing scuffle, it discharged, severely wounding him. Julia's story then concluded, as in the story Agnes told, with Rouvel fleeing the house, the others leaving soon after, perhaps in mere flight, perhaps in a desperate pursuit.

Marie-Josèphe emerged from Julia's telling as muse, mistress, now murderer. I flicked through it again. Hoping it might get better? I felt more than a pang of longing for the old wandering confusion, the demented vigour, the deep teasing incoherence of Sebastien Rouvel.

I looked at her, not saying anything at first. Daring her to comment.

Julia just arched an eyebrow.

—It's silly, Julia. A wild, silly story. Nothing more. Is this your idea of 'informed conjecture'? Will your editor really let you get away with this?

—Death, Nicholas? Stumbling off, and death in the desert so soon after? Is that so very silly?

—It could happen to anyone in that country, Julia. And especially to someone like Sebastien Rouvel. Getting lost. Stumbling around in the desert. It doesn't need a shooting to explain it. He could barely ride. As you say, he knew only the streets of this city. He could barely mount a horse.

—It's coherent. It makes sense. It addresses all the evidence.

I took a deep breath.

—You've got this lame idea, Julia, that the more a thing makes sense, the closer it gets to the truth. I've got another proposition for you. That there's more truth in the confusion. That the closer you get to the whole story, the more you are just backing off into your own version of events. Trust the mystery, Julia. It keeps you closer to the truth than your 'coherence' ever will. That's my proposition.

—So what is your explanation?

—I don't have an explanation, Julia. And I no longer seem to need an explanation. That's the point.

She just coughed scornfully, and reached for her bag.

—The real point is, Nicholas, that as long as your Tante Colette is alive and well—oddly enough, the fact that she is lying, Nicholas, tells us that she is still thinking very clearly—it doesn't really matter if my version is not true. The point is that it will make her tell the truth. The truth goes out. Or my version goes out. It's up to her, Nicholas. It's up to you.

We sat without talking for a time. Julia seemed to take out her aggression on her cigarettes. I tried to imagine her, her long legs crossed, in Colette's musty salon, talking of *Les Codicilles*. Talking of her conjectures, her hypotheses, to Colette's photographs.

—If there's any cruelty here, Nicholas, it's yours, not mine. You've forced my hand. I have no choice. I have to. I have to finish it.

In spite of everything.

—I know it's conjecture, Nicholas. Hypothesis. All a bit theatrical for your taste. A bit like a bad novel, perhaps. But it's conjecture with more behind it—the papers, and all that we know—than anything you have told me, or anything that Colette has said. But you should realise that it's also conjecture—a quite indulgent and unnecessary conjecture, I might add—that the shooting was any sort of accident. Your Tante Colette is lying, Nicholas. You've said it yourself. She lied about the deportations. About Marie-Josèphe, with her stories of how she simply followed him. *Coignard. Concubine. Déportation simple.* She lied about her mother. About her father. About Agnes. As long as she could get away with it. And she is lying, I can tell you, about Sebastien Rouvel. I know it. I have an instinct, Nicholas—a professional nose for these things.

She could see she was getting nowhere. She tried a softer approach. Pleading, almost, for my assent.

—There may well be some other story, Nicholas. Some whole aspect that I've missed. I really am interested in the truth, despite what you may think. I'm an historian. I don't want someone coming along in a few months time and making me look ridiculous by producing some whole new swag of evidence, telling some entirely different story. I have enemies, Nicholas. Believe me, there are people out there who will take me apart, if I get it wrong. If you can find any other way of putting this all together, I'll happily burn this version straight away.

—Then burn it now, Julia. It's nonsense. There is no evidence that Rouvel had any intention of leaving. From what the children remember, he had nowhere to go, anyway. He was sick, and tired and desperate and as miserable as a failed human being can be, and happy to stay on as long as anyone would feed him. And listen to him. His writings are evidence of sickness, that's all. Exhaustion. Sick fantasy.

—Is it fantasy?

She spoke more slowly, avoiding my eyes.

—If so, then it's a fantasy, Nicholas, that lots of others want to know about. I've been talking to Editions Grandet. They are already talking about advance publicity. Television. And interviews with Colette, as well. Eighteen seventy-one. Nineteen sixty-eight. The same disturbance in the streets. Someone who seems almost to span the two periods. There's far more interest than you think.

—With Colette? Julia!

—She's lying, Nicholas. Or, at least, she knows much more than she is telling you. She's probably almost the only living person to have met Sebastien Rouvel. She's the only one, apart from the other sisters, who has spoken to him, and you won't let me meet her. And I've worked on this for years!

—But Julia, do you imagine that Colette would just invite you in for tea? That she would sit and talk to you about Sebastien Rouvel?

—Of course she wouldn't. Her whole life has been built around avoiding that very thing. A good interviewer will soon winkle it out of her, though. And that is why, dear Nicholas, I'm giving you this.

She reached into her bag. Another typescript. A full carbon copy of 'The Aftermath'.

—You must give this to Colette. Read it to her if you have to. Tell her that unless she decides to tell the real truth about Sebastien Rouvel, everything she knows about Sebastien Rouvel and her mother, why they left and what happened on that day, then I intend to publish this, much as it stands. Saint-Germain-sur-École will be full of television reporters. Even *Paris Match*. With pictures. It's the kind of story they love. Look at what is happening out there in the streets, Nicholas. It's Sebastien Rouvel's moment.

—Julia, this is blackmail. Straight blackmail. Exactly the kind of thing Sebastien Rouvel would have done.

—It's only an hypothesis.

—Julia, Marie-Josèphe Coignard is not an hypothesis. She is real. A mother. Their mother.

—Colette is lying.

—This will kill her, Julia. It will kill all of them.

—I wanted to do it in some other way. I am an historian. I have a duty to the truth. An obligation.

—Then burn your wretched typescript. That's the best you can do to help the truth.

—You are just trying to hurt me, Nicholas, but I don't care what you say.

—Julia, just give me time. A little more time.

—She's had all the time in the world, Nicholas. Nearly eighty years of it. And when she dies, a world is lost. The whole thing is out of my hands. Editions Grandet has told me. Either it all happens quickly, or it doesn't happen at all.

The papers sat between us like a loaded weapon.

—Don't be so angry, Nicholas.

She placed a hand on mine, which soon dropped away. She risked a smile, which faded. She pushed the papers towards me.

—These people are mostly dead, Nicholas. And those that are living are very, very old. A few months ago, you didn't know of their existence. Why do they now mean so much to you? What difference can the truth make in their lives? Don't let it all die with them. That's all I'm asking, Nicholas. Is that too much to ask?

Seventeen

COLETTE WAS WAITING FOR me. I climbed the steps, let myself in through the open door and made my way across the hall and into the salon, where she was waiting in her usual chair. The room, though, was much lighter than before. The curtains were drawn back, more shutters were opened, the windows cleaned. A table with a floral cloth had been set for tea. The salon was dusted and aired. Colette was bright, happy to see me. Dressed, or so it seemed, in a lighter colour than before.

She took my hand. She chattered gaily—some complicated story of the *portugaise* who had not come that day of all days, the problems she had in finding the pieces for the tea. A loss of teaspoons. A tradesman's unexpected visit, in the morning. Of repairs, at last, to the house. Of

Geneviève, who was so much better, whom I would meet very soon, though perhaps not today. In all this triviality, a rich compliment to me.

—Our family, *Nicolas*. You. Such a pleasure. I said it to Madame Truchet just yesterday. The only family we have really known.

I had no choice but to break in.

—You must tell me, Tante Colette. You really must tell me now about your mother. About her time at Deception. It is now important, very important. About her time on the prison island—the truth of what happened there. And at Deception, in the end.

She said nothing for a time, the pleasure fading, her eyes taking in the cakes, the tea service. As though the bright cloth, the tea things, were accusing. As though all this, the dusted rooms, the opened curtains, had tempted fate too far. She started once or twice to speak, as though exploring and then retreating from a gap, a crevice, some fissure through which another story might be run.

She stopped short, gestured me to a chair, and looked out the window.

—The truth of what happened there? I only know what my mother has told me, *Nicolas*. I have no reason for thinking it is not the truth. Your books may tell you other things, but I know it as she has told me.

—And yet she was deported, Tante Colette. The prison island. She was a *déportée*.

It was the first time I had pronounced the word. She did not indicate surprise. She smiled ruefully.

—Yes, she was deported. Like my father. I have told you almost as much. If not in so many words. It has always been there, as you know. In the spaces. Like a kind of shadow, *Nicolas*, trailing all that I have told you.

—Why was she there, Tante Colette? After the amnesty—why did she stay?

—She enjoyed her work there, with a family named Dufour, in their grand house. Her work, at the new school of Madame Penaud. No doubt, you know all of this. By whatever means. Her fragile happiness, as she once called it, on the island. She was not unhappy, in those years, as far as we can tell, as far as she ever said. Her life was easier, it is sad to say, on the prison island and in Nouméa, than it came to be in your country, and up at Mount Deception.

—It is no disgrace, Tante Colette. Thousands were sentenced.

—Few women were. Few women were deported. Almost none of her age.

The window seemed to claim her attention. She would not now look at me, but only out at the light that streamed in through the panes. She had told me, she said after some time had passed, that her mother had followed her father to the Ends of the Earth. A strange expression this, but one which they had come in time to understand. Her mother followed him to the Ends of the Earth.

Her mother also told her of a burning city and her flight through the streets. In the streets, because her Tante Agathe was dead and the apartment in the avenue de Tourville in ruins, and she with nowhere to go. She told of how she had been stopped by the invading troops, and was almost shot on the spot. How she was taken down to the slaughteryards at the Tour Saint-Jacques, where she was kept all night with thousands—men, women and even children—standing within the sound of the cries and groans of those about to be shot, all shivering with the cold, in the light rain that had begun to fall on the city's fires, shivering with fear each time their tormenters moved up and down to thin the rows and choose their victims for the next round of executions.

—I will not ask you why you feel the need to know such things. How much of these things you might know already.

She turned her head towards me. Her expression this time almost lost to the light. She brushed her skirt. As though the thing that needed to be said, the thing that weighed most upon her, had now been released. That the attention must now turn to me.

—Do you wish to hear me say, *Nicolas*, that my mother was a criminal? That she was treated like a criminal, rather. That is closer to the truth. That I should tell all this, while you are still a stranger to us, as though it was just the matter for a teatime conversation, a colourful episode to amuse us through a summer afternoon?

—I need to know what happened, Tante Colette. That is all. I have seen her dossier, at the Château de Vincennes. Your mother's dossier, and the record of her trial. Most of the records have letters, depositions, lists of charges, statements from witnesses. But for her, there is just a single sheet. Just her name and sentence. Nothing from her family. Nothing more.

Colette insisted that the family simply had not known. That was what her mother had told her. They might not have acted differently if they had. They were told, later, and just before her deportation, and they did not then respond. The only compassion came from her Uncle Claude, who later gave her this house; he lacked the brutal piety of the others, who treated her as though it was she in person who had shot the Archbishop, who hacked to death the Dominicans at Auteuil. Her trial being no more than a farce, with no evidence, no witnesses, no crime that could be distinguished from the general riot of a city that was invaded and in flames. A quick and muddled hearing, the charges against her confused with the crimes of others, and she sent on to the prisons, and to deportation to the Isle of Pines.

Colette fell silent. She began tracing agitated patterns in the carpet with the end of her stick.

—You speak of records, *Nicolas*. You speak of dossiers. What the papers, the records tell. Let me tell you something of these papers. What they can tell, and what they may fail to tell.

She spoke more to the light, to the world outside, than to me. Perhaps, she said, there might be records of a trial, if there was such a thing to be called a trial, at a time when those inflicted with a certain malice might still find opportunities even from a prison cell to intrude on the process and to draw things to their will. Nothing of what she could say would ever be proven, and all she could say—all that even her mother could ever suggest—was that there seemed to be some obstruction in the process. That documents were mislaid. That letters which should have been sent to her family, to witnesses, to the neighbours of Tante Agathe, were never sent.

Such accusations must indeed sound foolish. Such notions live as vital and insistent truths within one's private thinking, but as soon as they are spoken must sound unlikely and extreme. Yet they do not vanish, just on that account. There had been more than a shadow, a hint, a trace of unseen influence. No evidence of any kind, nor anything that anyone could point to, but always, her mother had told her, there was an undercurrent, some unseen manipulation, a hand that seemed to move silently behind all that happened at that time, the hand moving even judges and their judgments upon others. An influence which did not end, it seemed, with Paris and the burning city, but which went on to blight the lives of all, of her mother and her father and all of those to follow.

Colette then turned from the light, to face me directly at last. Looking at me closely, as though trying to see again the stranger that lay concealed beneath the friend.

—And now through your hands, *Nicolas*, this need of yours to know, must touch us yet again.

—You had a visit, Tante Colette. A visitor to the desert.

She looked at me with no surprise. The house was quiet. Quieter even than usual. There was no sound or movement upstairs. As though Geneviève, too, was listening. Outside, very faintly in the distance, Clémentine was singing to her birds. Colette's voice was muffled, almost a whisper.

—So you speak, at last, of Sebastien Rouvel. Why do you not say the name?

—Sebastien Rouvel. Your visitor. Sebastien Rouvel. Tante Colette, I need to know.

—Yes, I recall Sebastien Rouvel. I know the man of whom you speak.

Colette turned from me, and once again, to the light. She said nothing for a time. Then she struggled to her feet, and drew the curtains. She set herself down in her chair again, brusquely refusing all assistance. She told, slowly but with growing vigour, of a ragged figure blighted by sickness who had blown in off a road that led nowhere. A sorry figure who limped about the house in filthy shirts and tobacco-stained rags, old things her father could no longer use, his eyes still young but his body giving off the rank smell of someone very old, blinking through his broken spectacles into the rawness of the light, peering through his thick spectacles with the shattered lens, his eye swimming eerily within the other, kicking at the scrounging cats who tried to trip him as he stumbled between his sheepyard cottage and the house.

Yes, she did remember Sebastien Rouvel. As vividly as if he were here with them, in this room.

There were tears in her eyes.

—Did you speak to him, Tante Colette? To Sebastien Rouvel?

—We were kept from him. We were not permitted to speak. By my mother. By my father.

But she could, she said, tell me something of this man. She alone, because Geneviève was ill and Clémentine's memories unsure. She could tell me about this person who stumbled up the road to Deception, as though he knew when their father would be away. Whose twisted nature seemed to lead him to believe that the misery he had engendered in the lives of others meant there was a bond to which he could turn, some debt or lien that he could now draw upon, his only knowledge of intimacy the memory of his cruelty, his only notion of kinship and affection the chance of inflicting further pain. Sebastien Rouvel.

—Do you know of his writing, Tante Colette? Do you know what happened to his writing when you left?

—We know only that he died soon after. That is all we know. His papers? Old scraps of things is all that I recall. Scattered to the winds, I do imagine. Blown out and away across the deserts. You do not need to tell me, *Nicolas*, about the writing of Rouvel. Even after so much time. If you had read what he had written, you would feel that you had all kinds of knowledge. It is like that—the power of the words, the power of mystery and confusion which feels so much like revelation. You tell me of his writing. I can tell you of the frenzy of a sick man—sick in his body, sick in his mind—his life ebbing away, and he still writing as though he owed it to the world to inflict on it this last shaft of malevolence. Writing which made as much sense as anything else to be found at Deception. Writing which made as much sense to the birds and to the lizards as it did to anyone else. So many, many lies, all strung together in ways designed to seduce the reader from all sense, all decent order. Unhinging, separating. All pandering to the cruellest expectation, more closely to the shapes of fear and of desire than any frail fact or real event could ever hope to match.

I leaned forward to her. I wanted to take her hand, but her fingers were clenched in defiance to the top of her stick.

—I must tell you, Tante Colette. That writing, some part of it at least, has survived.

Her pallor deepened in an instant. She choked off a cry. Her eyes grew misty, distant. Then determined. Defensive to the last.

—So it is to be Sebastien Rouvel, again. The infection is still with us. Why did you not mention this before? Why did you not speak of this writing?

—There was indeed a shadow, Tante Colette. Something in the way Agnes talked about him—what she felt about this writing. Something to cause pain. I thought I should wait. To see.

—It is by this waiting, *Nicolas*, that the pain is now so much greater. Where is this writing?

I fingered the package on my knees.

—It is with a friend. A friend in Paris.

—Is it someone you trust?

—Yes.

In helplessness.

—With others, it seems, you had no such inhibition.

—I'm sorry, Tante Colette.

She sat up straight, rigid, drawing back from me.

—You cannot please everyone. You must choose. You speak about the facts, about knowing, about finding the truth. But is there any kind of truth, *Nicolas*, that is more important than true passion for the fortunes, past and future, of your own flesh and blood?

On the way out of the house, I did manage, though, to speak with Clémentine. I had retreated in awkwardness from Colette's frightening silence, from the pages that had fallen from her lap and to the floor. Unwilling to pick them up and place them again in her hands.

Clémentine was with one of her cages, struggling to move it further from the house.

I tried to help her.

—Tante Clémentine, do you remember Deception? Do you remember your father?

The work with the cage was not easy. It had been constructed many years before, with a wooden frame. It was never meant to be moved. Certainly not now, when so much of the frame was rotten.

—At Deception we had birds. Parrots, I remember. Blue and red and green. But mostly galahs. Galahs, we called them. Grey and crimson. We taught them to talk. *Bonjour Arthur, Bonjour Arthur.* I remember Deception. Here. You must help.

I began to move the cage from one part of the overgrown rear garden to another. Inside it, her birds, one or two parrots and a number of wrens and finches, protested with indignant squawks and a great fluttering of wings with each jolt as I heaved and dragged and coaxed the cage across what must once have been an ornamental parterre to the place she had marked out.

—When we came home, Maman had promised that I could keep birds, just like the ones we had at Deception. I cried when we left, you see, because we could not take the birds. I have looked after my birds ever since. Haven't I, my sweet ones? Haven't I, my darlings?

She broke off into a bird-like babble of endearments to her damp and moulting prisoners, poking at them with her bony fingers, talking in an inane prattle in French and broken English.

We made our way back to the far side of the overgrown parterre. I spoke to her again. For just one last curious moment. One last chance at an explanation.

—Tell me, Tante Clémentine. Do you remember much of Deception?

I saw distress rise in her eyes, saw words hover for a moment on her lips, and then fade slowly away.

—Tante Clémentine, do you remember your last weeks at Deception? Do you remember the day you left?

—I remember the lambs. It was not long before we left. They would keep moving, you know, after they were cut off. The tails. We felt sorry for the lambs. We would cry and beg the men not to do it, not to the littlest ones, at least. They would keep on with their work until the yard was scattered with little tails, the last of them still twitching on the ground.

I heard a door slam. Colette had come out of the house, hobbling on her stick.

She called, once, twice, to Clémentine, who did not appear to hear.

—What else do you remember, Tante Clémentine? What else do you recall?

—Sometimes my sisters tried to help, to catch the lambs and bring them to the men. Colette got blood on her pinafore. My father sent her back to the house. She and Geneviève got rashes from the burrs in the lambs' wool and needed ointment, to stop the burning.

Clémentine. The smallest. All but forgotten in the milling of the sheep, the haze of heat, the dust.

Colette began to make her way down the steps, awkwardly, far too quickly, still calling abruptly to her sister.

—Do you remember who was there, Tante Clémentine? At the time you left? Do you remember why you left?

—I tried to help, too. Just once that I remember. I remember that I climbed down into the yard, with the sheep rushing about, and that I tried to catch a lamb, as I had seen my sisters do. And then there was a rush of sheep, and I fell over, and I remember Papa picking me up and taking me home, and I was covered in mud and filth, with bumps and bruises from the sheep.

—Tante Clémentine!

I whispered, almost hissed, with Colette coming near.

—Do you remember Monsieur Rouvel?

—Of course.

She replied without taking her attention from the cage, the scoop of seed that she was taking from a toppled bureau.

—Monsieur Rouvel was shot. That's why we left.

—Shot?

She kept on with her scoop and bucket. I took her shoulders in my hands and gently turned her about, forcing her to meet my eye. She looked up at me, startled, almost frightened by the pressure of my hands. Look back, Tante Clémentine, I whispered, almost begged. Look back, and see again, see more than you ever thought you saw, and tell me what you see. Tell me everything you saw, and especially the things you saw but did not understand.

—Tante Clémentine, you say that he was shot? That Monsieur Rouvel was shot?

Clémentine still looked up at me, searching my face as though I was the one who was confused.

—Oh yes. Monsieur Rouvel was shot. He was a wicked man. He ran off into the desert.

I thought of Agnes, watching Rouvel as he stumbled along the verandah. The doors crashing in the wind.

—How was he shot, Tante Clémentine? What happened on that day?

—Maman shot him. It was Maman who shot him. Colette saw it all. That's why we all came home.

—Your mother shot him? It was your mother who shot Monsieur Rouvel?

—That's why we left. Did Colette not tell you? That's why we all came home.

Agnes watched them playing with the lizard, Colette too old for such things but Geneviève and Clémentine in the full flood of excitement for the ritual to follow, their faces now more clearly to be seen through the crevices of Agnes's single telling, the uncertain slats of memory admitted and of memory denied, this scene of banging doors and rising dust and Colette gone off to look for wood, the lizard clinging in desperation to its stick and the visitor suddenly before them, breaking from the house against all the beating of the wind, stumbling along the verandah and clawing with awkward and urgent hands at the reins of Agnes's horse.

The horse was in a sweat. Agnes led her towards the house and tethered her to the gate, stepping inside for a moment to put the pistol in its usual place behind the door, their mother in the house somewhere and busy with the screens and shutters, and Monsieur Rouvel inviting himself across to sit on the verandah as he often did when their father was away, spreading out on one of the wicker layabouts next to the dripping coolness of the canvas waterbags, reading old newspapers or writing in his books, but now no longer to be seen; gone inside, perhaps, to speak to their mother and seek shelter from the wind.

But then it was that something happened.

This, Agnes could tell, clearly. This much she remembered and could tell. From over by the garden gate, she saw him stumble from the house, crouching and limping as he always did, but this time almost falling from one verandah post to the next, staggering out across the stone-walled garden, steadying himself for a moment on the far gatepost. He stumbled through the gate and began to untie the pony, pulling and tearing and cursing at the tethered reins, shaking his head and shouting something to them that they couldn't hear. She saw him move in front of the plunging horse and then to the wrong side, hopping for a stirrup that was far too short, the saddle straining perilously against the girth, the unwilling pony twisting and stooping into the weight of his foot so that he was forced to turn within the straining arc of the twisting horse. He managed at last to rise into the saddle, with a last look to the girls. Then he dragged Princess's head around, moving at first towards them and then down into the bed of the creek which led off towards the north and to the west.

She saw Colette come from the house. Some minutes later, Agnes said. Perhaps less. This time, she held the door carefully so that it would not slam in the wind. She sat on one of the wicker layabouts, the same where Monsieur Rouvel usually sat, as though this was an ordinary day, as though the sun was shining and she simply wanted respite in the shade. She had lost her hat, her hair floating in loose waves, her pinafore tossed and billowing around her knees. Little Clémentine began to walk towards her, but even she was troubled by the blank unsighted way Colette was sitting, bare and hatless in the wind. She stopped halfway across the yard as though not quite knowing why she did so, tugging at a falling stocking and looking back to see what Agnes would do.

A few moments later, Marie-Josèphe came out of the house, the door beating yet again in the wind. Looking as Agnes had never seen her look, her clothes in disarray, the wind drawing long strands from her tousled hair and tossing them about her face. Raising a hand against the dust, her dark eyes searching the yard and then falling on Colette, just to her right, sitting on the layabout. Agnes saw her lips moving, speaking as though in anger or perhaps in distress; and then she strode off, her dark skirt and fringe of petticoat flapping hard against her legs, to stop for a moment with each of the younger girls while Agnes watched, still from her place at the end of the verandah. Her long dark hair was all undone, her cheeks and the little creases at the corners of her eyes marked with mingled tears and dust. Coming over, at last, and taking Agnes's face in her hands. Beginning to say something about how Agnes must stay, that she was now almost an adult, and that she must look after Papa; and then stopping, and taking her in her arms. Then disappearing into the house, coming out just minutes later with her bags, their ancient suitcases stuffed full and trailing clothing, Marie-Josèphe struggling with the weight and calling to the older girls to help, her jaw set in a determined way that Agnes had not seen before, and ordering a protesting Fritz to bring up a horse, and pile the bags and other things into the gig.

No-one, not even Clémentine, asked Agnes to climb in, not when Fritz brought up the gig, nor when they climbed inside. She watched them, wanting to know why but saying nothing, just following them mutely to the outer gate. No-one said goodbye to her, all watching her as though they were just passing by, but with the horse rearing and panicking in the wind and sand, its eyes rolling and staring, and no-one, not the children nor Agnes nor old Fritz, really wanting to venture out into that wind. Not knowing where they were going, not knowing how long they would be gone. The little ones began to cry with dread at the confusion, the flying whip and rearing horse, but not Colette, who had not said a word but only gripped the side of the cart and stared back towards the house, as though it was still there but now a hundred miles away, with Marie-Josèphe standing in the gig, pulling on the reins to keep herself upright, but at the same time driving the reluctant horse towards the gate.

The dust was blowing up in coils of angry wind, a huge willy-willy running across the yard in a cloud of thistle seeds that looped and swirled around the cart. The horse, whipped and beaten in the unfamiliar wind, began to twist and rear within the shafts. Marie-Josèphe stood with the whip and flogging reins, the horse tearing from the grip of Fritz and stumbling at last across the flimsy wooden gate and vanishing then with all of them into the storm of dust that blew up from the south. While Agnes watched. Standing by the gatepost, watching and wondering what she would say; looking back across the yard to the place from where her own horse had vanished over the rise and to the north, to the empty verandah and the wicker layabout and the slammed door to the house, to the smouldering pile of rocks and the stick and the lizard that had looked so close into the glowing coals and now was nowhere to be seen, she must have wondered, as she was still wondering to her final moments in what way this could be told.

Eighteen

COLETTE WAS WAITING AT the top of the steps when I returned—summoned for a final time—despite the light rain and the cold wind that was blowing. It was late evening. The gates had been dragged closed. I left the car out in the road, and walked towards the house, towards the waiting figure on the steps, her garments blown and tossed, towards the voice that rang out to call me in, over the sound of the gravel moving beneath my feet, of the wind slapping the branches that reached across the drive.

—Wrong. You have misunderstood everything. Everything!

She shook her stick with menace as I approached. The wind tossed and flicked the long steel strands of her hair about her face as she struggled down to meet me at the base of the steps.

Above, Geneviève's window was closed. The first time I had seen it closed. The curtain had been caught in the closed window, the trapped flap dangling in the rain.

She hobbled towards me, taking my arm. Taking my arm as always, but this time with a fearsome strength. Letting me feel the anger. Telling me, as we climbed the steps, that I only knew enough to misunderstand. Enough to accuse. Not enough to forgive. That she would now tell me everything. Things that now Monsieur Jalabert must know, that everyone must know.

—Betrayal. Such betrayal! Of me, your family, even Monsieur Jalabert, who tells me that this was kept even from him.

I could see she had been weeping.

I was directed, by her shaking stick, towards the salon, towards the same overfurnished room that I had first been shown into just weeks before. That room. Much darker than on my previous visit. Where in the short blindness when entering from the light I was scarcely aware of the presence of others until Clémentine, waiting quietly, suddenly fidgeted and let something fall. Where Monsieur Jalabert also waited in his previous place, sunk deep into the frayed and musty tapestry of an ancient armchair, watching without a word or sign of recognition.

Monsieur Jalabert, for all his hints and implications, now nursing, perhaps, a rich betrayal of his own? Madame Truchet sat by him scowling.

Colette thrust me towards a chair and took her place, the tall chair in the corner, her face just a pallid vignette within the weak cast of the lamp, her robe now shrouding her in darkness, one hand grasping the hard knob of her stick and the other taut in anger on the armrest of her chair, letting the cool wind and the closed shutters and the discomfort of the damp say that this was unlike all the conversations that had taken place between us through the weeks that went before. Letting the dim light and the cold explain that this time there was no pleasure to be had in speaking, that the things of which she spoke were now beyond her power of choosing. Colette, a formidable stranger once again, with the night beginning to settle in, her pale skin above the dark must of her clothing now seeming to absorb what fragile light there was.

—All that I tell you is now written down, and in great detail. All day, I have worked. It is signed and witnessed—by all of us, even Clémentine—for we are told it may soon be a document of some legal importance. It has been most closely read by dear Monsieur Jalabert, who is, as you know, our oldest friend. Sometimes I think our only friend. He has told us that it will indeed be a document of legal consequence.

She reached to pick up Julia's papers from the table alongside. They slipped from her grasp, and fell to the floor. I made as if to rise to pick them up, but was fixed to my seat by a stabbing gesture from her stick.

—This writing. The truth. Part of the truth. To answer your obsession to know all. It is not, though, like the other writing. Not like the nonsense, the foul stories that your friend has written, up in Paris.

—Not like the insane things your friend has written.

She spread the papers further with her stick.

—Not like the foul stories Sebastien Rouvel wrote, these obscene scribblings you have brought with you from the ends of the earth, bred from disease and delirium and the desert: lies which you must now be tempted to think, because they are yellow with age and are now ancient lies, are not lies at all.

All listened in deep silence as she spoke, jerking her head forward now and then to mark a point or to repeat something that I may have missed, pausing now and then as though to check that what she said did not run beyond my meagre stock of words. No-one offered, through the growing darkness, to rise and trim the light, with old Monsieur Jalabert sitting silent and motionless in his chair, hunched forward over his stick and staring severely at the floor, and Tante Clémentine intently knitting in the last faint light from the window, clicking and sighing and even humming tuneless fragments from her seat close by the light. The tales of Colette running out past all her silent listeners and through the doors which no-one had thought to close, to tell at last the empty streets her knowledge of the dead.

—So we must begin with his writing.

She gestured at the fan of papers, all that Julia had written, spread out across the floor where it had fallen, poking at it as though it were a dead bird or a discarded piece of soiled clothing or some piece of rotting refuse that had found its way into the house. She turned the pages over, scattering them further across the widening damp. As though releasing once and for all the worst that could be said.

—I have seen in your friend's story some passages that are familiar, the stuff of ancient nightmares, now interwoven with the new lies concocted by this friend of yours in Paris. Two of a kind. Obscene. Obscenities then and obscene still, the words the same words I recall his reading to me as a child; words which meant nothing—nothing that was clear—at the time when they were read but which in the months to follow rose up to haunt me in the nights; lunatic images, drawn from one man's sickness and pain but which were written with a power that ran that sickness from the words, from those crumpled pages, and out into the world so that everything about us—the trees, the rocks, the call of the birds, the house, our hair, our very clothing—all began to speak to me of things that ran beyond my knowledge, began to shape the world in forms of suffering that ran beyond all pain I had to that time known.

We listened as she spoke to the deepening night, the shutters closed against the rain which beat against the peeling slats and spattered on the panes, breaking through the buckled shreds of cardboard where the glass had slipped away.

Fear, o fear the bright salamander as I walk yet again in triumph from the scalding heart of fire, who have crossed the fiery crucible, the cell, the tumbrel, stake, stocks and scaffold and the barren islands that sulk amid the desert sea, and even the highest heat of the southern desert that lies below the ramparts of baked rocks and boiling stones ...

I sat fixed at the centre, the sodden arc of Julia's papers spread about me by the motion of Colette's probing stick, the papers now circling me like some sorcerer's inscription that I must not dare to cross.

. . . nutrisco et extinguo, *who see flesh fall in bright flames from all around but am not myself consumed, rising in three days and three thousand years to feed upon the fire and always again after three days and three thousand years.*

She coughed. Looked to the others. And then to me.

—You say that I have lied. You do not say it, but in all that you have done, in all your friend in Paris has written, it is clear. I do not deny I have not told you all. In this, there was a reason. These facts you speak of are not sacred. So much is bred from fiction and illusion. So much you now call history is just shadow bred from shadow, blind actions set in motion by cruelty and insinuation, the motions then set out in further lies to tease the years to come. A triple fiction. A triple set of lies, to which your fourth is added. With your new friend up in Paris.

She sighed, and raised a glass of water to her lips.

—We had some foolish notion, *Nicolas*, that you would offer us a future. All I have done was an attempt to give to you a visitable past. A territory from which some kind of future might be wrought. A future for us all. All I have done is to create an amnesty, some knowledge of the dead that might accommodate the living. Is this a form of lying? Is it really lying, *Nicolas*, to try to rescue—for you—some poor shred of the lives of our loved ones, the lives that should have been?

—Not all your friend in Paris writes is wrong. Not all is lies. He had a power. A strength in what he wrote. A strength that brought on age before its proper time, that brought to me even at that age the pain and age of others, with something running out from that cottage, from the pen of Sebastien Rouvel, some power from that writing that touched all of us, that we all came to acknowledge in dread or hatred or fascination. And I can see in what your friend writes that these writings now are to be the truth; that those who are dead and cannot speak for themselves will now be known only through these enchanting lies of Sebastien Rouvel. That these papers will live, while they have died, and be the only evidence, the first infecting source of the disease long passed away and now with only the disease itself left to work its way, these pages providing the shapes, the matter indeed for almost any obscene thing one might wish to imagine. My mother is dead and my father is dead and Rouvel is dead and soon we will be dead as well, but these writings will, it now seems, live on. All those who sought to turn the injury of those times into some better feeling have long gone. The triumph of his sickness will be complete. This is the tragedy.

Colette sipped at her glass of water, then coughed to break the stillness that had fallen. She pressed forward to challenge me more directly.

—This is the tragedy. Sebastien Rouvel. Let me tell you

more of this Sebastien Rouvel. Just once or twice we saw him try to move, to reach beyond this ragged scrawl. This obscene nonsense. Just once or twice we saw him try to touch, and even to be kind. To be, to act, like other men. One evening, I do recall, he drew poor Clémentine onto his lap. It was some months after he arrived. Monsieur Rouvel would sleep during the day while everyone else worked, and then would take his meals with us in the evenings, moving in easy steps into the house and into all parts of our lives, filling the vast silences that seemed to have come on us all with the endless talk of France and of the islands; of everything, it seemed to me even at that age, my parents needed to forget.

—I remember little of what he said. It was of ideas, places, people who meant nothing to me then and who mean nothing still. I remember the easy flow of words and the long silence it brought to the table, with just a comment every now and then and very sparingly from Papa, who seemed bound in some way to Rouvel. Whether just by courtesy or by some other thing, I could never say. A deeper kind of silence descended on all of us at that time, and even Clémentine—no more than four years old—felt it, and spoke of it. As I will tell.

—I cannot tell you what occurred when Papa first arrived back from the south and found that Monsieur Rouvel had arrived, that my mother had been caring for him, taking him food and even, I believe, washing and dressing him during those first weeks when he was so very sick. I remember how she would return from his cottage—it was soon filthy, with his old rags and bottles and his papers—pale and sometimes red-eyed, and we wondered if Maman would not catch his sickness. I still recall the looks that passed between my father and my mother as Rouvel spoke and talked about the past, and made little jokes—his eyes laughed, at least, though no one else seemed to—about events of long ago. And I recall, too, that as the evenings drew on, Monsieur Rouvel would get drunk, and speak more loudly, and then we would be sent to bed.

—My sisters would soon be asleep, and I would lie awake, listening to his voice, louder and louder. Just waiting for Monsieur Rouvel to leave, to get up and stumble over to his cottage, where he would then read and write, sometimes speaking loudly to himself for long periods, each night until dawn. Almost a member of the family, he became. Never quite well enough to leave. He would not travel down to Port Augusta for new spectacles. But gradually he regained his health, and wore clean clothing from my father—because he did not work, better clothing, indeed, than my father generally wore—and made himself more comfortable down in his cottage, with books and furniture from the house, as though to stay forever.

—Even the little ones seemed aware of something broken, of our lives drawing apart, of our father drawing away from our mother, of me drawing away from Geneviève, of the whole life of our family moving into silence, with only Monsieur Rouvel's words and needs to take its place. Even the younger ones seemed in some way aware of it. It was the littlest, Clémentine, who told the truth for all of us.

—It was one night at dinner. Monsieur Rouvel drew Clémentine onto his lap. He had encouraged her to do so before, after the meal and just before the time when we would normally have left the room. She always refused, declining in a way that drew little enough attention. On this evening, though, Clémentine had walked over to him, carrying with her a favourite doll—a rag doll, it was, with a head of porcelain, the one we called Mathilde.

—Clémentine had approached him and whispered something to him, and he bent down and picked her up and placed her on his knee. Everyone was glad of it. There had been no conversation that evening. Clémentine was now looked to by all to build for us the centre, to fill the empty spaces.

—What is it, little one? he asked gently.

—We want you to go.

—She said it softly, and then more loudly. And then she began to squirm, and try to get down. Monsieur Rouvel at first tried to calm her, to laugh away her fear and his own sudden anger and embarrassment, but Clémentine would not be calmed, now squirming harder against the hands that tried to hold her in place, and then screaming in genuine fear.

—We want you to go, we want you to go!

—He looked about him for a moment, helplessly, his hands grasping the squirming child so fiercely now that she began to squeal with the pain. But everything that Clémentine had said was echoed in the silence, was mirrored in the eyes of everyone around the table. Then he snarled something, and threw an angry look at both my parents. He stood up from the table, sending Clémentine and the doll toppling to the floor, but softening her fall with a cruel grip to her arm.

—But I remember, as we all remember, the head of poor Mathilde, shattering into pieces on the floor. We remembered the silence as he swept out of the house. Though I do remember, too, thinking of unkindness, of how ugliness bred ugliness and anger bred anger, and I remember wondering, as he left the room, the door slamming behind, what anger we might not now reasonably expect, what further kinds of pain we must all now deserve, with Clémentine speaking in this way the silent thought of the room.

***

I saw the child on his knee, twisting and toppling to the floor, looked into the circle of those distant faces, the father, the mother, the other children lost in the menace of the silence as he broke from the room. I watched Clémentine as Colette spoke, now smiling at the repeated mention of her name, smiling with childish pleasure at this setting of new memory, her arthritic fingers cruelly twisted yet able still to wield the needles, knitting at some long and useless infant garment, soiled and shapeless after such long manipulation. I thought of Clémentine's world of cages and confusion, all past harshness slipped away. Accommodated, somehow, to it all. With a special amnesty of her own. Yet still intent as Colette spoke, intent upon her knitting as though the knitting matched the telling, yet with the awkward garment getting longer and steadily more shapeless as the night drew on.

I thought of the silent hours of her sister Geneviève, in her room upstairs. The young woman in her heavy cloche, her face always shaded from the light. I thought of Geneviève, no image coming to me but the shape, the shade, the heavy hat, the face lost in its darkness. With now and then a muffled sound passing through the ceiling. Of a chair displaced. Of crockery rattling on a table. The sound of feet, hesitant, moving unsteadily from piece to piece across the room.

***

—Sometimes, when he was well and even on the hottest days, he would set off to climb Mount Deception. Deception lay some distance to the west, the highest point on a jagged ridge that rose sharply from the plains—jagged, we used to say, like the horny spine of the lizards we would find among the rocks, the whole ridge rising from the plains and scattered rocks like a sudden violent wrinkle on the earth. We would see him set off in the early morning with nothing but a waterbag and his precious canvas satchel. A long and limping walk it was through the rising heat of the day, and sometimes we would follow him for some distance as he walked across the plain, creeping along the fissures and the creek beds to keep from his view. He would come back late at night, covered in sweat and dust, but always in a state of elation, with tales of something he was building there, some structure of stones, a cairn of some sort, right at the very top. A fruitless thing, it seemed to us, which no-one would ever see in such a place where no-one would ever go, but that was something that did not enter his thinking, any more than it seemed to matter whether anyone would read his writing. And in time, he was able to show us, through our papa's telescope, a small rising mound on the highest peak to the west.

—I remember how one day in December—a hot day it was, as he seemed to prefer for these journeys to the peak—we did set off with him, at his suggestion, Geneviève and I, with no intention to go far with him, but just talking and walking further and further beside him towards the mountains. For more than an hour we walked with him across the rocky plains, scattered with purple stones. Monsieur Rouvel talked, more and more strangely as we approached the ridge, of what we would soon find when we crossed, foolish teasing talk of vast silver seas and stately ships and distant cities in the desert.

—I remember how we stopped, a little way up the slope, with Geneviève now exhausted and fearful, and determined not to go on. She would wait for us there, in the shaded bed of a dry creek, until my return. I climbed up further with Monsieur Rouvel. I recall him climbing upwards through the loose shale and rocks and broken trees, limping always but with some new kind of strength as he pushed towards the summit far above. The rocks were loose; the whole mountain seemed composed of tiny pebbles and sharp fragments piled in fragile steps that quickly turned to cascades and rivulets of falling stone. It was too dangerous to climb close to him, and yet he seemed unheedful of the danger, his attention focused only on what he would find at the top.

—It was perilous, climbing in my heavy dress. I recall the perspiration seeping through the cloth, my whole body and its clothing soon thoroughly drenched, and a sharp pain, increasing with each step, within my boot. I stopped in the thin shade of a small tree. Some few trees had taken root amid the rocks and grew there, twisted and buckled and almost leafless in the wind. Below it was a pool of dust and dried kangaroo dung. It was a place where animals would come to rest, and there I sat, my foot stinging now with the sharpness of the pain. I sat and waited, and I remember Monsieur Rouvel turn and, seeing me, laugh and continue on his way, upward and upward, the stream of pebbles past me marking the path of his ascent. I sat, for hours it seemed, worrying about Geneviève alone and fearful far below, listening to the wind that rushed up the slope, singing in the needles and the stripped branches above. I looked out across the plain to the east, back towards the house that sat beside the distant line of tall gums that ran along the creek. Hours I waited, wondering whether to go back or to wait, as I hoped Geneviève was still waiting, for Monsieur Rouvel.

—At length he returned, his coming preceded by bounding stones and a long cascade of shale. He sat and we talked. He told me again of the things he had just seen, but this time of things that were real; how all the land on the other side of the ridge glowed bright red in the sun, except for the silver of the vast salt seas that ran out from the base of the mountains. How from the top of the ridge the land fell away from your feet, as though sliced away with a knife; that on the other side there were no foothills, no slopes, but only what seemed like gigantic cliffs looking out across the desert and the seas of salt that ran to the north and to the west.

—He gave me a long drink from his waterbag. I recall even now that strange raw taste the canvas gave, the special rawness in that place, amid the dust and dung, the water splashing from the upheld bag in rhythmic spurts about my mouth and chin, the cool of it running down my neck and seeping through the front of my dress. He turned his attention to my foot. Without a word, he knelt before me and took my boot in his hands, slowly loosening the lace, and easing my foot from the boot and then my stocking to follow, drawing it gently, slowly, from my foot, from the blister which had broken and bled. Then he took my bare foot and ankle in his hands. He knelt in the dust before me, and slowly caressed my foot, turned it and worked it gently in his hands, so that the easing of the tiredness and the soft touch of his hands drew me from thoughts of the pain. I tell you this so that you will know; so that you will not just know, but understand. How he caressed my foot, amid the dust, his head bent and the odour of sweat and the labour of the climb rising about us, clasping my ankle gently and slowly massaging my foot, working the muscles gently, and touching, at last, the ugly blister, raising at last the hurt foot to his lips, his eyes now fixed on mine, his eyes peering not through his broken spectacles but upward to me, through the dark hanks of hair that fell across his face.

I looked at Monsieur Jalabert, his head resting on his hands, his hands folded across the top of his stick, unmoving in the stiffening chill that crept into the room. I wondered if this was what he had hoped to hear, if this was at last the nakedness he so desired, this central file and his own life soon able to be closed? I watched him closely as she spoke, watched for some movement of the hands, the slightest gesture of response, hoping that he might lift his face so I might read these answers in his eyes. But Monsieur Jalabert was as mute as stone, never looking towards me, as though he and I had never spoken, as though I had never been an accomplice in this matter, as Colette slowly spoke on, pausing now and then for just a moment to raise a glass of water to her lips.

> *So through the underearth I crept, nails torn, tongue raw and splintered from scraping at the roots of trees, seeking the last deep moisture of the earth in this place where eyes dry and wither in their sockets and teeth fall loose within retracting gums, skin cracks and splits in broken tablets like plates of shrinking clay . . .*

I thought of Sebastien Rouvel's pointless cairn, high up on Mount Deception. I thought of his poetry of earth, his visions of the desert as the sea, his doctrine on the vast expanse of soul to be discovered among the empty rocks, the desert wilderness. I wondered if all that expanse and vision was just more failure to connect, a harsher form of truculence writ larger than before, across a bleaker landscape that did not reproach, with no hint of compassion. I looked at Monsieur Jalabert as he listened to Colette, as he must once have sat in that same chair and perhaps listened to the young Colette in bright boyish fascination; Monsieur Jalabert, his own life of shadow living now drawing to a close, shrunk back within suit, tie, handkerchief, perhaps wondering too if all this knowing, shrewdness, facts and files might best have been exchanged, and years ago, for one such passionate admission? One bartering of the truth, in all its fragments, for just one truly collected moment, one entire rush of feeling?

—He seemed then to be everywhere—to be, as even Clémentine seemed to feel, in all the corners of our lives. In the silences of our mother and the absences of our father, even there we felt his presence, who from his shack down by the sheepyards, from his incessant writing, seemed to be telling a life for all of us, it creeping out to shape and to infect even our thoughts; and soon it was not easy for any of us to say what it was that we thought, or how it was that we had felt before he stumbled in off the Hawker road, sick and exhausted, and then began to talk.

—I cannot say exactly what I mean. I can only speak of growing silence. I can only tell you how my own thoughts slipped and reeled through those few dangerous months, how some spirit ran from the pen of Sebastien Rouvel which touched me more deeply than anything before; how it was not just what he told me in his cottage in the nights—and I will tell you all, everything that happened, so that no more of these truths will be released upon us by your friend in Paris—but far beyond that, in the feeling and thoughts that he brought, which soon seeped into Deception itself and the creek and the desert mountains beyond.

—Before he came, we would go down and swim at the rock pool, Geneviève with me and sometimes Agnes. It was just a deep pool in the creek, formed against a steep rock wall, the only place along the creek where the reeds grew tall and the grasses near the edge of the water stayed green through the whole length of the summer. There we would play in the water and even, when the water level was high in early summer, jump from the rocks into the water.

—Geneviève and I and Agnes, when she was younger, would go there to swim. We would say we were going for a walk in the bush or a ride on the back of Princess, and then steal our way to the rock pool and pull off our clothes and swim and splash for hours in the cool water. We could only swim there in the early summer because it was soon the only place where the cattle could come down to drink, and they would foul the water. By the end of January the waters were usually a foul green, thick and smelly, and with a floating scum. But even after the water began to smell and took on a poisonous green hue, we would still go there to sit and play and tell stories because it was the one place in all of Deception that stayed green all year around, the grasses around the edge and even the foul green of the waters; the only place which seemed in some way like the things we had read of, what children did in books in other places, near waterfalls and streams and across green fields; as though it was those stories that were real and that our life, so far from anywhere and stranded amid the bare rocks and mountains, was made up, merely a fanciful thing.

—And I remember one time when we played there, when it was hot and Geneviève and I had pulled off all our clothes and slipped down into the cool waters. We played loudly and our shrieks joined those of the birds, the flocks of galahs that swept through the trees above us, the tall white gums. I recall how on that one day I was standing naked in the sun below the rocks and wringing the water from my hair—such long hair I had then—wringing it out and combing out with my fingers the leaves and bits of stick. It was then that I saw something catch the sun, something glinting among the rocks, and I felt sure that it was Monsieur Rouvel, that he was hiding among the rocks and watching us, perhaps on his way back from one of his slow limping solitary walks out towards Mount Deception or the dry country beyond, watching us as we swam naked in the waters.

—I hissed something to Geneviève, a warning that he was perhaps there, watching the two of us as we stood naked and exposed amid the desolation, the cool water glistening on our bodies and our hair streaming about us in long wet strands. We fell silent and slipped into the water, covering ourselves up to our necks, to cover ourselves from his gaze, and if he had indeed been there I think he must have heard me, must have realised that we had seen him, because the next time I dared to look around, the light was gone. There was no sign of him. If ever he was there. But so vividly I remember it, the rocks and our laughter echoing through the trees, and then the sun glinting from the rocks, glinting perhaps from the spectacles of Monsieur Rouvel as he watched us from the rocks. Or perhaps it was some other thing, just the memory, perhaps, of something that Rouvel had said, something he had read to me, which came to my thoughts and brought to me, so suddenly, my nakedness. The thought, the words, of nakedness.

—We slipped below the waters, and from that moment I was bare as I had never been before, naked to myself and to Geneviève, and naked even to the rocks and to the cattle, quietly chewing the cud in the shade and waiting: exposed and staying so from that day to this, in that my nakedness, within his writing, must now also become a real and lasting thing, not just the brief and laughing stolen schoolgirl moment it had been. That was the last time we ever swam in the rock pool, which was the scene of the little happiness I took from that dry place. We did not go back again after the scolding from Maman when we came home, our hair still wet and hanging in heavy tails with the thought of Monsieur Rouvel concealed among the rocks, and it creeping into the later part of that last summer anyway, the heat growing day by day and the waters shrinking and now the cattle gathering during the day around the shrinking green pool, fouling the waters. We never spoke to each other again about the grasses and the reeds or the green waters, as though the mere idea that Sebastien Rouvel had been there, that Sebastien Rouvel might now have written of those waters, was enough to pass away its full possession.

—There was, you see, some power. Your friend may call it vision. Some intensity of anger and malevolence, perhaps.

I do not have a simple word for it, but whatever it was I can feel it still, for all that we hated him. I say hated. That is not quite the truth. It was more that Monsieur Rouvel seemed to tell us something about ourselves that we hated, that we could not endure. I have told you that he was ugly, and repulsive. That is not entirely true. There was a strange allure in his rage, in the fury he bore about with him. Perhaps what we hated in ourselves was that attraction. All this, I would have told you. In time, I would have told you, when you could understand.

—There were times when one or the other of us had to take something to him in his cottage, and at first Agnes and Geneviève and I would argue over who would have to go. I remember how, when it was my turn, I knocked on his door with a small folded pile of clothing that I was asked to bring. His cottage—really not more than one small room—was filled with smoke and the thick and not unpleasant smell of old tobacco. I remember Monsieur Rouvel sitting with his back to me, still working by lamp-light though it was bright daylight outside. He merely grunted when I knocked, and I stole quietly into the room and placed the clothes on a chair—on a pile of papers, always the papers—and tried to slip out of his shack and back to the house again before he saw me or spoke to me.

—I was not fast enough. Suddenly, though he hardly seemed to know that I was there, he had stepped across the room and closed the door. Speak to me for a moment, was all he said, and I sat as I was bid, on the edge of his unmade bed, and clasped my hands in my lap.

—He began to talk in his usual fashion, an unbroken stream of words in which there was much that I did not understand. And all the while I sat, at first much wanting to go but at the same time pinned to that bed by the easy words which flowed around me and touched me in strange ways. Touching everything I knew—things that were familiar, that had normally no meaning to them at all—and clothing them with a new kind of life: my clothes, my hair, my skin. Attaching all that I had, all that I was, through his vast webs of words, to so many other things, beautiful and painful things that had happened elsewhere, and long ago. I had no words myself. All I was, all I knew, changed as he spoke. I sat in silent dread, and fascination. But not quite wanting to go. It was this that was so strange.

—Not all that your friend writes is nonsense. Not all.

—I can only tell you what happened. Again, I cannot tell you what it means. I was just thirteen years old. Most of Rouvel's words were of things I did not understand. Much of what I did understand seemed evil or at least impertinent, not for my ears at that time. And yet I was drawn, beyond myself, beyond any wisdom, all that I knew of right and wrong up to that time. At night, sometimes, after everyone in the house was asleep—no-one slept well in that house, in the summer heat—I would creep out onto the verandah. There I would sit and watch the light of his lamp, the glow of the lamp on the hessian curtains, down in Monsieur Rouvel's hut. Sometimes I would see him moving about, or hear his voice, mumbling in the darkness and the still of the night. I would hear him, talking to himself or reciting, as I was to discover, passages from the manuscript that he was writing, reading them to himself but aloud, and to the emptiness of the night.

—And then, one night, I went to Monsieur Rouvel. He smiled at me as I came in, and nothing more, and went on working. I curled up in the large chair that my father had sent down for him, sat in silence for hours it seemed, in my nightgown, and just watched him as he worked, as the sweat beaded on his brow and sometimes he had to wipe his glasses. I watched him as he wrote, and listened, as from time to time he would look up from his writing and bid me listen. I listened to the strange, the wonderful things that he wrote, which ran so far beyond that place, and beyond all things I had ever known. Passages which have now come back to me, interwoven with all the lies and dreamings of your friend in Paris.

—After that, and on many occasions, I would creep down there in the nights to watch him write. He would barely acknowledge me when I came in, but would simply gesture to the chair. In the dim light of his shack, amid the heat of the night and below the creaking iron, I curled up in his chair, my arms clasped about my legs and my nightgown soon damp with perspiration, clinging to my body; and I watched him as he wrote, his thick hair falling over his face as he bent over his papers, watched the circling of the moths and insects that were drawn to him in the night, watched him share the light with these other creatures of the night, waiting in silence until now and then and without warning he would speak.

—Now and then he would look up from his writing, look up at me and remove his spectacles, as if at such a distance he could see more clearly without them, and then he would recite what I imagine he had just written, recite the words without looking at the page, murmur the words while searching my face and my body, my bare feet and arms as I sat curled up in the shadows, to see how I would understand what he had written of me.

—Of me—because in those nights, in those secret times when I crept down to see Monsieur Rouvel, it was as though I became the thing he wrote, that there was no self, no face, no body but the body given to me by the words of Sebastien Rouvel, having no life or self or being, it sometimes seemed through the long and hot and eventless days that ran between, other than that given to me in the nights by the words of Rouvel. And so he touched me—touched me with those words, caressed me, graced me, naming and as though creating in his words each part of me, of my body. Impertinent, it was. Perhaps obscene. A kind of violation, indeed, but one that ran beyond all vulgar power of imagining such things. If you could read those poems—not as read by your friend in Paris, but as they were written, or rather as they were spoken—then you would know.

—Whether he was inspired, or simply cruel and mad, I could not tell. I read his words now, and they are cold and strained—forced, obscene, improbable. Like crude copies of far better things that have been written since. Like words just taken from the poems of others, strung together in old bits and pieces, like the cages of poor Clémentine. They seemed less so when he spoke. We must not deny him that. The power. If we deny him that, then everything else that happened becomes obscure. Inexcusable. Our whole lives. I have never sought either comprehension or excuse, to this moment. I had hoped for some kind of shelter, in understanding, in some kind of compassion. But now, I must tell you all, in sheer nakedness. And so, I tell you all.

—Yes, he was strange—at times, wonderful—not all your friend in Paris has written is a lie. Unless you understand this, there is no understanding to be had.

***

I saw her sitting on the bed in the heat of Rouvel's shack, watching him writing in the pale circle cast by the lamplight, the thick hair falling across his face, her legs drawn up, her arms clasped about her knees, her toes protruding bare beyond the hem, sitting in silence and out of time and place through these lost parts of the night, moths playing about the tousled aura of her hair, her hair unpinned and flowing about her shoulders and she clad only in her rumpled nightdress moistened by the heat of the summer night.

> *A child of great beauty but with flesh green like fresh spring shoots led me deep into these roofless catacombs, where she would hear such words as she would never understand, words to which she would listen in the night and to no other sound that creased the air between us.*

I watched him stop writing now and then to read such words to her as she would never understand. Words that were written perhaps for no person ever to understand, words written only to unhinge and break, to which she listened in the silence of the night, to no other sound that crossed the air between them, not the crack of the cooling iron above their heads nor the sound of a distant owl or curlew; the girl though hearing only, against all the vacancy around them and the deep silence of the night, some richer promise in the words he used, bringing a strength of feeling not to be equalled in all forms of knowledge since, with nothing at the end of such release but deeper silence, the world around her fast become a desert, and all her world to come.

—You ask me what happened on that day. Despite all, you seek an ending.

Colette shivered and wrapped herself more closely in her shawl, as though against some further hostile presence that had come in from the cold. She spoke as though to the draughts that blew about the room, as though to some further listener waiting beyond the salon and the dim hallway, the steps and dark tangle of dripping garden and the high wall and buckled iron gates that lay beyond.

—Our father was again away, taking stock south on the roads. It was, I recall, a hot and windy day, with the dust blowing up and the sand singing in our ears. One of the little ones—perhaps it was Geneviève—had found a lizard. A frightening beast, with a wide mouth and a large screen behind its ears which sat up and made its head look gigantic, to its foes. More like a rock, more like a stick, than any animal you would see here. We decided to kill the lizard. Children are like that in your country—perhaps everywhere. Cruel. Because the lizard was so ugly, no-one felt any need to be kind. In that harsh place, amid the sticks and dry leaves and broken rocks, there seemed no reason to be kind.

—Agnes was not with us at the time. We had built a fire in a ring of stones, and were going to roast it. I remember still the wretched lizard, clinging with all its might to the end of a stick, and Geneviève swinging it around, and the lizard still clinging grimly to the end. Thinking perhaps, This is bad. But if I let go of the stick it may well be worse. I recall, too, one of the workers, an old German with only one hand who was perhaps the last man on the place, wondering why it was that we needed to hurt the poor beast. Saying something about there being enough pain in the world without our adding to it. That the country was surely big enough for us and for the lizard, without it doing harm to us, or us to it. But the younger ones were now too excited to let it go; the wind was blowing and the dust moving and the sky bright red with all the soil that had been loosened and set in motion around us.

—Nothing was normal, nothing could seem real on days like those, when the sky was red and the whole earth seemed on the move, when you could reach into the air and clutch at it in handfuls and the sand tore at your eyes and skin, and snapped your hair around you like a whip. I looked over to the house once or twice, and to the layabout where, in the morning, Monsieur Rouvel had been sleeping. He was no longer there. The newspaper he had been reading was blown into pieces across the garden, its leaves wrapped around the last of the shrubs, or caught against the fence.

—I walked over to the house.

—Inside, all was silent, with only the banging of loose roofing iron, and the sounds of the wind. It was dark. In the summer, we would always draw the blinds and close all the windows and doors, and try to preserve the cool of the night within the house. I remember still the soft and shaded darkness, the sound of flies dying against the window panes, the coolness and relief felt for a moment when first you went indoors, the heat gradually creeping on you, the tingling of perspiration as it began to move within your clothes.

—I was hardly in the house when I heard the sound of voices from a room at the end of the long passage that ran the length of the house. Muffled voices, but I could tell that they were those of Maman and Monsieur Rouvel. There was no light in any of the rooms, though with each moment I could see more, my eyes adjusting to the half-light. There were voices coming from the room, my parents' bedroom, and an open door.

—I thought to call to Maman, but something in the sounds I heard caused me to pause. I thought for a moment to go outside, to rejoin the others. But there was something in Rouvel's tone—some echo of the way he had spoken to me in the nights—some softness in his voice that I could not now define, that drew me to that room, that drew me to those sounds, of Maman weeping, or so it seemed, and of Sebastien Rouvel, speaking softly, as though to reassure, her voice breaking now and then between his words, and his voice riding up over hers again.

—And so I crept down the passageway. Now creeping, not stumbling about and shouting as we often did about the house, but moving slowly and with care. I reached the door. There I saw him, with my mother, in the dimness of the light, the close air of that room. The first thing of which I was aware was Rouvel's back. Rouvel's back, his heavy shoulders moving, his thick black hair. He wore only a shirt, the shirt half removed, his shoulders exposed, his body bare, arched and moving in strength, and my mother pressed beneath him and he struggling, as it seemed, to hold her there, her legs bare and she pushing against him, pressing against him as though to throw him off and he thrusting her more deeply with each savage movement into the scattered pillows and the tangle of the bed.

—Do not speak! Do not speak! Only listen. You are here to listen. It will not be told again.

—He lay upon her, his body arched and straining with a force that made her cry. Her face was covered by a cloth, a corner of sheet perhaps or some discarded garment, her cries half-smothered by the hand with which he held her head down, by the fingers which he seemed to force into her mouth. Her dress was torn, her skin covered in perspiration, her breasts streaked red with the mark of his clawing hands, one arm pinned down and the other hand raking his back and even drawing blood, her face part lost in the cloth and the thick fall of his long black hair, she moaning still and pleading softly against his hand, against the fingers and the cloth thrust into her mouth, and with Sebastien Rouvel speaking slowly, gently, riding over her words, still smothering her words with his hand, speaking slowly through his teeth as he struggled against her, drowning what she tried to say with stronger words of his own. Words that seemed familiar. Words I had heard before.

—Neither of them saw me. And I said nothing. And for a time, I watched. And listened, for one last time, to his words.

Colette paused, and sat back from the lamp. Her voice had now grown husky. It was early morning, creeping towards first light. She waited for a time. Clémentine seemed to have lost all concentration, and merely smiled vacantly, clattering again with her needles. I listened to the rain outside, to the cascade of water that flowed down the walls and over the windows and spattered heavily on the sills.

—Perhaps you have such moments in your life; moments when you know that what you do will change, will break; and yet you know that you will never, in the length of the life to follow, blame yourself for that act. At thirteen, I knew that feeling. At thirteen years old, and walking back down that long passage, to do what I had to do to Sebastien Rouvel. To protect ourselves. You must understand. To protect myself. My mother.

—Agnes had left the crow pistol in its usual place, behind the front door. It was always loaded. I crept back down the corridor, and took it. Then I returned. This time, my boots beat heavily on the boards as I came back, the pistol raised in front of me at the height that was needed, so that I would hardly need to aim, the weight causing my hands to shudder, the hard pull of the trigger forcing me to use both my hands.

—And I realised, as again I realise now, that we must at last be known by what we do, and not by what we say; that we must be known by what we are and what we have done, and not just by what can be told. Looking on, in that moment, through the long years to come, I chose at once to move beyond that vast web of words where each word touches, each word caresses the other across a vast and intricate seductive maze but reaches further from the act, the thing, from what I saw and what I did. But in the end we will be known by what we do, the act and not the words, the act which it seems must become known even so many years later, even generations later; and after so many words from us all, from your friend in Paris and from Sebastien Rouvel himself, from you and even beyond all the stories I have told you of the life before and since that time, we come at last to the centre, to the very centre of it all, to the act itself. And mostly, of course, I did not think at all, but acted by a certain knowledge, acted by such deep conviction of necessity as sustains me even now, that has sustained me against all that has happened in the time that has since passed.

—After the deed, it was my mother's time to weep. I was as dry as stone. She begged me then to weep, with the mark of blood still upon my dress, and for years afterwards, but I would not. Your friend demands the facts. The feelings are our own concern, to live with through the long years that have followed, to speak of to no other person; to die with my mother, and soon to die with me.

Colette moved forward one last time to the light. She moved forward, her shoulders straight, her eyes keen in the softness of the low glow of the lamp, now bright with what they had known in that other time, now looking at me, with all the keenness and intensity of her thirteen years, with all the resolution of those thirteen short years.

—What I have told you is the truth. It is written. It must now be taken to the proper authorities. There to contend with other forms of writing. There is, now, no concealment. Only nakedness. A conclusion. A brutal ending for us all.

Looking at me, as she had looked at no thing since that time. Moving back into her chair. Sinking back from the light. Touching for the first time the steep back of her chair.

—It is told. And you may go. *Allez!*

Nineteen

Lucien was sleeping. He was in his favourite square, below the walls of the Bibliothèque Nationale. It was very early morning. He had found another tattered coat somewhere and slipped it on over the top of his old ones, to face the colder weather that had come upon us with summer passing into autumn. He was slumped, a greasy pile of reeking drapery, across one of the iron benches, his head dangling painfully over the side, a smile on his lips like the smile of a sleeping child.

I sat next to him on the bench, not wanting to wake him. Taking in his filth, his fetid truths, his reassuring stinks, with a new kind of tenderness. When he finally woke, I brought him a coffee in a paper cup, and sat and watched him drink.

There was a new kindness in his voice after I told him what had happened. When a patisserie opened nearby, we shared a roll. I had no appetite. Most of my share went to Lucien, and to the early morning sparrows.

—You know, Lucien, I'm starting to think you are the only sane person I've met in this city.

—I know.

I told this sane person the whole story, or almost the whole story. About the stories, the letters and the papers. He listened carefully, warming his hands and breathing in warm fumes from the coffee.

—And so she shot him.

—She says she shot him. She believes, at least, that she shot him. But I can tell you, Lucien: there were no bullets in that pistol. Agnes once told me about it. It was packed with black powder, and a wad of paper. Enough to hurt, perhaps. Enough to scare. She could not have killed him.

—She tried to do so. She has confessed as much. It is enough.

—It was the shock, Lucien. He left in shock. And got lost. You don't know that country. How every tree, every rise, looks like the last.

—That may be so. But now, and because of you, my friend, there is something. Pursuit and punishment. Your friend's book. Because you would not let your sleeping dogs lie.

—Lucien, it's all my fault.

—Yes.

—I should have told you more of this. Much earlier.

—Yes.

—I have to fix it, Lucien.

—Does she know why she shot him? Do you think she understands?

I did not reply. We had the facts. But only the facts. The rest was locked up with Colette, more firmly now than ever.

—And you? What do you want?

—I know enough, Lucien. I want to leave it now.

—I think that you know less than you did before.

—That may be so, but it's far more than I need to know.

—I don't think you have your answers. Or your book.

—I have more than I can understand, Lucien. More than I can bear.

We sat in silence again. Listening to the sounds of early-morning traffic. Occasionally, Lucien would scratch himself, or cough his misty clouds into the morning air.

—You have waded in deep, *mon vieux.* No way of getting out without pain. New enemies, and lots of pain.

—The pain will be there anyway.

—You know what your problem is? You're too young. Much too young. You think that eighty, a hundred years is a safe length of time. That you can dig these people up and take a look at them, and then just put them back again.

He peered at me. A last, bright-eyed and penetrating gaze. He looked out across the square, at the gathering sparrows, the early widows with their bread.

—You still think that you can know things, and not be changed by what you know.

Beyond Lucien, the breaking of his awful cough, there stretched only the loneliness of the city.

—But I can tell you something. I can tell you what it is that you must do.

He put his hand on mine, rubbing it roughly, and with affection.

—And then, my young friend, you must promise, you must absolutely promise, to leave this place. To go home.

Julia. It promised to be another day of crazing heat. Of sweat, and pressing crowds. I wanted, though, to meet her in the street, in a café. Perhaps, as for the first time, in the place de la Bastille, or even just down at le Monge, looking out over the place. Instead, she called me up to her apartment.

She was roused from her sleep. She was dressed in her bathrobe, naked beneath it, wiping the sleep from her eyes. She greeted me with a yawn, a cold kiss that scarcely touched, and showed me to my old place on the bed. Dislodging the cat. It was still early morning. The atmosphere was fusty, close, the curtains drawn. On her desk, her typescript sat in a neat pile, and beside it were Rouvel's papers, bookmarked, thickly interleaved with all the notes that we had written.

—A coffee? I've hardly slept. I need a coffee.

—Don't trouble, Julia. I can't stay long.

She sat at her desk, swivelling towards me, pulling the flap of her robe over her bare legs. She smiled. The old smile of excitement, of anticipation. The best of Julia.

The smile fading, as she looked at me more closely.

—Have you shown it to her, Nicholas? Has she read it?

—She has read it, Julia. Every word.

—And?

—Colette has written the real truth of what has happened. Carefully, and in legal form. In great detail. Their family lawyer has assisted. She has written it all, her own memories, things her mother told her, things she learned from Sebastien Rouvel's own lips. His secrets. All that he did in those lost years.

—She has written about all this?

—Everything. All that she can remember.

I pulled it from my bag and waved it at her.

—You say she'll swear to the truth of it?

—In court, if necessary.

—And may I have it?

I rose from the bed, as though I was going to hand it to her. Instead, I took up Rouvel's pages, turning them over in my hands in an abstracted sort of way.

—I'm afraid you can't, Julia. That's what we've decided.

—We? Who has decided? You and those old women?

—What we have decided, Julia, is to make the truth public ourselves. But only after your own book is published. When your book comes out, Colette's story, so very different from your story, will go to the press—to the police—to anyone who wants it. To *Paris Match*, if necessary. With photographs. Whatever you write in your book, it's going to look very silly within weeks.

She gaped. Then laughed.

—This is ridiculous. You're such a fool, Nicholas. You try not to hurt anyone. So you end up by deceiving us all. And the damage just goes on and on! Do you really imagine you can bring everything—my whole life—to a halt, just by that stupid threat?

—It's not just *Paris Match*, Julia. There is a further step.

—What step?

—The papers. If they belong to anyone, they're mine.

Rouvel left it behind. Agnes inherited it. She gave it to me.

Which was when she came to realise that I had the pages in my hands.

—I'm going to have to destroy them, Julia. It's what Colette wants. It's what Agnes wanted, too. She just couldn't quite bring herself to do it.

Julia had gone very pale. Her eyes were now fixed on the pile of papers in my hands.

—Nicholas, you can't. You couldn't possibly. You can't do that.

—They have done so much damage. In your hands, Julia. And in mine.

—Nicholas, you can't do this! You've seen the work. The time. My life!

She stared at me. Thinking quickly, thinking frantically. Then she made a desperate leap for Rouvel's papers. We fought, as I had dreaded we would, as even Lucien suggested that we might, struggling across the room and tripping over the bed, peering for one dreadful deadlocked moment into one another's eyes as though searching for some glimmer which would rise up and save us from each other, the squalid writhing battle over the papers sending once again the file boxes, the folders and the coffee cups flying, until finally she tripped and went sprawling to the floor.

She sat in humiliation and fatigue, her bathrobe fallen open in sexless disarray, weeping with exhaustion and pain. I wanted desperately to stretch out a hand, to help her to her feet. To comfort. To explain. To talk with Julia of other answers, of other ideas, of how our lives, our very bodies, had somehow both been hijacked, of safer and of gentler ways in which each of us might make our visits to the past. Wanting to tell her how I would gladly have sold the lot of them to deep oblivion—Rouvel, Paul, Marie-Josèphe, and even Tante Colette—for the chance of one more moment of precious intimacy, here amid the papers in the rue de la Clef. One whisper of real tenderness. Thinking of all the things that might have been, that should have been and now could never be.

Instead I gathered up the last of the torn and scattered papers in an awkward bundle, and made quickly for the door.

—They're mine, Nicholas! He was my great-great-uncle. My family. Nicholas, wait! There has to be another way!

I ran down the stairs, clutching the papers, with Julia struggling to her feet and coming after me, leaning over the rail and shrieking after me, threatening, begging, crying.

—I'll change it. The story—anything! We have to talk. It's just not possible. Nicholas!

At the base of the stairs was the fat concierge, scratching her elbows, watching me in silence as I stumbled down the stairs, crashing from the banister to the wall and back against the banister, pursued by Julia's voice.

—It's mine! I'll write it, Nicholas. I'll tell it, anyway!

I pushed past the concierge and broke out into the street, scattering papers and stooping to retrieve them, with Julia's screams, *voleur, voleur*, following me down the street. Feeling cruel and angry—a cruelty and an anger with nowhere now to travel, not now and for the long years to follow, except towards myself, with bits of Rouvel's writing still dropping, blowing about me as I pushed through the crowds and down the street, blown like leaves across the city streets in the first cruel autumn winds.

Epilogue

I DID COME BACK TO Paris. After many, many years. With most of life safely passed. Standing once again on a bridge, looking out along a river. The same bridge where I once saw, or imagined as vividly as if I had seen, a young woman running through the burning night, her clothing blown about her by the hot and troubled winds. A city crackling with rifle fire and the steady boom of guns, with bodies in the streets and burning buildings, the steady creak of wagonloads of the dead. A city now gone back to the mill of tourists, the peaceful business of buying, showing, selling.

This time, I stood in daylight. In the early morning, amid the carbon monoxide and the thick growl of traffic. Looking down at the waters of the Seine, ignoring the looks of the passers-by hurrying on their way to work, distracted for a moment by this person on the bridge, pensive, stooped and pondering the flood below. Surveying a city still familiar, and yet also greatly changed. After thirty years of travelling, with only this great city cautiously avoided, a life of much begun and much unfinished, of circling back and forth and always with a wide berth around this unhopeful site of real attraction, this place of such rich promise, of such cruel failure to deliver.

There was no Lucien. Death had come quickly, and shortly after we last met. It was on one of his expeditions up to Montmartre: miles of painful uphill shuffling, but as sacred to him as a pilgrimage to any hallowed shrine. He had completed his monthly orisons, and was on his way to whatever it was that he called home. He was run down by an official cavalcade, travelling as always too fast and noisily along streets that were much too narrow. Lucien had become quite deaf, or perhaps he was just unimpressed by the wail of sirens, the furious tooting and the shouts from passers-by just before the cavalcade hit, swerved, and banked up one against the other in a long staccato crunch of torn metal and the shrieking of official tyres.

It was the Canadian who told me the story—the Canadian, now an old man, long retired and living half the year in Paris, still paddling around in Condorcet. I met him outside the new Bibliothèque Nationale. Yes, he vaguely remembered me. And poor Lucien. It had happened more than twenty-five years ago. There was a short obituary in *Le Matin*, and a little ceremony for Lucien in the square Louvois—hosted, oddly enough, by the same officialdom that had banned him from the libraries of Paris. Our scholar tramp. Lucien would have enjoyed that less—the tender orations of his oppressors—than the sight of the long ribbon of broken metal and drooping flaglets that he left banked up along the rue Montmartre.

No doubt poor Lucien only heard the first impact, the sound of his own flesh and blood hitting and parting and spreading out across the first official radiator grille, and perhaps, mercifully, not even that. So it is not such a sad story—after all, 'the *clochards* don't live very long'. The *clochard* in question, *Le Figaro* noted with approval, died instantly. That the Canadian remembered. The speeding dignitary was a little late for his reception, but quite unhurt. His wife and her dog were treated at the scene.

I went down, on that same visit, to Saint-Germain-sur-École. To the cemetery where they had buried Geneviève, just months after my last visit, next to her mother. The stone showed that Clémentine had lived on until 1973. Colette died in 1976, and was buried beside Geneviève.

The graves were untended, the headstones looking older than they were. Of the house, I imagined only signs of more decay, some thirty further years of neglect, expecting to peer down through the ragged trees and past the ramshackle cages towards the weedy steps, to the broken shutters hanging off their hinges, the windows still closed on the room where Geneviève lay ill, to the door through which Colette had first called me into the darkness, and to the wild shrubs and ruined orchard and overgrown parterre that lay beyond.

The place of course was renovated, through and through. A developer had surrounded it with neat suburban villas in the same but scaled-down style, the old house now just the grandest of them all. All sombre stories, all tales beyond those of assured suburban comfort and net personal worth, were swept away by the gleaming façade, the newly paved and swept driveway, the electronic monitor at the gates. The only sign of human messiness in all this geometric splendour a plastic child's toy, a three-wheeler in gay blue and red and yellow, upturned in the middle of the driveway.

I thought of how it must have been, with Marie-Josèphe and the three children making their way for the first time from the train in an open cart and with their few meagre belongings from the station over at Ponthierry or perhaps Boutigny-sur-Essonne, the gates perhaps still closed at the time of their arrival, the long drive unweeded and unswept but still showing the pathway that ran down to the steps. Of how it must have looked to three small girls, still reeling from the motion of the boat, coming at last on this long fabled country, to this home that they had never known as home, to the deep green tangle of the garden and the soft light and moist air and the cultivated fields, their faces pressed against the cold bars of the gate while their mother sought a neighbour to unlock or break the chain.

I looked up at an open window on the upper floor, the blowing curtain and the silence within, and thought for a moment of a cruel birth, on the edge of the desert and below the baking rocks. I thought of what Colette might have worn on that same day, a long dark dress beneath a pinafore with white petticoat below, her hair perhaps worn in long curls and a large hat on her head, her Australian freckles not yet disappeared even after the long weeks at sea: the two of them and little Clémentine, looking in wonder at this house which was to be their home, with their mother standing over them, the young woman from the Studio Penot now so much older, seeing in that old house with its straight walls and tall white shutters and ordered gardens an end at last, protection from all unwelcome forms of knowing, this beautiful house with its cool and sheltering darkness now secure against all talk of histories and the past, the mother now extending her arms over the shoulders of the three of them, and saying, this is our house, this is the house in which I spent so much time as a child, this is the place in which I was happy; and now and from here on and *in aeternitatem* you will live in this place, nowhere from now but in this place, and you too will know what happiness is. Her hands upon their shoulders as they came closer, as they stared up at the façade.

Standing on the bridge. On the bridge with my now ancient satchel still bulging with papers, braving the wind on this wintry day, looking out over the decks of a passing *bateau-mouche* slipping by beneath, and down the river towards the vast expanses of the Grand Palais. With the crowds hurrying past, sometimes sparing this lonely stranger a glance, most of them thinking, surely, this is an odd sight at this early time of day, to see this person standing alone on the bridge, pressed by the winter winds. But with just a few of the wiser among them thinking, though perhaps later and from the kind of distance that one needs to judge in fairness, yes, this did look very odd, but perhaps only because we came in late upon the story; that if we knew more, we might see that this is entirely the right place, the right time, the right thing to do.

There was no book on Sebastien Rouvel. Not by Julia

Dussol, or by any other. A morning at the catalogues in the new Bibliothèque Nationale showed a few more general works by worthy historians, picking over the usual bits of evidence, setting out an excuse here and laying on a little more blame there, with interest in Rouvel largely fading on the collapse of the Commune, his death still mentioned only as an afterthought, somewhere still vaguely just *au centre de l'Australie*. There was no mention of a woman. There was no mention of poetry. Editions Grandet itself went out of business in 1973, swallowed up by some larger house, the imprint now used for publishing lifestyle manuals and travel books.

Did she decide that this was a story that should simply not be told? There was as much truth in her version, perhaps, as there was in any other. The facts, as Colette herself once said, do not give us the feelings, and it is in the feelings we find the truth. And what use is truth, when it can aid only the dead? What use are facts that impede the living, that lead to an end to passion and the need for greater lies? Better to seize upon a fiction that helps one to go on living—extract the moment in its freshness from the toll of past and future, from the awkwardness of unpromising beginnings and from cruel and heartless endings; rescue the best part of the pleasure, of Julia Dussol, leafing for the first time, bright-eyed, through the manuscript in the place de la Bastille, or Julia lying with her arm across my chest, our discarded clothing lost amid the papers that were strewn across the room, the perspiration on her body still glistening, drying slowly in the softened light that flowed in from the place?

He thrusts his hand into his satchel, this lonely foreigner on the threshold of the last part of his life, beginning now to feed handfuls of paper to the river, Colette's papers, Julia's papers and clutches of his own, glimpses and fragments and half-formed fantasies; and then, after such hesitation, an older set of pages, yellowed and breaking in his hands, to let the paper take its chances as it floats off towards Le Havre and the oceans beyond. Wondering if Julia Dussol has fared better than he, without this departing ending to her story? Daring, at last, as Agnes had always wanted, and against all the claims of History, to bring this sorry telling to an end. Wondering how Sebastien Rouvel would have felt to see this publication to the waters, his papers coursing down the burning river past the boats that float in glowing mercury and the fires that blaze along both sides, the deep glow of the Hôtel de Ville to the west and the vast blaze of the Tuileries to the east, watching such a conclusion to what might have been a love story or perhaps a murder story, or a story of obsession or of blackmail and intrigue, the Salamander and the Cell of Banded Light, the Leviathan and the Palace of Justice and the Tales of the Anvil, the Castle of

Rocks and the Prophets of the Desert; watching as the fragments sweep into the currents that split and run out from the bridge, the papers cascading and turning and mingling with each other, to be scooped up perhaps in muddy handfuls somewhere on the long journey between the city and the sea, the mysteries to be carried on in someone else's life, some curious Sunday angler on the banks down by Rouen, or some schoolboy paddling in the shallows beyond Le Havre, perhaps, amid the sandbanks in that place where the river meets the coast.

11/13

Lucy Robbins Welles Library
95 Cedar Street
Newington, CT 06111-2645